M000286693

The
Telegrapher

September 13. 2010

To Aunt Frances,

—

Hope you enjoy reading more
about our family!

— with love,

Also by Thomas L. Wiley
The Angels of Lockhart

Morse Code

A	• –		U	• • –
B	– • • •		V	• • • –
C	– • – •		W	• – –
D	– • •		X	– • • –
E	•		Y	– • – –
F	• • – •		Z	– – • •
G	– – •			
H	• • • •			
I	• •			
J	• – – –			
K	– • –		1	• – – – –
L	• – • •		2	• • – – –
M	– –		3	• • • – –
N	– •		4	• • • • –
O	– – –		5	• • • • •
P	• – – •		6	– • • • •
Q	– – • –		7	– – • • •
R	• – •		8	– – – • •
S	• • •		9	– – – – •
T	–		0	– – – – –

The Telegrapher

By
Thomas L. Wiley

Monarch Publishing House
2573 Lake Circle
Jackson, MS 39211-6630

Copyright © 2010, Thomas L. Wiley

ISBN: 978-0-9797861-1-2

Library of Congress Control Number: 2010921960

All rights reserved. No part of this book may be reproduced or transmitted in any form or by any means, electronic or mechanical, including photocopying, recording, or by information storage and retrieval systems, without the written permission of the publisher, except by a reviewer who may quote brief passages in a review.

Printed in the United States of America

*With love to my wife
Merrie
For her endless encouragement and
support in making
"the second book" a reality.*

Acknowledgments

A work of this nature—a family saga—is impossible without the help of family. Sadly, the two who gave me most of the firsthand information about the Parker family are now gone. Gussie and Hodges Riggan, my wife's aunt and uncle, both in their late eighties, died before publication. Their wealth of information and the stories from almost a century ago were invaluable. A special thanks to Dick Brown, Merrie's cousin, for his insight into the family and recommendations on how to make the story better. To my children and their spouses, David and Elaine, Brent and Betsy, Eric and Julie, Davy and Laurie, and to my mother, Pearl Wiley: thanks for your encouragement. Brent, thanks for reminding me that the home team always bats last.

I also wish to thank Ann Giompolleti, Larry Goldstein, Rexine Henry, and Sherry Rula for your suggestions. They were invaluable. To Sue Bray, Marsha Pyanowski, and the rest of the crew at BookMasters: thanks for the editing, cover and book design, and all the other details that finally brought the story to print.

And to my wife, Merrie: you were my sounding board. The "second book" is as much yours as it is mine. Thanks.

Contents

Chapter 1

The Beginning

Meridian, Mississippi
December 31, 1945

The dream is always the same. I'm lying on the kitchen table. Mamaw is standing beside me, wiping my forehead with a cloth. Papa and Dr. Knox are talking softly.

"Can the arm be saved?" I hear Papa ask.

"It's too damaged. If we don't amputate, infection will set in and he will die."

I hear the soft clink of metal as Dr. Knox lays out his instruments. He turns toward me with a cloth in one hand and a bottle in the other. He places the cloth over my face and opens the bottle.

"Ollie, the ether has a strange smell, but it will help you rest. Now, breathe slowly and deeply."

"No! Papa! No!" I scream and try to get up. "Please make him leave me alone! I'll be okay! Please! Papa! Please!"

"No, son," Papa says as he and Mamaw hold me down. "There is no other way. Dr. Knox is right. Mamaw and I are here. We will be with you."

The room begins to spin. I struggle and cry out, "No! Papa! No!"

Then everything is dark.

It's been years since I had that dream. I guess I've gotten so used to not having my arm that my mind doesn't replay it anymore. But recently the dream has returned. It is a terrible, frightening dream. But then, it's not a dream; it's a flashback. I'm again experiencing that horrible day fifty-five years ago when I lost my arm.

Years ago I would wake up fighting with all my might to keep them from taking my arm, crying for Papa to stop; but then I'd realize it was over—had been over for days, then months, then years ... As I woke, a feeling of total uselessness would engulf me. How can I be or do anything? What kind of worthless life is in store for me? I would think of the old Civil War soldiers, sitting around Papa's general store, maimed and broken, unable to do much of anything, fed and cared for by their children and grand-children. I would bury my face in my pillow and cry myself back to sleep, begging for God to make me whole again.

In the past few weeks the dream has returned with a vengeance. I guess as I look retirement square in the face, my emotions are getting stirred up. The uselessness of retirement must be striking a familiar chord in my mind, bringing back memories of long ago.

For months—or has it been years?—my fellow workers have been hinting that it's time for me to retire, time for the one-armed old man to relax, slow down, and enjoy life. Time to let someone with a little less gray hair take the torch and run with it. Or in my case, someone to take the Morse key and keep the never-ending stream of dots and dashes flowing through the wire.

When they bring up the topic of retirement, I try to make light of it. I usually laugh and tell them that I'll be there long after they're gone. But deep down, their comments do bother me—bother me a lot more than I let on—because I know they are right.

Fifty-four years at a desk is a long time, and as much as I hate to admit it, age is taking its toll.

Over the past year or two I've come to realize that I am not as sharp as I used to be. I find myself having to ask for messages to be repeated—something that a few years ago I would never do. And the tapping on the Morse key seems to have gotten fainter. Noises that at one time never bothered me make messages hard to hear. Was that dit-dah or was it dit-dah-dah?

Sometimes I worry that messages are not complete, that I've left out a word or two. No big problem for a message from one loved one to another. But in a two-page contract, an error can be disastrous.

Anxiety and doubt are starting to creep in, overshadowing my love for my dots and dashes, telling me that it is time to stop.

But I don't want to retire. I love my work. I can honestly say that I love it as much now as I did in 1891, when Mr. Matthews let me tap out my first message over that magical wire: My NAME IS OLLIE PARKER IN LOCKHART. STOP. CAN YOU HEAR ME. STOP. I can still remember the excitement, the rush, when a few minutes later a message returned from Meridian: MESSAGE RECEIVED. STOP.

Telegraphy is my life. For over five decades I've viewed the world, not through a window or a book, but through a wire—a copper wire not much bigger than a piece of string. Messages sent in the form of dots and dashes. Cryptic communication to most people, but to me messages as easy to understand as reading the front page of the local newspaper.

The entire concept of telegraphy continues to fascinate me: the mechanics, the miraculous speed of communication, and the messages. Messages that let me see the far reaches of the Earth, and messages that allowed me to see into the very hearts of men.

Every day has been an adventure—each day as new and bright as the day before.

And to think: the summer before I was introduced to my beloved dots and dashes, the summer of my thirteenth year, I was convinced that my future was over, that my hope of having a life worth anything had been snuffed out, lost forever, victim of a foolish teenage prank.

Chapter 2

The Telegraph

I discovered telegraphy at age fourteen purely by accident. Or should I say "literally" by accident.

A year earlier was when it happened: I lost my arm and almost died. The recovery from the accident was slow and difficult. For two months I was confined to the bed, and for several more months I didn't leave the house. During those times of helplessness and pain, Mamaw was there, caring for me day and night.

Mamaw was my grandmother—Papa's mother. My mother had died five years earlier when I was eight, and Mamaw had moved in to raise my two sisters and me. During those years Mamaw and I developed a closeness, a bond that lasted until her death twenty-two years later. For all practical purposes, she became my mother—my encourager and my confidant. Even after Papa remarried two years later, Mamaw remained my "mother."

For months after the accident there were the dressing changes. With the trauma to my arm and shoulder, the amputation had left a pretty large area of raw surface. There was no such thing as a skin graft at that time, and the wound had to granulate in, a very slow process. "Wet to dry" dressing changes were done twice daily. Mamaw usually did the honors, and each time she changed it she would say, "Ollie, I'm sorry. I wish I could make this easier. I know it hurts, but I want you to know that it hurts me too."

I know it was hard on her, those hundreds of dressing changes, but she never acted as though it were a burden. She never had an expression of disgust or repulsion, even though it was definitely a repulsive job. Only feelings of love and acceptance appeared on her face. Never did she want me to feel less of a person because of my injury.

For the first two months, I was too weak to do anything. I couldn't even sit up without getting dizzy. Dr. Knox said that I had lost a lot of blood and needed iron—liver being the best source. Mamaw took him at his word and served it twice a day, or at least that's how it seemed to me. And between meals, there was a tablespoon of cod liver oil. To this day the sight of liver makes me nauseated.

Slowly I gained my strength and started getting out of bed and then out of the house. It was six months before I was strong enough to go back in school, and then only for half days. The accident had occurred in the summer of 1890, and it was the spring of the next year before I could last all day.

That next summer I started working again at the railroad depot in Lockhart—the same place where the accident had occurred a year earlier.

Lockhart is my home town, a small farming community ten miles north of Meridian. Nothing much remains of that tiny hamlet: the town a victim of good transportation and the bad luck of existing too close to a booming, growing city. In fact, about the only thing left in Lockhart is the old Methodist church and its cemetery.

The summer of the accident, when I was thirteen, I had worked at the depot with Junius and James, loading and unloading box cars. Junius and James are my stepmother's younger brothers. The work was hot and sweaty, but we had fun doing it—made a game of it as boys tend to do. If it were sacks of feed we were loading, we would compete to see who could load the most. The losers would buy a piece of gum or candy for the winner. And getting paid and having a little spending money wasn't bad either.

The next summer, the summer after the accident, Mr. Matthews asked if I'd like to work inside the depot doing odd jobs. We both knew that working on the loading dock was not an option for me. I was still weak, and lifting a fifty pound bag of horse feed is not a one-arm job.

I quickly found out that there wasn't a lot I could do inside either. I couldn't sweep, couldn't do much cleaning. Two hands were needed for almost every task in the station.

For most of the first day I found myself standing behind the counter, shifting from one foot to the other, watching the teller sell tickets. I was only fourteen, and the teller wasn't about to let me help count the money. (A side note—counting money with one hand is not an easy task either.)

This boy with one arm soon realized that he was of little use, and at the end of the day I was exhausted, not from work but from boredom and despair.

That night I couldn't sleep. I was worrying and crying: What kind of useless life was in store for me?

Again I thought of the Civil War veterans who sat around Papa's store, their lives shattered by their injuries. As far as I could tell, none of them ever did anything productive—their lives a total waste after the war. Was I destined to join their ranks, playing checkers on the top of an old barrel for the rest of my life? And even worse, I didn't even have old war stories to tell as they did!

The next morning I sat quietly at breakfast—too upset to eat, trying to decide what to do. I dreaded going back to the depot and had just about talked myself into staying home when Mamaw walked in. After Papa remarried, Mamaw moved out of our house and into a little cottage down the road but she was in and out of our house all the time.

"Ollie, glad I caught you before you left for work," she said as she poured herself a cup of coffee and sat down beside me. "How did everything go yesterday?"

Everyone else had already left the kitchen, and it was just the two of us. I sat silently, not knowing what to say, trying to fight back the tears.

"Mamaw, I don't feel good today. My stomach hurts, and I think I'll stay home. And besides, I don't think they really need me." I began to cry.

Mamaw placed her cup on the table and put her arms around me. For the first time in my life, I realized that my hugs would forever be deficient. With one arm, I could not hug her back. I began to sob.

"Mamaw, I don't know what to do! I'm so useless! I can't do anything and it makes me so mad! Mamaw, I'm a cripple, and I don't like it! I want my arm back. I've been praying to God every day to give me my arm back, hoping that I'll wake up and it will be there. I tell Him that I'll do anything to have it back!"

Mamaw put her hand under my chin and turned my face toward hers and smiled. "There are some prayers that can never be answered the way we want them to. Ollie, I would give my very life if it would bring back your arm, but that won't happen. And there comes a point where you have to accept what has happened, and go on with life. You've heard the saying 'take the lemons and make lemonade.' Well, right now you have the lemons. They are being sliced and squeezed, and the juice is still sour. But I promise you that the day will come when sugar will be added, and you'll be able to say things are not so bad. I can't tell you when that will happen, but it will. For now, though, you have to do the best you can.

"And, Ollie, I've learned that if you feel sorry for yourself, before long people will pity you, and that's not what you want. I know that you want people to treat you the way they did before the accident. Well, for that to happen you have to act the way you did before."

Mamaw stood up. "Ollie, I'll walk with you to the station."

We walked along silently. Just as we got to the depot, Mamaw leaned over and whispered, "You go in there with a smile on your face, enjoy the opportunities that God has given you. Look at every day as an adventure. If you look for it, something wonderful will show up."

She kissed me on the cheek, patted my behind, and gave me a little push. "Now go!"

I reluctantly went inside, not convinced by her little talk that things would be better.

When I walked in, Mr. Matthews was at the telegraph. As he finished what he was working on, he looked up and said, "Hey, Ollie. Have you ever seen the telegraph key? Come over and I'll show you how it works. It's really fascinating."

There on the work bench was a metal contraption about six inches long and two inches wide, hooked up to two wires. It was mounted on a piece of wood and had a lever that would move by itself every so often, emitting a clicking sound. Surprisingly the clicking could be heard throughout the depot. (In my boredom and despair, I had not appreciated it the day before.)

"It uses electricity and magnets," Mr. Matthews said as he stood up. "Have a seat and I'll show you how it works."

I sat down and he pointed to the lever and said, "Depress that thing," which I did. "You have just made a clicking sound on a similar unit in Meridian."

I remember the wonderment. "You're kidding me! That's ten miles away!" I exclaimed.

"No, it's true. When you depressed the lever you completed an electrical circuit. See those little metal points?" He pointed with a pencil. "When they come in contact with each other, electricity flows through the wire. If they don't touch, no electricity flows. When the electricity gets to the key in Meridian—and it's instantaneous, quicker than the blink of an eye—it causes a magnetic field to be formed around a piece of metal. A wire is wrapped tightly around the metal, and as the electricity flows through the wire, it turns that piece of metal into a magnet, an electromagnet. You've seen a magnet, haven't you?"

"Yes, sir," I replied. "Junius has one—the neatest thing. It'll pick up pins and nails. You can place it on the side of the stove and it won't fall off."

"That's right," Mr. Matthews said. "A magnet attracts iron. As long as you hold down this lever and electricity is flowing, the piece of metal at the other end in Meridian is a magnet and will pull the other contact to it. Let it go and the circuit is broken. The magnetism is no longer present, and the contacts come apart. The contacts coming together make the clicking noise you hear. Ollie, the telegrapher in Meridian can do the same for us—cause our key to click when he makes contact.

"Now comes the fun part," he continued, "communicating with those clicks. We use a sequence of dots and dashes to form letters which in turn form words. Tap the lever fast and it is a 'dot.' Hold it a fraction of a second longer and it is a 'dash.' "

Mr. Matthews clicked it twice. "Dot-dash, or as we say dit-dah. That's the letter *A*. Dah-dit-dit-dit is *B*."

He reached into the drawer and pulled out a piece of paper. "Here's the entire alphabet and numbers too. We call it the Morse code, made up by Samuel Morse and his assistant, Alfred Vail, around fifty years ago.

"I was in my teens at the time, about your age, when all this was being developed and I found it fascinating. I read everything I could about it. Fell in love with it and have been enjoying it since. As you can see, I have made it my life's work."

Mr. Matthews scratched his head. "Now that I think about it, Samuel Morse would be one hundred years old this year if he were alive. Born in 1791. He was an interesting fellow. He was from a very prominent family and went to Yale where he studied philosophy.

"Morse was also an inventor. In his twenties, he obtained several patents on different types of pumps. But it wasn't until he was in his forties, in the 1830s, that he got interested in telegraphy."

Mr. Matthews paused a moment and said, "Ollie, I don't want to bore you with all this."

"No! No!" I interrupted. "This is fascinating. Tell me more."

Mr. Matthews pulled up a chair and sat down beside me.

"Ollie, the desire to communicate rapidly over a long distance has been around, I guess, for as long as man has been around. In the past, smoke signals, flags, and mirrors were used. But with all of those the receiver has to be within sight of the sender, which limits the distance. With the discovery of electricity, and especially with the development of the electromagnet, things really changed.

"Ollie, do you know what 'telegraph' means?"

"No, sir, I don't," I answered.

"It comes from two Greek words *tele* which means far and *graphein* which means to write or to draw. 'To write far' is its literal meaning. 'Photograph' uses the same root word. 'To write, or draw, with light.'" He held up his pencil. "And see the lead in this pencil? Well, it is actually carbon, not lead. We also call it 'graphite' because we write with it."

He chuckled and then continued, "The derivation or origin of words has always fascinated me. I could go on with other words, but let me get back on the subject.

"Telegraphy has been around for years but had never been practical. In fact, in the late 1700s a telegraph machine was invented, but it required twenty-six wires, one for each letter of the alphabet. It depended on sparks from each wire burning into paper to communicate.

"Ollie, the electromagnet is what made telegraphy practical. Samuel Morse wasn't the first to use it in sending messages, but he was the one who developed a practical working model.

"It's interesting how it happened. In the 1830s, Morse was on a ship, traveling back to the U.S. from Europe when he overheard some men talking about the velocity of electricity. One man referred to Ben Franklin's experiment using several miles of wire. Franklin found that there was no appreciable time lapse from the current at one end and a spark at the other.

"Mr. Morse had also studied electricity while at Yale—in addition to philosophy—and he soon joined in the conversation. Before long they were talking about electromagnetism. That conversation piqued his interest and over the next few years he was able to develop the telegraph as we know it now.

"His first telegraph patent, if I remember correctly, was in 1837, and the next year he was able to transmit a message over two miles. Initially a pen attached to the magnet was used to make marks on paper, a very slow process. Morse and his assistant soon learned that it was easier and faster to listen to the clicks rather than have the machine mark the paper. They developed the Morse code, a sequence of dots and dashes specific for each letter and number, which we still use today.

"Ollie, a good telegrapher can send and receive forty to fifty words a minute. The really good ones don't even have to write it down. They say it flows into their head just like the spoken word does. They don't even have to think about it.

"Well, Mr. Morse continued to work on his new project, and in 1844—I think it was on May 24—the first city-to-city telegraph message was sent. He strung a wire from the Supreme Court building in Washington, D.C., to the Mount Clare train depot in Baltimore. As everyone gathered around, he sent a message: 'What hath God wrought?'. Ollie, do you know how he came up with that phrase?"

"No, sir," I said. "But it sounds like it may be from the Bible."

"That's right. It is in the Old Testament: Numbers 23:23. Annie Ellsworth, the daughter of Patent Commissioner Henry Ellsworth, had suggested it."

Mr. Matthews laughed. "Morse was pretty smart and knew who to please. He wanted the Patent Office on his side and pleasing the commissioner's daughter was just the trick!

"After that demonstration, telegraphy took off like a wild fire. Western Union was established in 1851, and by 1854 they say there were enough wires in the United States to circle the Earth—24,000 miles of it—and that was just the start. Within a few years telegraph wires actually did circle the globe. In 1866 a cable was laid across the floor of the Atlantic Ocean and by 1870 there was a cable connecting Britain with India.

"It's still hard for me to comprehend," Mr. Matthews shook his head and continued, "in a matter of seconds a message that I send from little Lockhart, Mississippi, can be picked up in Meridian, and then transferred to the East Coast and on to England, and from there sent halfway around the world to India. It would take the post at least three months to deliver a letter that far away."

Mr. Matthews reached over and began tapping on the key. "Ollie, let me send a quick message to Meridian letting them know that we will be playing for a few minutes..."

His eyes were bright with excitement as he sent the message. He was like a child showing off his favorite toy—having the greatest time telling me all about the history and workings of this truly amazing invention. In fact, I'm not sure who was enjoying it more—him or me!

"There," he said after a few moments. "As I said earlier, all letters and numbers are made up of different combinations of dots and dashes. The dot is a quick tap, the dashes a longer tap. In fact, a dash is three times longer than a dot. A dot is one unit; and dash is three units."

He tapped the key. "Dit-dah, *A*; dah-dit-dit-dit, *B*; dah-dit-dah-dit, *C*; and so forth." He pointed to the sheet he had pulled from the drawer. "You can look at this for the rest of the letters and numbers. Now, the space between letters equal to three units and space between words is equal to seven units.

He tapped again and said, "Now listen closely. Dah-dah-dah, *O*; dit-dah-dit-dit, *L*; dit-dah-dit-dit, *L*; dit-dit, *I*; dit, *E*—Ollie. Dit-dah-dah-dit, *P*; dit-dah, *A*; dit-dah-dit, *R*; dah-dit-dah, *K*; dit, *E*; dit-dah-dit, *R*—Parker. Ollie Parker. In Meridian the telegrapher just heard your name.

"Wow!" I exclaimed as I picked up the sheet of paper with the code on it. "This is fascinating! Can I take it home tonight and look over it?"

"Yes, you may. In fact, I have an old key that is just about worn out. It still makes the clicks, and you are welcome to take it home and play with it."

That evening I couldn't wait to get home with my new toy. After supper I pulled the key and the code out on the kitchen table and began studying and tapping. I was totally captivated by these dots and dashes!

Mamaw had cleared the table and was washing and drying the dishes. When she heard the clicking, she came over, dish towel in hand, and asked, "What have you got there?"

She leaned over to get a better look but then jumped back and threw her hands up, "Ollie Parker, get that mousetrap off this kitchen table! Have you lost your mind? That thing is filthy!"

"Mamaw, it's not a mousetrap. It's a Morse code key. And it's the neatest thing. They use it to send telegrams at the depot. Mr. Matthews showed me how it works today and let me bring it home to practice. I haven't had this much fun since ... well, since the accident."

I then explained to her as best I could how the telegraph works. She nodded several times and said, "Ah, I see," but it was obvious she didn't understand a thing I said.

When I had finished, Mamaw said, "Well, isn't that something!"

She then placed her hand on my shoulder and smiled. "Didn't I tell you this morning that if you kept your chin up and looked on the bright side, something wonderful would show up? God has a way of knowing when to put something good in our paths when we need it."

She looked closer at my new toy and shook her head. "That contraption still looks like a mouse trap to me!"

I stayed up late into the night studying and practicing. The telegraph key with its dots and dashes was the most captivating thing that I had ever come across, and I didn't want to stop and go to bed. At some point during the night I could hardly keep my eyes open. I thought, *I'll just turn the lantern down a bit and rest my head on the kitchen table. Close my eyes for a minute and then continue.*

The next I knew Papa was standing over me, shaking me gently.

"Ollie, Ollie," Papa said. "It's time to wake up."

I opened my eyes and slowly lifted my head. "What? What?"

"Ollie, it's six o'clock. You've been here all night. Time to get up. Time to get ready to go to work." He began to laugh. "Son, if I slept like that, I'd have such a crick in my neck—I wouldn't be able to straighten up for a week."

That morning I could not wait to get to the depot. I gobbled down my breakfast and headed to the door just as Mamaw walked in.

"Good morning, Ollie," she said. "Why, you seem to be in a mighty big hurry this morning. What's going on?"

"Nothing special," I answered. "Just don't want to be late to work."

Mamaw stopped me long enough to give me a hug and a kiss on the cheek. "Life looks better today than it did yesterday, doesn't it? You go and have a wonderful day!"

Chapter 3
A Gift

Over the next few weeks, I continued to play with the key at home, tapping out words and memorizing the code alphabet. At the station I listened to the clicking, trying to decipher messages as they came in. Initially the clicking made no sense at all, just a jumble of dots and dashes. I wondered how in the world anyone could make any sense out of this. But then I began to recognize the letters, and before long the letters became words, and then the words became sentences. I was picking it up fairly quickly, more quickly than I realized.

On the Fourth of July, I really surprised myself and everyone else at how well I was grasping the Morse code. That morning the depot was busy. Almost everyone in town was headed to Meridian for the holiday festivities. Lockhart was too small to put on a show, but Meridian knew how to do it right. The mayor and city council had planned a big day that everyone bragged would rival Chicago or Philadelphia—food, horseracing, a parade, and a huge fireworks display as soon as it got dark. There was even a carnival set up at the city park.

Rather than making the two-and-a-half-hour buggy ride to Meridian, many of the town folk were taking the morning train to Meridian and returning on the late train that night. The M&O was kind enough to delay the last train back to Lockhart; it usually left

Meridian at five o'clock each day, but on that day it would not leave until eleven o'clock. Everyone could enjoy the fireworks and not worry about traveling in the dark.

I had thought about asking off for the day and going with James and Junius to Meridian, but decided against it. Even after a year, I didn't have all of my strength back and found that by late afternoon I was pretty exhausted. I didn't think I could keep up with them, and I didn't want to slow them down. So I stayed and helped out at the station.

The regular teller was off for the day and Mr. Matthews and Richard were at the window selling tickets as fast as they could. Richard was the assistant station manager and the only person, except for Mr. Matthews, who was proficient at Morse code. Usually there was not a line to buy tickets in our tiny depot, but today there were at least thirty customers anxiously waiting to catch the train. While Mr. Matthews and Richard were busy with selling tickets, I was behind the counter helping with seat assignments, making sure everyone had a seat.

Suddenly the telegraph began to click out a message. At that very instant Mrs. Hobgood, who was next in line, slammed her handbag on the counter and began complaining to Mr. Matthews—she was a rather large lady, and liked to push her weight around. (figuratively, not literally!)

"Mr. Matthews," she said, "we have been waiting entirely too long and if you don't hurry, we are going to miss the train."

Her husband, a slight, quiet sort of fellow, was standing behind her with hat in hand staring at the floor, apology written all over his face.

"Everything is going to be fine," Mr. Matthews reassured her. "We won't let the train leave until everyone is on board."

As soon as the Hobgoods were taken care of Mr. Matthews called out, "Richard, I missed that message. Did you get it?"

"No, sir, I didn't," he answered.

"Mr. Matthews," I chirped in, "that was Meridian. They wanted you to remind everyone that the last train back tonight would leave at eleven o'clock sharp. All the hotel rooms in town are full, and if anyone misses the train, they will most likely be sleeping on the ground."

Mr. Matthews and Richard both stopped what they were doing and looked up with their mouths open, astonishment written on their faces.

"Ollie?!" Mr. Matthews said.

"Yes, sir?"

"Did you do that in your head?"

"Yes, sir."

"No pencil or paper?"

"No, sir."

They both shook their heads in disbelief, and then went back to selling tickets.

As soon as the train left and the station was quiet, Mr. Matthews sat down at the telegraph key and motioned to me. "Ollie, come over here for a minute."

"Yes, sir," I replied.

He tapped out a message. "There," he said. "Now listen to this." He began to tap out another message. "What did I say?"

"Well, first off, you sent a wire telling them to disregard messages for the next few minutes. Then you said that you wish that you could have gone to Meridian today. That the celebration and festivities were going to be a lot of fun."

"Unbelievable!" Mr. Matthews exclaimed. "How long have you been studying this? Three weeks? Ollie, it took me years to do what you just did!"

He stood up and motioned for me to sit down. "Have a seat. Now, you send a wire. Let's see how well you transmit."

I tapped out slowly, My name is Ollie Parker in Lockhart. Stop. Can you hear me? Stop.

"Not bad at all," he said as he clapped his hands. "In fact, that was very well done. Ollie, you have a gift. There are very few people who can master telegraph that quickly and even fewer who have the ability to do it without writing it down."

At that moment the key began to click: Message received. Stop.

"Wow," I exclaimed. "They were listening in Meridian! They heard what I was saying!"

"Yes, they heard it all," he said. "Something to always keep in mind. Don't send anything over the wire that you don't want everyone in the world to hear. There's nothing private on the wire. Everyone in the station can hear it."

That was advice that did me well for over fifty years.

"Ollie, would you like to take over the telegraph? Send and receive all the messages for the rest of the summer?"

"Yes, sir!" I exclaimed. "I would like that very much!"

Chapter 4

The Struggles

That was the beginning of my life as a telegrapher. For the rest of that summer, I was responsible for the telegraph, sending and receiving messages—getting more proficient with each passing day. And I loved it! I couldn't wait to get to work each morning, and I hated to leave each afternoon. That fall I worked most afternoons after school and most Saturday mornings. This continued for the next four years, until I finished school, and then I was hired full time by Mr. Matthews.

I had found my life's work. Through the prayers and cares of my family, primarily my grandmother, and the encouragement of Mr. Matthews, life was good. I had something to pour my life into, something that was fulfilling.

But still I felt inadequate. Learning to function, to do simple everyday tasks with one arm, was a struggle. A simple thing like washing my hands—or rather hand—was no simple duty. I soon found that cleaning the *back* of my hand would not happen. Lather up the palm and fingers and rinse. That was it unless someone else washed my hand. And washing my face? A one-handed face wash just doesn't do it!

Dressing was a little difficult, but I quickly learned how to slip my arm into the sleeve, lift my arm up so that the shirt would slide down, and then reach over my armless shoulder and pull the shirt around. It looks a little awkward, but it works.

But tying my shoes? Impossible! I used to leave my shoes tied loosely, so I could easily slip my feet in. I never did get used to loosely fitting shoes. Then ten years ago, in the mid 1930s, when Mr. Bass and Mr. Spaulding imported the idea of slip-on shoes from the Norwegians, I thought I had died and gone to heaven! I now wear my Weejuns everywhere I go.

And tying my tie? I surprised myself! I became quite innovative, and soon could throw a fairly decent half-Windsor. And it's not a bad looking knot, even if I say so myself!

I also found that eating was going to be a challenge. While I was recuperating in bed, family members initially fed me. I was too weak to do almost anything. As I got stronger and fed myself, my food was served to me cut up into bite-sized pieces. When I was strong enough to get up and eat at the table, I learned that I still needed help. I couldn't cut up my food: it takes two hands— both a knife and a fork—to get the job done. It took me a while to get over my hesitation of asking someone to do it for me, but now I will even ask a stranger if I'm in a bind.

And a sandwich? Oh how I miss grabbing it with both hands and chomping down! It just doesn't taste the same with one hand! And a steak? A steak isn't a steak when it's in little bite-sized pieces on a plate. But I do what I have to do.

Heavy, manual labor—the "real" work that separated the men from the women and the weak—was out of the question. I remember watching Junius put both hands to the plow behind an old mule, or toss a bale of hay up on a wagon with his hands. My stomach would knot up, not from jealousy, but from feelings of inadequacy and uselessness. Simple tasks that he did easily were impossible for me.

And then there is the cosmetic side of amputation. I found this to be as hard to deal with as the physical limitations of my loss.

When someone is different—different for any reason—looks different, walks differently, acts differently, dresses differently, or is missing something, eyes naturally shift to him. And most of the time the one receiving the stares doesn't like it. He doesn't like being different, and he likes being noticed even less. It must be human nature to want to fit in and look like everyone else—to be part of the crowd.

Around friends and family it was not a problem. Everyone got used to the way I was and soon stopped staring. I think the term used now is "conditioned." They became conditioned and no longer focused on my defect—or even saw it. (I remember a lady at church years ago who had a large, ugly, hairy mole on her chin. I had gotten so used to seeing that thing week after week, that after a while I no longer "saw" it. One day after church someone commented about her mole, and with all honesty and with a straight face, I said, "What mole?")

When I was among strangers, I was very self-conscious. I felt as though I were always the object of stares and whispers. Children tended to be the worst, and the most vocal. They are naturally curious and haven't learned the social skills to keep their thoughts to themselves. Their stares are not subtle: they will walk right up to me, stand two feet away with their mouths open, and stare. And then there are the questions. If I have heard it once, I have heard it a thousand times, "Mommy, why does that man have just one arm?" I remember one child staring at me for a moment and saying, "Mister, you can't clap your hands."

But adults can be just as insensitive, and nosy. Why is it that total strangers feel that it is okay to stop me and ask what happened to my arm? I sometimes think that a missing appendage equates to fair game for conversation. It doesn't matter that my face is buried in a newspaper, or that I'm trying to take a nap on a train. "Excuse me, sir. Ah, excuse me. Do you mind telling me how you lost your arm?" And there is the most bizarre question of all. "How does it feel to have only one arm?" I have been asked that question hundreds of times, and I still don't know how to answer it.

Another problem is what I call the "baby bird" effect. In a nest of baby birds, there is sometimes a discrepancy in the size and health of the little fledglings. The strong are able to fight more effectively for food, and with time the strong get stronger and the weak get weaker. The strong will eventually push the weak out of the nest. They are not being cruel: they are just increasing their chances of survival. Thankfully, I rarely saw this "baby bird" effect—domination of the weak by the strong. With us humans, we call it "being a bully." Lockhart was too small and everyone knew me and treated me with respect.

But it did happen one time. It was in the fall, two years after the accident. School was back in full swing, and I had settled into life without my arm and was able to function fairly well. I was slowly learning to do things with one hand that everyone else did with ease with two—or learning to accept that I could never do them. All of my friends had become accustomed to my new appearance and had begun treating me as one of the crowd.

In early October, a new family, the Crameses, moved into town, and the next day Lester Crames showed up at school. Lester was big. He must have been six inches taller than the rest of us and outweighed me by fifty pounds. When he walked into the classroom that day everyone knew he was trouble. There was a scowl on his face that said, "You bother me and you will pay for it."

The entire morning Lester acted bored, not paying attention to anything the teacher said, slouching in his chair. He continually tapped his pencil on the desk, seeming to dare the teacher to say something.

As the morning progressed, he started looking at me. Every minute or two he would glance over at me and sneer. I didn't know what to think, but it began to bother me. This guy doesn't even know me but already seems to dislike me.

As we were walking outside for lunch, Lester came up behind me and pushed me down the steps. He began laughing and said, "Hey, freak. Don't you know how to stand up?"

Thankfully, the only thing that was hurt was my pride.

Suddenly James, Junius, and a couple of the other guys were on top of Lester like warts on a hog, and were beating the stuffing out of him. If the teacher had not broken it up, I think they would have killed him.

After his little attitude adjustment, Lester never bothered me again. In fact, his manners and attentiveness in school improved greatly, and he eventually settled in as one of the crowd. He and I actually became good friends.

As far as I can remember, that was the only time in my life that I was ever bullied because of my handicap.

The desire to be whole is a very strong emotion, and functional wholeness is what we really desire—the ability to do the physical things that everyone else is doing. But if functional wholeness is not possible, then we will sometimes settle for cosmetic wholeness—we want to at least look like we are whole. That's where prosthetics come in.

Artificial limbs have been around since antiquity. As long as there have been missing appendages there have been attempts to replace them. Fingers, hands, arms, legs—you name it—have been carved out of wood or pounded out of metal to try to mimic what God so wondrously and effortlessly made. Not too long ago

I read that a mummy unearthed in Egypt had a wooden big toe. I doubt that it was very functional, but if painted the right color, it probably drew less attention than an empty spot in that fellow's sandal.

Thanks primarily to wars, and occasionally to accidents, there has been no lack of need for replacements. In 1866, the year after the Civil War ended, one fifth of the budget for the state of Mississippi went to supplying artificial limbs to maimed veterans.

Most early prosthetics probably had more to do with function than with aesthetics. A peg-leg is primarily for function. But then, there is some cosmetic benefit: a pants leg looks much better over a piece of wood, as opposed to just flapping in the breeze.

The artificial hand and arm are different. Until recently it has been about the cosmetic effect. Function, for the most part, was out of the question. There's a big difference in using a wooden leg to prop a fellow up as opposed to getting any realistic function out of a wooden hand. Now, there has been the hook in an attempt to give some function, but it comes up woefully short, and sharp.

But because of the recent war, the functionality of the artificial upper extremity is getting a boost. (I hate to say thanks to the war, because no one should be grateful for the maiming and dismemberment that this horrible war has brought.) This year, 1945, the Artificial Limb Program was started by the National Academy of Sciences, and promises to bring utility to artificial limbs that in the past has been only a dream.

In 1905, fifteen years after the accident, I decided to purchase an artificial arm. Prior to that I had not even considered it. Yes, I would have liked to have blended in a little better, looked more like everyone else, but the idea of a heavy wooden arm strapped to my shoulder ... It would have been more trouble than it was worth.

But I came across a book, by A. A. Marks, *Manual of Artificial Limbs, Artificial Toes, Feet, Legs, Fingers, Hands, Arms, for Amputations and Deformities, Appliances for Excision, Fractures, and other Disabilities of Lower and Upper Extremities, Suggestions on Amputations, Treatment of Stumps, History, etc., etc., etc., 1905,* and it got me thinking.

Mr. Marks of New York had been in the business of prosthetics for over fifty years, and his son, George Edwin Marks, was now running the company. Their company had been one of the largest suppliers of artificial limbs in the United States and the world for years. The manual had two hundred and fifty-seven pages of descriptions, illustrations, and recommendations for use of their devices, followed by one hundred and fifty-eight pages of testimonials—*almost eight hundred of them*—from satisfied customers and doctors.

The testimonials were fascinating. There were letters from all over the world—Mexico, Canada, England, South Africa, Holland, and even Tokyo, Japan. All of them proclaimed the benefits of their prostheses, encouraging others who had suffered as they had to join them in experiencing the wonders of modern medicine. The people ranged from the Honorable D. B. Henderson, Speaker of the House in Washington, D.C.; to a North Dakota Sioux Indian chief, who went from being an invalid to serving as leader of his nation thanks to his new leg; to the everyday run-of-the-mill factory worker, housewife, and child. There was one from a policeman in New York City, who stated that on more than one occasion he had used his arm as a club with very good results. The recipient of one of the blows felt as if he had been hit with a cannon ball.

I studied the chapters on prosthetic hands and arms, and read and reread the testimonials of the arm and hand amputees. Each seemed to have one observation in common: their artificial appendage looked so natural that many people never noticed or realized that it was not real. Oh, the thought of at least appearing whole again! Hope welled up within me!

The shoulder-joint prosthetic arm looked so real in the illustration. A leather harness and straps secured it to the shoulder, and under a shirt or coat, it appeared indistinguishable from the natural. The hand was made of rubber and could be removed and replaced with a hook, a grasper, or several other functional devices. And surprisingly, the entire structure weighed only two and a half pounds and cost only seventy-five dollars.

For weeks I mulled over whether to order it. I filled out the order form in the back of the catalog, but could not bring myself to mail it. Ambivalence and apprehension stopped me dead in my tracks. Yes, I wanted an arm, even if it was fake. Yes, I desperately wanted to look like everyone else. Why, I even dreamed about walking down the street and riding on the train with a new arm, and no one was staring at me.

But my problem was that I worried about what family and friends would say or think. I had been without my left arm for fifteen years—longer than I had had it. I could function quite well. In my work, a prosthesis would be of no real use. The telegraph key needs only one hand to operate it. My friends and family had gotten used to me without it, and they treated me as normal as the next fellow. Thus my dilemma—everyone would know that my new arm was a cosmetic purchase, just for looks. Would they think I was being silly? Would they make fun of me behind my back?

I kept thinking about Mr. Dockins and his toupee. Mr. Dockins was an older gentleman in Lockhart who had been slowly losing his hair for years. It was such a gradual process that no one really seemed to notice it. But he had become quite slick-headed. His baldness didn't bother any of us, and we assumed that it didn't bother him either.

Well, one day a man showed up at church with a head of hair so thick and black that it looked as if a horse's mane were growing on his head. Everyone was whispering, wondering who this odd-looking new arrival to our town could be. Papa, always the gentleman, went over and introduced himself to this stranger, and lo and behold, it was Mr. Dockins!

That Sunday I don't think anyone, including the preacher, remembered what the sermon was about. The church was too much abuzz with whispers and snickering, no one giving any thought to the Scriptures. Even the preacher was having a hard time staying on track. As we left the church, everyone was quiet. No one dared speak, especially to Mr. Dockins, in fear of bursting out in laughter.

The talk of the town the next week was Mr. Dockins and his horsehair rug. I think there were enough jokes made up about his new head warmer to fill a book. Well, he wore that thing for another two weeks, and then it disappeared as suddenly as it appeared. I suppose with no one commenting on his newfound hair, and with the smiling glances upward as people spoke to him, he realized the toupee was not a good idea.

For several nights I lay awake worrying that I would get the same response as poor Mr. Dockins. I so wanted to look whole, but the idea of being ridiculed or made fun of was overpowering. I decided I needed a little free advice from my grandmother. She always seemed to have the right answer to life's troubling questions.

I stopped by Mamaw's cottage one afternoon after work for coffee and a piece of cake before heading home—a practice that I had started years ago while still in school. She always had something fresh out of the oven for me to snack on.

As she cut me a generous piece of cake, I poured us both a cup of coffee, and we sat down at the table to visit. Conversation, for the most part, was small talk about my day at the depot and about what was happening around our little town. I was a little hesitant to bring up the topic of the arm, afraid of what she might say, but I knew there was no way I was going to order an arm without getting her opinion.

As I finished my cake, I said cautiously, "Mamaw, I was looking through the neatest book the other day—a book of prosthetics..."

"Well, I'm glad to hear you are reading your Bible," Mamaw interrupted as she stood up, walked over to the stove, and picked up the pot of coffee. "There's no better reading than the Good Book, and the books of prophesy in the Old Testament are wonderful reading. I try to read through each of them at least once a year. The book of Isaiah is my favorite—with all those predictions about the coming of Christ.

"Now, which of the books of prophesy are you referring to?" she asked as she warmed up my coffee and sat back down.

"No, ma'm," I said. "Not prophetics. *Prosthetics*. A book of prosthetics—artificial limbs—wooden and rubber arms and legs and such."

"Oh," she said, sounding a little confused.

"Mamaw," I said, then I took a sip of coffee, trying to show as little apprehension as possible. "What would you think about me getting an artificial arm?"

She thought for a minute and said, "Ollie, the important thing is what do *you* think about it?"

Mamaw was always good at turning the tables and making me make my own decisions.

"Mamaw, this book is so neat." I pulled it out of my pocket and started showing it to her. "The arms look so real and lifelike. And the testimonials in the back of the book—everyone seems so happy with their product."

Mamaw took the book and looked through the pages on arms. "Why, these are truly amazing—so lifelike."

"I can't decide whether to get one or not."

As she closed the book, she looked up at me, and with a curious tone in her voice asked, "What is your concern?" She must have sensed my apprehension.

I lowered my head. "Mamaw, I'm afraid people will make fun of me."

"What?!" she said with an astonished look on her face. "Make fun of you because you have an artificial arm?"

"Yes, ma'm. I hate the stares that I get when I'm out and about. Mamaw, you don't know how much I wish that I could blend in—just be part of the crowd—even if the arm isn't of any use. Right now I stick out like a sore thumb. But if I show up with a wooden arm, what will my friends think? I'm afraid they will think I'm being self-conscious. Do you remember when Mr. Dockins had his toupee? I don't want people laughing at me like that."

Mamaw let out a loud sigh and shook her head. "Ollie, if you think that will happen, you are selling your family and friends very short. There's a big difference in a poor-fitting wig and a replacement for a missing arm. Why, I can't believe you have gotten yourself all worked up over this. You have nothing at all to be concerned about. We care about you too much. I dare say that no one, and I mean *no one*, would have anything but positive thoughts and remarks. Buy one of those things, and enjoy it!"

She then laughed, "But then, if someone does laugh at you, you have my permission to take that piece of wood off and beat him over the head with it!"

The next day I took the order form to the post office, obtained a money order for seventy-five dollars, and mailed them both to A. A. Marks Company in New York. Three weeks later my package arrived, and I had my new arm.

When I first removed it from the package, I remember thinking how strange—and how fake—it looked. The arm itself was made of wood and was painted the color of flesh. There was a leather harness at the shoulder end and a removable rubber hand at the other end. The elbow was slightly bent to give it a "natural look" when walking.

I remember Mamaw burst out laughing the first time she saw it lying on my bed. She covered her mouth, shook her head, and apologized, but couldn't stop laughing. She said she was imagining that harness strapped to the face of a horse.

Could this thing really fool anyone? Surprisingly it did—even without a coat. When I walked down the street, most strangers would not give me a second glance—so unlike the reaction I used to get.

Initially the contraption was a little difficult to strap on, and I needed assistance to get it on properly. But with a little practice, I was soon able to do it by myself.

And Mamaw was right. No one ever laughed. I never once felt that my family and friends were anything but supportive.

But a funny thing: after a few months I stopped wearing it at home. Even though it was light, it was a little cumbersome and in the way. So around the house I would take it off. And after about a year I stopped wearing it to work—and to church—and to shop. Eventually I wore it only when I was going on a trip or expected to be around a lot of strangers. In those circumstances, I would strap it on, sit back, and enjoy my ability to blend in with the crowd.

I still have that old wooden arm, somewhere. In fact, it's the only prosthetic I ever owned. The harness and hand did have to be replaced a few years back. The leather had become brittle, and the rubber hand had turned black. Otherwise it's had very little maintenance. For going on forty years it's done me quite well. Come to think, though, I haven't had that thing on in at least four or five years. I guess in my old age self-consciousness has pretty much disappeared.

Chapter 5

The Bicycle

Two summers after the accident, the summer of my fifteenth year, I was introduced to the bicycle. Or rather it was introduced to me. Junius bought one.

Junius was not only my step-uncle, he was my best friend. I first met Junius when I was nine on a hot Sunday morning in the summer of 1887. A new family had recently moved to Lockhart from Tennessee—big news for a community of fewer than a hundred citizens—the Bludworths: T. W., his wife Charlotte, and their seven children, Lizzie, Lottie, James, John, Timothy, Thomas, and Junius.

I remember thinking, "Junius! How odd! Never heard anything so strange." As children, we kidded Junius about his name. "Where in the world did your parents come up with such a crazy name? Couldn't they find at least one more Christian name to go with your brothers? Junius! They must have thought you looked like a Roman gladiator when you were born."

I learned later that the name, Junius, was a common family name of the Bludworths going back for generations. I also found out that Junius *is* a biblical name, but spelled Junias in Romans 16:7.

At the Lockhart Methodist Church that Sunday in July 1887, while I was meeting Junius, Papa was meeting his sister, nineteen-year-old Lizzie Bludworth. Papa, at age thirty-one, had been a widower for about a year and a half and was in need of a wife.

Mama had died in 1886 at age twenty-six, leaving Papa with three young children to care for. I was eight and my two sisters, Maude and Gussie, were four and eighteen months. Prior to her death our existence had been idyllic, or at least that's the way I remember the early years of my childhood: parents who loved me dearly and a home filled with laughter and peace. Mama and I were very close, and I don't think I have ever truly gotten over her death.

I remember those first few months without Mama were so lonely and unhappy, almost unbearable. Papa was distraught with losing his beautiful wife, the girls cried constantly for their mother, and I felt as if my very heart and soul had been ripped out. Papa tried as hard as he could to be both father and mother, but with little success on the mother side. Thankfully, Mamaw moved in with us, took over the motherly duties, and became the glue that put our family back together again.

Within a few months of their meeting, Papa and Lizzie were married, and Lizzie became mother to my sisters and me.

For the next twenty years Lizzie had babies—seven of them. Sadly, not a single one of those angels lived past infancy. Times were hard back then, especially for little ones: no antibiotics, no vaccines—just prayer and loving care. Illnesses that we now look at as minor problems were the cause of many a heartache and sorrow, as was the case with our family—at least that is the story the family tells. I often wonder how our family survived those times of grief. Lizzie never speaks of those little ones; it's as if those years and those babies never existed. Their only reminder is a row of tiny gravestones in Lockhart Cemetery.

Junius, his brother James, and I were the best of friends from the moment we met. In a small town like Lockhart, there usually isn't an overabundance of children of the same age, so kids within a year of each other usually become best friends. But I think that the three of us would have been best pals even if we had lived in a city of a million. We had such great times wandering the deep pine forests of Lauderdale County, fishing, and swimming all summer long.

Having step-uncles my same age was sometimes a little confusing. Junius, James, and I used to have so much fun with that little fact. We were always together, and people who didn't know us very well would ask if we were brothers. Junius would smile, pump out his chest, and say, "James and I are, but this little fellow here is my brother-in-law's wife's stepson." People would say "Oh," scratch their heads, and walk away with the most puzzled look on their faces.

We stayed best of friends, even after the accident.

For months all Junius had talked about was getting a bicycle. He read everything he could about this strange machine that was rapidly taking the world by storm. Every advertisement and article about bicycles in the *Meridian Star* he cut out and studied and reread. He saved every penny he earned working at the depot and finally took the train to Meridian one Saturday morning and came back that afternoon with a brand new Crescent bicycle.

I was working at the depot that afternoon when he arrived with his trophy, and it seemed that everyone in town was there to greet him. This was the first bicycle in Lockhart, and it was big news. Everyone wanted to get a glimpse of it.

Now, it wasn't as though no one had ever seen a bicycle. There were plenty of them in Meridian, and several bicycle clubs had been formed which roamed the countryside on weekends.

Every so often one of the clubs would come riding through Lockhart and stop at the depot or the general store for a rest. Occasionally on a hot summer's day a worn-out rider would buy a one-way ticket back to Meridian and load himself and his cycle for a much more relaxed trip home.

But Junius was the first person in Lockhart to actually own one.

Later that afternoon Junius came over to the house to give me a closer look at his new purchase. It was something to look at. The frame was painted a bright red, and the handlebars were shiny silver.

As I studied it, I shook my head and said, "Junius, isn't this thing dangerous? I've heard about people falling off of these things and breaking bones, and even being killed."

"Naw," Junius replied as he stroked the handlebars. "These new bicycles are as safe as can be. Now, the old ones were a different story."

Junius reached into his pocket and pulled out several wrinkled pieces of newspaper. One was titled *The Bicycle—Transportation of the Future*. It was a short history of the bicycle and had pictures showing prototypes from the earliest stages of development to the latest.

"See this one," Junius said as he pointed to one of the pictures. "This was one of the forerunners of the modern bicycle. It's called a velocipede, or a dandy horse. As you can see, there are no pedals. The rider would push himself along with his feet and glide. On a flat surface it could go about eight miles in an hour. Down a hill, it could really go. But watch out! There were no brakes."

He pointed to another picture of a strange contraption with a large front wheel and a small back wheel. "This one is called a penny-farthing. It's also called a bone-shaker because the ride is so rough. It has pedals and can go pretty fast, but it can be fairly dangerous. See how high up that seat is? You fall off that at any speed and you're liable to break a bone." Junius began to laugh. "In England a wreck on one of these is called taking a header, because you usually fall forward and land on your head."

Junius pointed again to the paper. "Now, here is the first modern bicycle, a Rover. It came out seven years ago in 1885 and looks just like mine."

He folded up the paper and put it back in his pocket. "Mine is a Crescent, made right here in the U.S.," he said as he stroked the handlebar again. "As you can see, it has both wheels the same size and pedals with a chain attached to gears on the back wheel. And look at these tires—pneumatic tires, full of air. A guy named Dunlop came up with it in 1888. Makes for a much softer, smoother ride than a metal wheel, or even a solid rubber tire."

Junius and I circled the cycle several times admiring it. He was mighty proud of his purchase and enjoyed showing it off.

"The bicycle is selling by the hundreds of thousands in Europe and in the U.S., and in a couple of years they expect the bicycle to replace the horse."

The horse was replaced, but not by the bicycle. The automobile was making its emergence at the same time and with the development of an affordable and reliable automobile less than two decades later, the horse—powerhouse for man from the time of creation—was relegated to sport and pleasure riding, and the bicycle—to a recreational vehicle for children.

Junius climbed onto his bicycle and circled the yard a couple of times. It looked so easy and so much fun. Oh, I wished that I could ride one! Envy began to creep into my soul.

Junius stopped in front of me and said, "You want to try it out?"

My envy suddenly disappeared and fear replaced it. "I—I better not."

Riding a bicycle looked like a two-armed task, and I did not want to make a fool of myself, or get hurt.

"Ollie, it's not hard. Once you get going it kind of rides itself. Get on and I'll run along beside you and help balance it until you get the hang of it."

"But I can't—I can't hold on with just one arm. I'll fall," I said.

"You'll find that it is easier than you think, even with one arm," Junius said. "We'll start out slow. Just sit on it for a minute. Get the feel of it."

Even though I was scared to death, I really did want to try, so I mustered up my courage.

"Okay, but please don't let me fall."

After another moment, I took a deep breath, grabbed the right handlebar with my hand, and swung my leg over and sat down on the seat.

"There," Junius said. "That's a start. Now, just sit there and get used to it."

I sat there for a minute and thought, *This isn't too bad*. But we were not yet moving.

"Now, if you had two hands, you would lean a little forward, putting weight on the front as you ride. But with only one, you're going to need to sit up straight and use your one hand to steer it.

"Push the handlebar back and forth," he continued. "That will make you go left or right."

The way he was instructing, I would wonder if he had been practicing one-handed bicycling before he came to visit.

"The next step is to start rolling and put your feet on the pedals. I'll hold on and not let you fall."

He placed his left hand on the left handlebar and his right on the back of the seat and gently pushed me forward. I started rolling. I was terrified! What if I fall and break my one good arm? I will really be in a fix.

"No, Junius, stop! I'm going to fall."

"Ollie, I'm here. I won't let you fall. You're doing just fine. Put your feet on the pedals and start rotating them. If you go a little faster, you will feel more comfortable. It's strange, but the faster you go the more stable it feels."

He was right, as we got a little faster, I did feel more comfortable—or rather less terrified.

"Junius, don't you let go."

"I won't. You're doing great."

For about ten minutes I rode up and down the road with Junius running along beside me. My fear was slowly disappearing and I thought, *This is not bad.* I was actually starting to enjoy it. I would say that the wind in my face felt great as we raced along, but we weren't going that fast.

"Ollie, I'm going to let go of the handlebar and let you steer by yourself. I'll still have my hand on the seat. I won't let you fall."

Fear seized me again.

"Junius!"

"You're okay. Trust me."

He let go and surprisingly nothing happened. I didn't fall. I didn't even wobble.

Junius continued to run alongside of me with his hand on the seat. "Ollie, you're doing great. You've got the hang of it."

After another minute he said, "Now I want to tell you a couple of things. One that is obvious, the other is a secret. The obvious: I am about to collapse. You are running me to death, and I can hardly catch my breath!" He was panting pretty hard as he ran along. "The secret: I'm not supporting the bicycle at all. I am only resting my hand on the seat and doing nothing more. You don't need me anymore, and I'm going to let go."

With that, he let go and stopped running. He bent over and rested his hands on his knees and caught his breath.

Panic again grabbed me. "Junius!"

"You don't need me," he said as he panted. "You're fine."

Surprisingly, I *was* fine. But not *just* fine—I felt great! I did not fall, I didn't even falter. I couldn't believe it—this one-armed guy had mastered the bicycle! I had done it! I continued to pedal and the bicycle continued to move. After a few minutes I circled back around to where Junius was standing and stopped.

"Junius, thanks so much! That was fantastic! And thanks for having the faith and patience to teach me. I haven't had that much fun in ages!"

I climbed off the bicycle and said, "Here you go. But you've got to promise to let me ride it again." I stroked the handlebar the way Junius had done and thought, *I sure would like to have one of these.*

I looked up at Junius and was caught off guard with what I saw. His lip was quivering and there were tears in his eyes.

"Ollie," Junius said as he tried not to cry, "I want you to have it. It's yours."

"No, Junius!" I exclaimed, completely shocked at the offer. "This is yours! You worked for it. You saved for it. You can't just give it away."

"I'm not just giving it away. I'm giving it to you. To my best friend. You don't know how much it would mean to me for you to take it." He began to cry. "Ollie, I'm so sorry! I can't bring your arm back, but I..."

I wanted to say, "Junius, please, not again. How many times do I have to tell you it's okay. I have forgiven you..."

But no, that is not true. I can't say that I have forgiven him, because I never blamed him in the first place. It was not his fault. Sometimes things just happen. Circumstances out of our control lead to horrible unfortunate outcomes. No one is at fault. Yes, sometimes, as with the case of my accident, someone or something starts the event that proceeds to disaster, but it is not that person's fault. Junius didn't mean to slip. And what was I to do? Stand there and let him get killed? I had never really blamed him and never will. He was my best friend!

I stood there trying to decide what to do. I was caught between my feelings. I was frustrated at him for asking me for forgiveness for the hundredth time. I was angered at the pity that I felt he was displaying. But then, I was overcome with love and admiration for my best friend who was offering me his most prized possession. He was still so burdened and overcome with guilt. And above all, I did not want to hurt him by refusing his gift. I knew his offer was genuine and to refuse would be the easiest for me, but the hardest for him.

I began to tear up. "Junius, it's okay." Little did I know that I would be repeating that statement again and again for the rest of my life.

I put my hand on his shoulder and said. "I will take it on one condition. We both start saving right now and when we have saved enough, we will both go to Meridian and buy one for you."

Junius perked up and began to smile. "That's a deal."

Six months later, on a beautiful Saturday morning in late fall, we loaded up "my" bicycle on the train bound for Meridian and rode back to Lockhart on our matching Crescents. As we raced along, the wind in my face truly felt great!

Chapter 6

Sam

His name was Sam—Sam Parker. Sam had been around as long as I could remember. In spite of the same last name, we weren't related. In fact, when he was born he was just Sam—the "Parker" was added sometime after the Civil War ended and the slaves were freed. Sam had belonged to my grandfather.

My grandfather, John Woods Parker, was born in 1807 and settled in the Lockhart area around 1830. In September of that year one of the nation's largest Indian relocation programs was started when the Treaty of Dancing Rabbit Creek was signed in present-day Noxubee County, Mississippi. Eleven million acres of Choctaw land in Mississippi and Alabama was ceded to the United States government, and fifteen thousand members of the Choctaw nation were moved to Oklahoma.

My grandfather happened to be "where the rabbits gather to dance" when the treaty with Chief Greenwood LeFlore and Chief Musholatubbee was negotiated, and he was able to buy up quite a large section of the ceded land in the northern part of present-day Lauderdale County.

He and his first wife carved a plantation out of the wilderness and within a few years were farming several hundred acres of cotton with the help of a small army of slaves. His first wife died in

1850 without providing an heir, and within a year he married my grandmother—Mamaw, Augusta Byron, twenty-two years his junior, who gave him a steady supply of healthy children. My father was the second, born in 1853.

I don't really remember much about my grandfather; I was only four when he died in 1882. But I do remember his pipe and his smell—the strong, sweet smell of good, aged tobacco. Even after the War, when there was very little money, he would settle for nothing but the best tobacco he could find. On the bowl of his pipe was carved a family of deer: a doe with her fawn and a buck with a magnificent rack, all looking up. In my four-year-old imagination, they were looking at the clouds in the sky when the pipe was lit. I often wonder what happened to that old pipe.

The Civil War was unkind to my grandfather. Like so many landowners in the South, he lost everything. His home was burned by Sherman's men after the fall of Vicksburg as they marched to Atlanta, and at the end of the War his land was divided in parcels by the occupying forces and auctioned off to "pay taxes." He and his young wife and children were forced to move from Lockhart to Meridian to find work. His former slaves, including Sam and his family, were left to fend for themselves.

The Parkers remained away from Lockhart until my twenty-three-year-old father returned in 1876, purchased the general store, and married my mother. When Papa returned to Lockhart, he found that Sam was still there, working a small plot of land, barely able to keep his family from starving. Sam soon took over the workings of our small farm, doing most of the odd jobs needed to keep it going while Papa ran the general store. He essentially became my father's right-hand man. After the accident, he became *my* left hand.

Sam was a big man. He was at least six-foot-three, and weighed two hundred and seventy-five pounds. To a thirteen-year-old like me, he was a giant. His arms were as big around as my waist, and his shoulders were so wide that he had to turn sideways to go through most doors. I never saw him in a shirt that fit; they were all hand-me-downs from much smaller white men. Even in his sixties, he was as strong as an ox.

Sam was black, one of the blackest men I had ever seen. Papa once said that he was as dark as the inside of the cellar on a moonless night. His hair was starting to turn white but still as thick as wool. I used to kid him that with his "crown of silver" he could never hide from me in the dark.

Sam taught me the art of milking, as well as other skills of the farm. Papa was often too busy with the store, and Sam was there to fill his place. The two of us spent many a hot summer day working in the barn or in the garden, and many a late afternoon fishing on the banks of Ponta Creek.

After my accident Sam took on an even greater role for our farm. The chores that I had been doing—milking the cow, feeding the chickens, weeding the garden, and such—were turned over to him. And when Dr. Knox finally said that I could get out of bed, it was Sam who carried me downstairs until I was strong enough to come down by myself.

Late one afternoon in early October Sam helped me downstairs, but instead of stopping at the couch in the parlor as he usually did, he took me outside and rested me on the porch swing. Mamaw had gotten Dr. Knox's permission to let me go outside, hoping that some fresh air and sunshine would help the melancholy that I had been experiencing. I had started feeling pretty sorry for myself, and the confines of the house didn't help. This was the first time I had seen sunshine since the accident.

"Mister Ollie," Sam said as he fluffed a pillow behind my back, "is this gonna be okay? We can get some more pillows if you want."

"Thanks, Sam," I said. "This is fine."

It was a little cool, so Sam went back inside and came out with an old quilt. He placed it over me and tucked it around me.

"This will keep you from getting cold," he said. "We don't need you getting a chill."

Sam then sat down in one of the wicker rocking chairs and slowly began to rock. The boards on the porch began to creak as he went back and forth.

"Mister Ollie, cold weather is gonna be here soon. That breeze from the north says it's on its way. The sun, too, it's getting low in the sky, starting to draw the heat away to the south." Sam rubbed his hands together. "I like the cold, especially after such a hot summer. Give me that cold over the heat any day. You can wrap up in a blanket when it's cold, but you can't take off your skin when it's hot."

Sam was probably waiting for a response, but I really didn't feel like talking. I just sat there, staring out into the yard.

Sam continued to rock; the creaking seemingly getting louder and louder. After a minute he said, "The fish ought to be biting soon. A cool breeze brings them to the surface, gets them jumping good. Mister Ollie, we'll have you down at the creek with a pole in your hand before you know it. They'll be grabbing your hook before it has time to hit the water."

I felt my stomach knot up. Sam was right about one thing. It would always be "my hand" and not "my hands." I sat silently. The fresh air and sunshine were losing out to self-pity.

The creaking continued to get even louder, almost deafening.

"And Mister Ollie, the rabbits will start moving, too. The cold brings them out of the thickets. We'll have you down in the pasture in no time, shooting us a big one. Can't wait for a taste of your grandma's rabbit stew!"

Me and a gun? He's got to be crazy! I can't hold a gun against my shoulder, much less aim it and pull the trigger!

I had had enough. I couldn't stand it any longer.

"Sam, would you please be quiet! Your talking is driving me crazy! I'm not going fishing, and I'm not going hunting—not ever again! And would you please stop rocking that stupid chair!"

Sam stopped rocking. "Mister Ollie, I'm sorry." He looked down, and his big shoulders drooped.

Shame suddenly grabbed me. Why did I say that? Sam was only trying to help. All he wanted to do was lift my spirits. That big fellow would never do anything to hurt me.

I started to cry.

"Mister Ollie," Sam said, "I'm sorry. I didn't mean to upset you."

"No, Sam," I said as I wiped my eyes. "It's not you. It's me. I'm mad and upset at the way I am, and I don't know what to do. I want to be whole again. I want to be able to do everything I used to do. I can't do anything: I can't go fishing; I can't go hunting. Why, I can't even bait a hook, much less shoot a gun. And I keep thinking about the rest of my life. I don't see how I'll ever amount to anything. I'm not worth a thing."

Sam sat there for a minute not saying a word. He then slowly got up and came over to me and said, "Scoot yourself over and let me sit down beside you."

I scooted over on the swing, and he sat down. He then put his big arm around my shoulders. "Let me tell you a story. It's a long story, but it's a good story, because it's about me.

"Mister Ollie, when is your birthday?"

I was a little confused. A story about Sam and he's asking me my birthday?

"Sam, you know when my birthday is," I said. "Why, it's December fifth."

"What year was you born in?"

"Sam, you know that, too," I said, perturbed at his question. "You know as well as I do that I was born in 1877."

"Yes, I know it. I know it as well as I know my own..." He stopped in mid-sentence and looked over at me.

"Mister Ollie, I have to tell you something. I don't have any idea when my birthday is. Why, I don't even know for sure what year I was born."

I looked up at Sam, surprised and shocked. "I thought you were born on Christmas Day? That's what you told me."

"Well, I made it up. You see, when I was born, my mama was on a plantation somewhere in Carolina. All Cups could tell me—now Cups was my mama's name—well, all Cups could tell me was I was born on a Saturday and it was wintertime. She didn't know anything about months and keeping up with years—well, there was no reason. All she knew was cotton: planting cotton in the springtime, chopping cotton in the summer, and picking cotton in the fall. That was her life. She knew days of the week because Friday came before Saturday which came before Sunday which was the day of rest, 'the Lord's Day.' And Monday was back to the fields and Tuesday the next day in the fields. There was meaning to days of the week. Months and years meant nothing.

"When I was young, Cups and I was sold to your grandpa. Years later he told me he bought me in 1831 and at the time I looked to be about six years old. And Mister Ollie, everyone needs a birthday—a day that is special for you. So I picked December 25, 1825. Who better to share my birthday with than the Savior himself!

"As I said, I was born in Carolina. Never knew my pa, but Cups says his name was Ezra. They had been together only a year when he was sold off—sold off before I was born, and she never saw him again.

"And I don't know much about Cups's family either. She told me her mama lived her whole life in Carolina working in the fields, same as her. But her mama's mama—Cups's grandma— she was different. She had marks all over her face and back, curvy marks like an old quilt. 'Trouble marks' is what Cups would say. Trouble marks she got before she was stole from her family, put in chains, and put on a boat. She was a proud woman, and a fierce woman. Had been born free, like a wild stallion, Cups said, ridden down but never broke."

"How did she get into trouble back in Africa?" I asked.

"Oh, no, Mister Ollie, she was never in trouble," Sam shook his head. "They put trouble marks on them to tell where they come from."

Suddenly it dawned on me. He was not meaning "trouble" but "tribal"—tribal markings.

"Well, as I said, Cups and I was sold to your grandpa and brought here to Lockhart. We was here when there was nothing but piney trees as big around as a house. The men cleared up the land and soon there was fields of cotton and corn.

"For as long as I remember, I worked the fields beside Cups and the rest: planting, and chopping, and picking. It was my life.

"But there was times when the cotton and corn just needed to grow, or the picking was done, when we could wander the woods—fishing and swimming and hunting. Why, we used to play in your swimming hole down on Ponta Creek. And that rope swing down on the bank in that big oak tree, we put the first one there over fifty years ago. We sure had a lot of fun in the creeks and woods.

"We went hunting, but never did have a gun. We set traps, catching rabbits, birds, and foxes—small animals. But sometimes we trapped something that was more than we could handle.

"I remember one time—Why, I must have been about your age when this happened—I had a trap down there at the far end of the pasture," Sam pointed off in the distance. "It was twenty or thirty feet into the woods and I was always catching coons and possums in it. I went down there late one afternoon to check and, lo and behold, there was a wolf cub with his paw caught in the trap! Wolves were common in these parts back then, but we almost never saw them—they know how to hide good. But many a night we heard them howling in the distance—lonesome cries that would bring a chill right up your back.

"Well, I thought it might be fun to have a wolf cub as a pet. He was young enough to where he didn't snap and growl, and I reckoned I could keep him tame if I treated him right. So I walked over to him and was getting him loose when I heard something behind me. All of a sudden I realized I had made a dumb mistake. Where there's a baby animal, there's usually a mama animal."

Sam shook his head. "Mister Ollie, that's a mistake you don't ever want to make. Always remember that a mama's always close by."

He then began to laugh. "And that's good to remember when you start going courting after young ladies. But you'll find it's the papas that you have to watch out for, and not the mamas!

"Well, Mister Ollie, when I heard that noise, I knew I was in big trouble. I slowly turned my head and there thirty feet from me was the biggest, meanest looking animal I ever saw, growling at me with teeth as big as railroad spikes.

"I was scared to death and I didn't know what to do. There was no chance to run and no way to fight. Why, I had heard how a wolf can outrun a deer and then kill it with one bite to the neck. The only thing I could think of doing was to pray for Mighty Jesus to come save me.

"Well, just as that she-wolf was about to come after me, there was a loud crack! behind me, and she fell right over dead! I looked around and your grandpa was standing there with a gun still up to his shoulder.

"He slowly lowered that weapon and said, 'Sam, kill that pup before you become attached to it. It may sound harsh right now, but some wild things can never be tamed. That pup will bring you nothing but trouble.'

"To this day I still get the chills when I think about how close I came. Why your grandpa was there and why he had his gun with him..." Sam visibly shivered. "The good Lord was looking after me. And I never made that mistake again!

"Time went on and I soon grew to be a man. I worked the fields with Cups and the others, working hard and doing what I was told. Mister Ollie, I learned that's the best way to stay out of trouble—work hard and do what you're told. You do that and things go easy for you; don't do it and trouble will get you. It was hard work, but we was treated good.

"One day your grandpa made me boss of a work crew, and after awhile he made me boss of all the crews. I was mighty proud of that. I also married me a wife and began raising children—I had everything I needed or wanted.

"Well, your grandpa was buying up all the land around here and needed more hands to work the fields, so he went to Georgia and bought some new families of workers. He took me with him to help bring them back.

"Oh, was that something! We got on the train in Meridian and was in Atlanta before we could blink. You know, the tracks had just made it to these parts—been put down through Meridian only six or seven years before the War. Before that we would have been on a wagon for more than three weeks to get there.

"I was in with the bags and mail, but there was a window—trees and fields were going by so fast my eyes blurred. Mister Ollie, that's the only time I ever been in a train, and I don't plan on it happening again.

"The new hands settled in and worked the fields with the rest of us.

"After they was here for awhile, whispers started that one of them could read and write. We didn't know what to think because we never seen a slave who could read. He was about my age and could pick up a book—just like a white school boy—and read right from it. Well, he kept it a secret—didn't tell nobody, 'cause he knew it would bring him trouble. Mister Ollie, there was laws against slaves learning to read.

"He said he would teach me to read, but…" Sam shook his head. "I didn't need no trouble. There were tales of whippings and fingers getting chopped off for learning.

"He was plenty smart and told us 'bout things he heard in Atlanta. There was talk about freeing all the slaves. He told us that some slaves up north was already free, working and living just like white folk. There was to be a vote for a new president, and if a man name Lincoln won, all us slaves would be free.

"When he talked like that I was troubled. What would I do with freedom? I had everything I needed. Good work, good family, a boss that treated me good. But the more I thought about it, the more freedom got in my blood.

"I thought about Cups. Old and feeble. And her mama before her. They worked their whole lives in the fields and had nothing to show for it—nothing but a stooped back and hands no better than claws. But then I thought about Cups's grandma. A warrior woman who had known freedom—freedom that had been snatched away from her—freedom that kept her proud. I wanted to be proud like her. Go where I want, do what I want. Nobody to tell me different.

"In no time there was trouble in the air. There was talk of war, and then there was war. All the white boys were soon gone off to fight, and the only ones left was women, old folk, children, and slaves. Your grandpa was too old and your papa was too young, so they stayed.

"Those was hard times, but we still had food to eat and a roof over our heads. But that was about to change.

"One day the Yankee soldiers come through. They burned your grandpa's house to the ground. Took everything they could tote, and what they couldn't tote they tore up. They even burned the fields. Then the soldiers told us we was free—that we wasn't slaves no more. We could do whatever we want and go wherever we want.

"We was mighty happy with that news—for about two weeks. Then it started settling in—what was we to do with freedom? I learned fast that freedom don't mean nothing when you don't know what to do with it.

"Your grandpa and his family soon moved away. They had nothing but their own worries and had no time to worry about us. We was left with nothing but ourselves. Nobody to tell us what to do. Nobody to look out for us. Mister Ollie, we didn't even have land to work.

"Most everybody moved away, not knowing where to go or what to do. I don't know what came of them. I hope they made out alright. For me and my family, I didn't see no use leaving. If I was to starve, I would starve in a place I know.

"I started asking around for work. Well, Mr. Rawls—you remember him, he died a couple of years ago—he had a few acres that he let me work. Half of what I grew went to him. It was a high price, but it kept me and the family from starving. As I worked those fields, I felt no different than when I was a slave. I was free but there was no freedom in my heart or soul.

"Then, thank the Good Lord, your papa come back and bought the store. For me and my family, that was like Jesus coming back to Earth. Your papa hired me on and I been working for him since—now going on fifteen years. He treats me and my family real good, like your grandpa did before the War."

Sam sat silently for a minute. He then stood up and walked over to the porch rail. He leaned over it, looking out at the road that ran in front of the house—straining as though he were searching for something or someone. He then slowly turned his head to the right as though his gaze was fixed on someone walking along—walking along until he disappeared in the distance.

"Mister Ollie, I'm a free man—been free for going on twenty-five years. And being free, I can stop work anytime I want. I can pick up and leave anytime I want. I have freedom to do anything I want."

Sam turned around and looked at me. "Or do I?"

Sam let out a big sigh and shook his head. "Mister Ollie, it strikes me peculiar, but truth be known, I'm not a free man—no more free than I was thirty years ago, and no more free than when I worked for Mr. Rawls for those twelve years. People tell me I'm free, and I talk like I'm free, but in my soul I know I'm not. I'm a slave no different than I was before.

"You see, I can't leave, I'm sixty-five years old. I'm an old man. I can't read or write. I don't know nothing about business or numbers. All I know is hard work and farming—work where someone tells me what to do and when to do it. If I pick up, where do I go? And what do I do to feed myself? Nobody's gonna hire an old black man whose done wore out. No, I'm a slave to this place—always have been and always will be.

"Now, don't you hear me wrong, Mister Ollie. Your papa's been mighty good to me. He treats me right, even gives me respect. And if I want to pack up and leave right now, he wouldn't try stopping me."

Sam paused seemingly searching for the right word. "Opportunity. That's it—opportunity. That's what it boils down to. The problem is I've got no opportunity to do better. I've been placed right here with no way of ever getting out. And it's nobody's fault. I don't blame nobody for it, unless I want to blame the Good Lord for having me born a slave—and I'm sure not going to do that."

Sam was silent again. He rubbed the back of his neck as if he were hurting. He then looked over at me and chuckled. "Mister Ollie, I reckon you're wondering why in the world I told you my story."

It was beginning to cross my mind.

"Mister Ollie, I see me and you as having the same problem, but different. Right now you feel trapped. Your troubles have you around the neck, strangling you, and won't let go. You don't see how things will ever be good. But they will—because you have opportunity. That's where we are different. You have opportunity; I don't.

"Even with what happened to you—and it was terrible and I don't ever want go making light of it—you are gonna make something of yourself. You gonna get over this thing, learn to manage, and get on with life. I know you will because I know you, and I know you will take opportunity and use it.

"With what happened to you, you won't never be a farmer; you won't never work the fields. You won't never make a living by the sweat of your brow. And that's not all together bad. You see, times are changing. In the past that's what it took—sweat and dirt and hard work with your hands. But now it's different. The man who makes it good in this world does it with his thinking.

"And Mister Ollie, you can read and write, you got a good head on them shoulders, and you got goodness in your soul. Why, you are a success right now and don't even know it.

"Now, me—opportunity's not gonna ever knock on my door. At one time that bothered me—bothered me a lot. I was handed freedom, and it didn't taste good. It only meant hard times, and harder work, and more worry. I wondered what was wrong. Why didn't freedom treat me good like it did the white man? Opportunity—that was the answer. There has been no opportunity for me to do better.

"But that's okay. Life is good and I'm not to complain." Sam then smiled and pumped out his chest. "And the truth of it, there is hope and there is opportunity—for my grandchildren. Why, I can look at them and know it will be there for them and their children. They gonna have opportunities, plenty of them, Yes, opportunities that I could never dream of. Why, even now those little ones is in school, learning to read and write. They pick up a book and read like it's nobody's business. My, don't that just beat all! Makes me mighty proud! No, I'll never feel freedom in my soul, but they will."

As Sam finished, the front door opened and Mamaw came out pulling her shawl tight around her shoulders. "Ollie, it's time to come back inside. That wind is picking up a bit and we don't need you getting a chill. Supper will be ready soon, so no need in you going back upstairs. Sam, you can help him to the parlor for now."

Sam picked me up. As he carried me inside, he said, "And Mister Ollie, as far as fishing and hunting… It's not the baiting and cleaning that's the fun. It's the sitting on the bank or lying there in the shade of a tree, enjoying God's creation. It's feeling that tug on the line when you think you got a big one. That's what fishing is all about.

"And same for hunting. It's the woods, and the sound of the birds, and the wind in the trees. It's those cold mornings when you're all alone, no one there but you and the Good Lord. Why, you don't even need a gun. Truth be, there's never been a dead deer as pretty as one that's standing there with his head held high, sniffing the wind. That's what it's all about."

As Sam helped me get settled on the sofa in the parlor, I asked, "What happened to the wolf pup?"

A pained look came over his face and he was silent for a minute. "Mister Ollie, the hardest thing I ever did. But what made it harder is I didn't do what your grandpa said. I kept that pup—until he got in the hen house and killed several chickens. Then I had to do it. And it was like killing my own brother.

"I tried to let him go wild, but he wouldn't go. No matter how far away I took him, he always showed back up." Sam shook his head. "That wolf was kind of like me. He had never known freedom and didn't know what to do with it."

Chapter 7

The Swimming Hole

As a youth I always enjoyed swimming. James, Junius, and I had our favorite swimming hole up on Ponta Creek, a couple of miles north of Lockhart.

Ponta Creek was usually dry during the late summer, but at the junction of Lost Horse Creek and Ponta Creek, there was a deep pool that was present year round. In the winter the creek was a fairly swift running stream that flowed east to join the Sucarnoochee River. The Sucarnoochee then joined the Tombigbee River in Alabama, which flowed south to Mobile Bay one hundred and forty miles away. When the water was flowing, the pool was clear and clean, but in the summer it was a stagnant, muddy hole.

Just above the swimming hole there was an old Indian mound, the last remnant of Coosha Town, once a large Choctaw farming community that spread up and down Ponta Creek. Coosha Town disappeared back in the 1830s when the Choctaws were forced to migrate to the Oklahoma territory—"the Trail of Tears" the migration became known as. A few of the Choctaw people who escaped extradition were still scattered around, but we never saw them. Oklahoma, nephew of Pushmataha and the mingo, or chief, of the Coosha people, is supposedly buried in that mound.

We would sometimes find arrowheads and pieces of pottery scattered in the fields around the mound and often imagined ourselves as Indian braves on the warpath against the invading white settlers.

Swimming was part of life, and during the long, hot summers we would spend hours splashing and laughing in the warm, muddy water. Everyone knew how to swim. There were no lessons: you just jumped in and swam. Occasionally, though, you learned to swim because you had no choice.

On one lazy July afternoon when I was twelve, the three of us were sitting on the bank of the creek—catching our breaths after a game of water tag. James suddenly started laughing.

"What's so funny?" I asked.

"Oh, I was thinking about when Junius learned to swim," he answered. He began to laugh uncontrollably with his hands on his stomach. "Junius, you remember that day, don't you, little brother?"

"How could I forget?" Junius shook his head. "And James, it is not a laughing matter. I could have drowned!"

"Yea," James retorted, "but you didn't! And you did learn to swim!"

"What happened?" I asked.

"It was back in Tennessee," Junius began as he picked up a rock and skipped it across the water. "I was five and James was seven. We lived on the banks of the Tennessee River—one of the prettiest, cleanest rivers in the whole world. Beautiful rocky banks with high bluffs and deep pools. It's a whole lot different than this hot mud hole here."

"Hey," I chuckled. "Don't talk about my favorite swimming hole like that!"

"Cool, clear water as far as you could see," Junius continued. "I hadn't learned to swim yet, but I loved to wade up to my waist and splash around. I made sure I stayed close to the bank.

"One day I was standing on the bank watching James and some of the older guys swimming out in the deep water. I was so envious of them—out there swimming like a school of fish. Well, unknown to me Rupert Carter sneaked up behind me. Now, Rupert was a little touched in the head. Pop said he was a forty-year-old man with the mind of a three-year-old. The town idiot a lot of people called him.

"He was always spying on us and would often show up out of nowhere and play tricks on us. He would then start laughing and run off. I had gotten over being scared of Ole Rupert a long time ago. He was harmless. The older kids would sometimes throw rocks at him." Junius shook his head. "That wasn't right. He couldn't help being simple.

"Well, all of a sudden, Rupert grabbed me and tossed me out in the water. I almost died from fright when he grabbed me, but then I *really* thought I was going to die! When I hit that water, I started sinking like a rock. I didn't know what to do! I was choking and coughing and crying as I fought to stay afloat. And you know what happened then?"

"No, tell me!" I exclaimed, captivated by his tale.

"Well, I drowned!"

Junius and James burst out laughing.

"Awe, come on," I said. "Tell me what happened."

"I learned how to swim," he said as he leaned back on the bank and put his hands behind his head. "It was either sink or swim, and I chose to swim. I told myself to calm down and stop fighting the water. I started moving my arms and kicking my feet, and suddenly my head popped up out of the water. I took a deep breath and kept kicking. Before I knew it I was close enough to the bank to touch the bottom.

"Boy, that scared me! I got out of that water as fast as I could, sat down on the bank, and cried like a baby. But I did learn to swim that day."

"What happened to Rupert for doing that to you?" I asked. "Did they lock him up or whip him?"

"Naw, he didn't know what he was doing," Junius said. "He just thought he was being funny. And punishing him would do no good. Simple people are like that. But I did start watching my back a little closer."

Junius suddenly jumped up and shouted, "Last one in is a rotten egg!"

The three of us were back in the water, splashing and laughing, before you could say "jack rabbit!"

After the accident I did not go swimming for almost two years. The first summer I was still weak and didn't do any heavy exertion—tapping the Morse key was the extent of my exercise. Also there was still a fairly large area of raw surface on my shoulder and getting in warm, muddy water was out of the question.

One afternoon in early May of 1892, Junius and I were walking home from school. It was a fairly warm day. Spring was almost over and summer was coming. Junius was kicking a rock down the road.

"Sure is a beautiful day today," Junius said as he picked up the rock and threw it out in the woods. "Want to go for a swim? James and some of the older boys were heading to the creek this afternoon. He said we could join them if we wanted." He picked up another rock and tossed it down the road. "Sure would be a lot of fun. I bet the water isn't too cold, with all these warm days we've been having."

I felt panicky. "Ah," I stammered, "I don't think so. Not today. Maybe later. I—I've got too much to do at home this afternoon. You go ahead."

"Are you sure? We could do something else if you want."

He probably sensed my hesitancy, and my friend was trying to be my friend. Yet I could tell he really wanted to go. "Yea, you go ahead. I've got plenty to do at home."

I had not even thought about swimming in almost two years, and the idea suddenly frightened me—frightened me for two reasons.

First off, the only people who had seen my scar were family and Dr. Knox. It was a horrible, ugly scar, and I didn't like the idea of showing it to anyone. What would my friends think if they saw it? Would they stare? Would they look in disgust or even turn away? I did not want to find out.

Second, could I still swim? A one-legged duck trying to swim is a pitiful sight, and I could see myself flailing in the water with one arm, going around in circles.

But then, I had always loved the water. Some of my best memories of childhood were at Ponta Creek—swimming and splashing with the guys, swinging out over the creek on our rope swing and dropping into the deep water. And the rope swing! Could I ever do that again? It took two hands and even then I would sometimes slip. Why, just climbing the tree to get to the rope swing was now a seemingly impossible task! How could I ever do that again?

After I left Junius that afternoon, I stopped by Mamaw's cottage. A piece of cake and a warm glass of milk were waiting—plus the best advice in the world for whatever was bothering me.

"Mamaw," I said as I took a bite of strawberry cake. "Do you realize I haven't been swimming in almost two years—not since the accident?"

"No," she answered and laughed. "I'm afraid that's not something I've been keeping track of."

"Junius asked me to go swimming today and I said no."

"Why is that?" she asked.

"The scar."

"Oh, I see." Mamaw took my dish and placed it in the sink. She then sat down beside me.

"Mamaw, I don't want anyone to see it. It's not that I'm afraid they would make fun of me. That would be easy to handle. It's the look, that look of disgust. I don't think I could bear that from my friends."

Mamaw was in deep thought for a minute and then said. "Ollie, when I was a little girl, I had two pair of shoes. One pair I wore in the fields and barn whenever it was cold or wet. Now, in the summer we rarely wore shoes, but in the winter I liked keeping my toes as warm as I could.

"Those old shoes were a sight! Filthy, mud-caked, smelly shoes that I left on the back porch. I don't think I could have ever gotten them looking decent. In fact, I would suspect that if all the mud was removed, they would have fallen apart.

"The other pair—oh, they were beautiful! Bright shiny black with white laces. I was so proud of them. I kept them under my bed and only wore them on Sundays.

"On one cold and rainy Sunday morning in January, I was getting dressed for church and reached under the bed for my shoes. They weren't there! My Sunday shoes were nowhere to be found! I looked everywhere. I know I had put them under my bed, but they were gone. I accused my younger brother of hiding them, but he wouldn't admit to it.

"I had three choices on that chilly day. I could wear my old dirty, stinky shoes to church; I could go barefoot; or I could stay home."

Mamaw got up and walked over to the sink. "Ollie, the way it looks to me you have three similar choices. You can go swimming as you always have and not worry about it. You can cover up your scar—wear an old shirt so no one can see it. Or you can stay home and never go swimming with your friends again. I don't think any of those choices are wrong. Whatever you decide will be okay. But I'm not going to tell you what you should do. You make a choice and be happy with it."

She was right. The choice was up to me.

As I was leaving, I said, "Mamaw, what did you do?"

"What?" she said with a puzzled look on her face.

"The shoes. What did you do about the shoes?"

"Oh, the shoes. Well, I stayed home. I didn't want my toes to freeze, and I didn't think people would appreciate me wearing those stinking shoes in church.

"And guess what? The very next Sunday my shoes were back under my bed as if nothing had happened." She began to laugh. "I think my brother still has the knot on his head that I gave him that day!"

And my choice? An old shirt. None of my friends ever saw the scar. And as far as swimming—it was never the same, but I did enjoy it. I learned to tread water with one arm and was able to swim in a straight line!

Chapter 8

The Ponta Creek Monster

In August of that year, the three of us, James, Junius, and I, were up at Ponta Creek swimming, me in my old shirt and them in their ... well, in what most kids swam in before there were swim trunks.

As the summer had progressed, I had become more comfortable with swimming with one arm, and my friends had gotten used to the way I was and, for the most part, were treating me like one of the gang.

It was a hot summer, one of the worst in years. Daytime temperatures had been close to a hundred, and at night it was not much better. It was impossible to sleep. The humidity was stifling and the sheets stuck to us like a wet washcloth. There was no breeze—just stagnant, hot, wet air.

The only relief was the swimming hole, and it was not much better. It had not rained in at least three weeks and there was no flow in or out. The dark brown water was hot, and it felt as though we were swimming in a tub of muddy bath water.

After a short swim, Junius got out and sat on the bank. "This is not any fun. I've had one bath this week, and I don't care to take another. That water is awful."

"I agree with you," James said.

"What do you want to do?" I asked as I struggled to get out of the water. The muddy bank made it a little slippery and with one arm it was a little hard to keep my balance.

"Oh, I don't know," Junius answered. "Why don't we walk up the stream bed? Maybe we can find a pool of water in a shady area that's not as hot as this."

"You know this is the best hole for miles," I said. "You won't find anything deeper."

"No, but maybe we can find one cooler."

We put our clothes on. If we ran into someone, we didn't want to shock the poor soul. We then headed northeast along the creek bed.

The walking was fairly easy. The bed was mostly sand, but there were areas of gravel where the stream changed courses. In places, we walked along in knee-deep water, and in others the creek was bone dry. There were quite a few small pools and an occasional larger pool, but Junius would say, "Keep walking. We'll find a better one."

Frequently we had to climb over or under a fallen tree or over some rocky outcrops. These obstacles tended to slow me down, and so I pulled up the rear, letting James and Junius lead. I didn't want anyone having to wait on me.

As I was crawling under one log, I happened to look down, and sticking out of the sand was the most beautiful flint spear point I had ever seen.

"James! Junius!" I shouted. "Look at this!"

The point was six inches long and in perfect condition. Usually when we found one that big, it would be broken. It was perfectly shaped, the color of cinnamon, and glistened in the sunlight. The edges were sharp enough to cut a leaf cleanly in two.

James and Junius came running back to see what I had found.

"Wow!" exclaimed Junius. "That's a beauty! As good as that looks, it must have been a ceremonial point. I wouldn't be surprised if it had belonged to old Chief Pushmataha himself!"

I gently laid it up on the bank. My plan was to pick it up on the way back. The less I carried it around the less likely I would drop it.

We journeyed farther on our quest for the perfect swimming hole. Suddenly James, who was leading, stopped dead in his tracks. "Look up ahead," he whispered.

There sunning on a rock was a water moccasin. It was coiled up and appeared to be asleep, unaware of our approach.

"Do you suppose we should turn around and go back?" I asked, not wanting to take a chance of disturbing the snake.

Junius picked up a good size stick and slowly advanced. "The only good moccasin is a dead moccasin."

With that he slammed the stick as hard as he could right on the snake's head.

"We can go ahead now," he said calmly.

We continued along the creek bed. Even though it was late afternoon, it was sweltering hot, and sweat was pouring off us. Mosquitoes began to attack, and we began to attack back, swatting our necks and legs. Thankfully, I had on a long sleeve shirt— it's impossible to swat a mosquito on your arm when that's the only arm you have.

I was ready to turn back, but didn't want to be the first to cry uncle.

Finally James said, "It's getting late. Why don't we head back?"

"Not yet," Junius said as he continued to lead.

"Junius, we've come a long way," James said, "and we'll be at the Sucarnoochee River pretty soon. That's a far piece from home.

If we don't start back now, it'll be dark before we get back, and I don't want to be crawling along this creek bed in the dark."

Panic gripped me. The idea of navigating this creek in the dark with one arm scared me to death. Plus we already knew there were snakes around.

As we rounded a bend, I said, "James is right. We need to head back."

Junius suddenly stopped. He pointed ahead and said, "What in the world is that?"

About twenty feet ahead was a shallow pool. It appeared to be a foot deep, two feet wide, and about ten feet long. In the pool was what looked like an old log, but it was moving.

We didn't move. Whatever it was it was alive, and it was big!

"Is it an alligator?" I asked.

"There's never been an alligator seen in this creek," James said. "They don't get this far north."

"Then what is it?" I asked.

"I don't know," James said. "Let's get a little closer."

Nobody moved.

"Somebody has to be first," James said.

"Okay," Junius said, "I'll go."

Junius slowly started walking. With his courage going before us, we followed. As we approached, the thing began to wiggle.

"Watch out!" James yelled.

We all jumped back, ready to run. After a moment it settled down, and we started advancing again.

"I wish I still had that big stick," Junius said.

"I think it will take more than a stick for that thing." I said.

As we got closer, we could see it better. It appeared to be about seven or eight feet long and had large bony scales, like an alligator, but it didn't have any legs. It was as big around as my waist, and it had a fin on its back and a large fin on its tail. Its face was long and elongated.

"It's a fish!" James exclaimed. "The biggest fish I ever saw!"

"Is it a catfish?" I asked.

Occasionally someone would catch a large catfish in the Sucarnoochee River, but never one to rival this monster.

"Nope," Junius said. "It looks like a shark!"

"A shark in Ponta Creek?" James exclaimed, and began to laugh.

"Well, have you got a better idea?" Junius smirked.

"No, but a shark would die in freshwater."

We stood there looking at it for awhile, but kept our distance.

"What are we going to do with it?" I asked.

"Nothing," said Junius. "If it's a shark, I don't want to get close. It might bite my hand off!"

"Then you would be like me," I said.

As soon as it came out of my mouth, I knew that I shouldn't have said it.

Junius's shoulders dropped and he looked over at me. All of the excitement and adventure were gone; sadness and hurt had replaced them.

"Junius, I didn't mean anything. I was just trying to be funny."

"Ollie, I'm so sorry," Junius said, almost crying. "It should have been me. I wish that I hadn't..."

"No, Junius, it was not your fault."

We were silent for a minute. Thoughts of the Ponta Creek monster and the perfect swimming hole had disappeared.

Finally, James said, "Whatever this thing is, shark or not, it won't be going anywhere until it rains again—unless it can crawl."

The ice was broken, and we all began to laugh.

We headed back up the creek and were home just as it was getting dark.

Sam was coming out of the barn. He had just finished milking the cow and was headed to the house with a pale of milk.

"Sam," I exclaimed out of breath, "you're not going to believe what we saw on Ponta Creek. A huge fish with scales like an alligator. Never seen anything like it."

I began telling him all about our adventure.

"Sam, I want you to come with us tomorrow and look at it. Tell us what you think."

When I finished, Sam nodded his head for a minute and said, "Well, it sounds like you boys are imagining sea monsters! Or else you're trying to make a fool out of Old Sam."

"No, Sam. I'm not kidding! Cross my heart and hope to die!"

The next morning Sam reluctantly joined us. As we approached the monster, Sam jumped back and exclaimed, "Good night, hallelujah! What a fish! Why, that's the biggest sturgeon I ever saw. That thing must weigh three hundred pounds."

Sam walked over to it and bent down like he was going to touch it.

"Watch out, Sam," Junius yelled. "That thing might bite!"

Sam laughed and reached down. "Bite me with what?" he said as he patted the fish. "This thing ain't got no teeth. I guess he could gum me to death if he wanted to."

"What's a sturgeon?" I asked.

Sam laughed, "Why, it's a fish!"

"Come on, Sam. We figured that out. But what kind of fish is it? We've never seen anything like it. Where did it come from?"

"Most likely it come up from the river," Sam answered. "We used to see some of these in Ponta Creek years ago, but never one like this. Mostly they was two or three feet long."

Sam scratched his head, "Come to think, I haven't seen one of these in fifteen or twenty years. It must'a gotten turned around, come up this creek, and got stuck.

"And it is a strange looking fish. It don't have scales like most fish and ain't smooth like a catfish."

After a few minutes, we got up the courage to get close to the sturgeon, and with Sam standing close, we touched it and rubbed his back.

"It's almost like rubbing an old washboard," Junius said.

Suddenly the monster jumped and began to flop around in its little watery hole.

"Watch out, he's coming after you!" Sam shouted.

We jumped back, scared out of our wits. Sam began to hoot.

"Sam, don't scare me like that," Junius said. "You'll make me die of a heart attack!"

"Boys, you'd be scared of your own shadow if it snuck up on you!"

After it settled back down, we eased back over to it and began to touch it again.

"Are they good to eat?" James asked.

"Only if you are mighty hungry, and I ain't been that hungry in years. And this one, as big as he is, he's probably as tough as leather. I wouldn't be surprised if this thing's over a hundred years old."

"What are we going to do with him?" I asked.

Sam shook his head. "Well, as hot as it is, and with this pool as low as it is, I'm surprised he's still alive."

Junius had a pained look on his face. "If we're not going to eat him, we can't just leave him here."

"Yea," James added. "It might not rain for another two or three weeks, and the water won't be flowing good until November."

"We can't just let him die," Junius said. "That wouldn't be right."

Sam shrugged his shoulders. "The way I see it, the Good Lord put him right here and no need in us meddling with the Lord's business."

"Why, Sam," Junius said. "I'm ashamed of you. What if this was a cow? You wouldn't leave her to die, would you? You would be doing everything you could to get her out. It would be your Christian duty to get her unstuck, wouldn't it? Same thing with this fish."

Sam lowered his head. He had a look on his face as if he had just been to church and every one of his sins had been laid bare.

"Okay, Okay," Sam said as he shook his head. "What you got in mind?"

We looked around, and about fifty feet farther down the creek bed there was a good size pool. It must have been at least thirty feet long and twelve feet across—a pool like our swimming hole which most likely lasted all summer long.

"If we could get him down to that pool," Junius said, "he ought to do just fine for another couple of months until the rains start."

"You gonna throw him over your shoulder and tote him down there like a sack of feed?" Sam laughed. "Why, he ain't got handles for us to pick him up."

"Sam, be serious," Junius said.

"What about hauling him down there on a tarpaulin?" I asked. "We ought to be able to slide a tarp under him and pull him along, especially with Sam here to help."

Later that afternoon we were back with an old tarpaulin, and with a little coaxing and pulling we gave that sturgeon a new home for the rest of the summer.

As he slid into the deeper pool and out of sight in the muddy water, Junius wiped his brow and said, "Well, at least you could say thanks."

We began to laugh and headed back home.

"Makes me feel good," Junius said as we walked along. "Doing the right thing always makes you feel good."

"Even when you don't get no thanks," Sam laughed.

"Junius," I chuckled, "we can come back here and go swimming with our new friend, if you want to. His pool does seem to be a little cooler than ours."

"You've got to be kidding. Why, knowing something like that was swimming around underneath me—it would give me the heebie-jeebies."

Sam began to laugh. "Boys, as muddy as your swimming hole is, there could be one of them in there and you'd never know it."

It was three weeks before we set foot in our swimming hole again.

As I went to bed that night, I suddenly remembered—the spear point! In all the commotion with the fish, I had forgotten about my prize. I would go get it first thing the next morning.

After breakfast, I headed down to the creek. When I got to where I had left it, the spear point wasn't there. I was positive that was the spot, but it was nowhere to be found. I looked up and down the bank for at least an hour, but to no avail. I couldn't believe it. What could have happened to it?

When I got back home, Junius was sitting on the front steps of our house.

"Hey, Ollie. Where've you been?" he asked.

Before I could say a word, he said, "Hunting for this?"

He pulled a cloth out of his pocket, unfolded it, and there it was!

"The spear point!" I exclaimed.

"Yea, when I got here this morning, your papa said that I'd just missed you. I went down before breakfast and got it, and I've been sitting here, waiting for you to get back."

"Thanks! Junius. But you didn't have to."

"Ollie, I wanted to," he said as he handed it to me. "There's nothing I wouldn't do for you. You're my best friend—you saved my life."

Chapter 9

The First Love

A deficient area of my life that soon became apparent was my relationship with the fairer sex. I was too self-conscious to get serious about any girl. I could easily imagine the girls laughing and saying, "Me? And you? One-armed Ollie? You've got to be kidding!" The fear of rejection loomed heavily over me.

But then, there *was* one girl: Silk. Her real name was Abigail Brown, but everyone called her Silk. The first time we met, we were thirteen. It was the spring before the accident. Her father had been working at one of the logging camps close by, and the family had recently moved from Porterville to Lockhart to be closer to his work.

When she walked into the school room that morning, everything got quiet, everyone stared. She was a thirteen-year-old beauty, already becoming a young woman. But to say that she was a beauty ... well, it would be like saying that an eagle can fly, but not telling how it can soar through the sky effortlessly. Her features were flawless; her skin was the color of cream. But her most striking feature was her hair—soft golden yellow-white waves flowing perfectly to her shoulders—"the color of corn silk," Junius had leaned over and whispered. Thus she was christened Silk from that day forward.

There was an aura about her that drew everyone's eyes to her. The one word that would describe her is stunning. But there was one problem with Silk. She knew she was stunning, and she enjoyed it. She enjoyed her beauty and the attention it brought—but not really in a bad way. She was a good person, always pleasant, always friendly, and when she talked with people, she really seemed to care. But she savored the glances and the comments about her looks, and she used them to her advantage. She was not self-centered, but she had developed a self-confidence that let everyone know that she would one day rule the world.

I've often wondered—are beautiful people born with this self-confidence, or do they develop it because they are treated differently from the rest of us?

Her family had nothing. Her father barely kept them fed. The house where they lived should have been torn down years ago. Her dresses were old and worn, obvious hand-me-downs, but she would have made sackcloth look like queenly attire. That she was poorer than poor did not bother her: she had herself.

Silk and I became friends. Or rather I became one of her many friends—one of many who vied for her attention. I often wondered if I was kidding myself, but I truly felt that she took a genuine interest in me. At lunch break the few of us who were the same age would visit. At age thirteen we were too old to "play" at school. We told stories, teased each other, and laughed together—honing courtship skills that would come into play in later years.

One day a few weeks after Silk arrived, we headed outside for lunch. Our school also functioned as the Lockhart Methodist Church on Sundays. No need in having a building sit idle for six out of every seven days. It was a single large room with several rows of pews that were pushed to the back for school. There was a single pot-belly stove in the corner for heating, and several windows for cooling. The church was only five years old, but already had a sizable cemetery out back with several granite and marble tombstones. One of them belonged to my mother. She had been there for four years.

We brought our own lunches to school and would usually sit in the shade of an old oak nearby and enjoy our meal. But on days when it was not too hot, as on that spring day, we would sit on the ground in front of Mama's stone and share stories of family. I would tell Silk about Mama—how beautiful she was and how much I missed her.

That day Silk was dressed in one of her three threadbare dresses. We sat down and opened up our lunches. Mine was fried chicken and potato salad. Silk's was cold collard greens. Nothing else. Just greens. Being a not-so-tactful young male, a species known for not thinking before talking, I asked, "Is that all you're having?"

"Yes, it is," she replied with an air of confidence that let me know that nothing phased this young beauty. "This is all there was at home. There was nothing else to bring. But it is very delicious. Would you like a bite?"

I was dumbfounded but gained my composure quickly and said, "Why don't we just share our meals. We will both come out ahead, won't we?"

I had never really seen poverty. My family was fairly well-to-do by the standards of the day, as were most of the people in Lockhart. I never wanted for much of anything. My father owned the general store in Lockhart, and we always had plenty to eat and clothes that fit and looked nice.

Silk's family lived "hand to mouth"—whatever income came in was quickly spent just to keep the family fed, and sometimes that didn't get done. There was never any money left over, or at least that's the way it seemed. I found out later that that was not entirely true. There occasionally was a little money at the end of the month, but the family never saw it. Moonshine whiskey took the rest. Her father had a weakness that caused the entire family to suffer.

This was so foreign to me. Alcohol had never been allowed in my home. Papa always said he had never seen a man be a better person with a bottle in his hand but had seen many a man better himself by putting it down.

Silk's family poverty was also made worse by the number of mouths to feed. There were six children in the household: two older sisters ages sixteen and seventeen, and three babies ranging from a few months old to three years old. I had assumed that the three little ones were Silk's siblings, but I was soon shocked to find out they were not.

One day we were having our usual noon meal together at recess and were talking about family—about our brothers and sisters. Junius, with four brothers and two sisters, expounded on the pros and cons of a large family.

"With seven kids at the table, you have to be quick at meal time or you will come up with nothing but the short end of the wishbone."

"You must be pretty slow," I said, "as skinny as you are!"

"Well, I am the youngest," Junius chuckled, "but I'm learning to reach a little faster!"

Everyone began to laugh.

"You know," Junius continued, "There were only nine years difference between my oldest sister, Lizzie, and me. Lizzie said she thought Mama had always been pregnant and would always stay pregnant."

Junius looked over at Silk. "Your ma did it a little differently, didn't she? After you, she waited a good ten years before having another."

Silk reached over to Junius's lunch and picked up one of his sliced carrots. She began nibbling on it and matter-of-factly said, "Those babies are not my brothers and sisters. They belong to my sisters."

Junius seemed a little confused and scratched his head. "Really?" he said. "Where are their husbands?"

An awkward silence descended on our little group. Junius kept scratching his head, while everyone else's jaws dropped and eyes bugged out. Silk continued to nibble on the carrot and with no embarrassment at all said, "They don't have any."

"But I thought..."

"Junius, be quiet," one of the girls said. "Don't be stupid."

"My oldest sister, Opal, has two babies. Jess is three and Phoebe is five months. Jasmine's baby is two."

Silk picked up another carrot and continued to nibble. "My sisters were foolish. They have sealed their fate and they don't even know it. They will never be able to get out of this place. As God is my witness, that will never happen to me." She rested back against my mother's tombstone and put her hands behind her head. "Someday I'm going to be somebody."

In July, the accident happened. I was in bed for several months, and for several more months I did not leave the house. For the first weeks, Dr. Knox would not allow visitors. He said that I needed absolute quiet and rest—visitation would stress my healing body too much. Several times as Mamaw was tending to my wounds, she would tell me that a pretty little girl named Silk had come by to see how I was doing.

Once visitors were allowed, friends began to call. Silk was one of them, sometimes coming with Junius, sometimes by herself. The well-worn dresses were the same—no new garments had been handed down. Silk would stroll in as if she had been there a hundred times and sit on the end of my bed. Our home was no mansion, but by comparison to hers, it was palatial. If she was intimidated at all with our "wealth," she did not show it—she seemed as comfortable here as if it were her own home. Self-confidence and self-assurance radiated from her.

As I got stronger, I was allowed to sit in the parlor and receive guests. Maude, my nine-year-old sister, would often act as hostess and serve tea to my visitors and me. Silk would sip and converse as if this was what she did all day long. Except for her clothes, she would have passed as one of the daughters of some of the "old money" families in Meridian, here for her weekly Sunday afternoon visit—inborn elegance and grace with no care or worry about what tomorrow brings.

I thoroughly enjoyed her weekly visits and looked forward to them with great anticipation. Her visits probably did more than anything to lift my spirits and keep me from wallowing in self-pity. In fact, Silk would not let me feel sorry for myself.

"Ollie," she said one day as we visited and sipped tea, "everything happens for a reason. Remember that. And if you cannot find a reason, see it as an opportunity or a learning experience. Success is built on those two things: opportunities and learning experiences. An opportunity not taken advantage of is a waste. A learning experience that does not make you wiser is foolishness. The past can never be changed, but the future is built on the present—what you do now."

In November something happened that was almost as traumatic as losing my arm. Silk came by one afternoon alone. As we talked I sensed that she was a little uneasy, not her usual confident self. In fact, that was the only time I saw her when she did not seem to be in total control.

"Ollie, how are you doing this week?" Silk asked as she sat down on the sofa. She picked up one of the linen pillows, smoothed it with her hand, and placed it in her lap.

"Doctor Knox says I should be able to go to church on Thanksgiving. He said if I behave and take it easy, that should not be too much of a strain. I asked him about school and he said we needed to take it one step at a time. I'm ready to get out of this house. I haven't left this house in months."

After we visited a while, she looked off in the distance and calmly said, "Ollie, We're leaving. Papa has found work in Macon. We are leaving tomorrow."

I was in shock! I wanted to blurt out, "No! You can't do that!" But instead I said, "What?"

"We're leaving. This is the way it always is. Never in any place for long. Papa's always saying that things will be better in the next place. He's chasing a rainbow that does not exist." She rested her head back on the sofa and sighed.

We sat silently. My heart felt as if it had stopped pumping. My stomach hurt. The world suddenly was foggy, and I couldn't focus my eyes. *What is happening to me?* I thought. *I have said good-bye to friends before, but it never felt like this. But now, I feel like I am going to explode!*

I was only thirteen, but love was tugging at my heart—love that would soon disappear.

I didn't know what to say, but I was in no position to let my emotions get the best of me. I swallowed and said, "Will you write?"

Silk continued to rest her head on the back of the sofa. She crossed her arms and said, "We'll see."

The answer meant "No."

She stood up, walked over to me, and kissed me gently on the cheek. "Ollie, thanks for being my friend."

Silk straightened her back, confidence and poise again reigning supreme.

"And in case you haven't heard, Jasmine is going to have another baby—due in about four months. We tend to move when that happens."

She opened the front door, turned around, and smiled. "Good-bye, Oliver Eras Parker."

She closed the door behind her and was gone.

It would be eight years before I would see Silk again. During those years I often thought about her. I wondered where she was, what she was doing—whether she was married, if she was happy.

It was in the spring of 1899. I had finished school three years before and the M&O Railroad had hired me as the official telegrapher for the little hamlet of Lockhart. It was a typical day, nothing exciting.

I was busy with several wires to Meridian when Mr. Matthews called out to me that I had a visitor. I had not realized how quiet the station had gotten, but when I looked up, you could have heard a pin drop. Everyone was staring at the most beautiful human being any one of us had ever seen. But to say that this person was beautiful … Well, "it would be like saying that an eagle can fly, but not telling how it can soar through the sky effortlessly. Her features were flawless; her skin was the color of cream. But her most striking feature was her hair—soft golden yellow-white waves flowing perfectly to her shoulders—the color of corn silk."

It was Silk! It was really Silk! I couldn't believe that she was standing there. Memories that had been hidden for the past eight years suddenly came pouring out. My heart began to pound, and I felt short of breath. I couldn't move. I was frozen in my seat.

"Hello, Oliver Eras Parker. How have you been?"

"Silk! Is that really you?" I exclaimed.

"The one and only," she said as she walked over. The self-confidence was still there. But there was one striking difference in Silk. Instead of the threadbare hand-me-downs of the past, she was dressed in the most elegant traveling attire that I had ever seen, and it fit her ... perfectly. Queen Victoria would have been proud to own it.

I reached out my hand, and she took it in both her hands and said, "Ollie, it's so good to see you. It's been a long time. Why, you have grown up! And it looks like you're doing well these days."

I've grown up? Gulp! I dared not say what I thought about her!

Everyone in the station was still focused on us, or rather on Silk. I felt a little awkward carrying on a conversation in front of everyone, so I asked Mr. Matthews if I could leave for awhile.

Mr. Matthew grinned and said, "No problem. Take all the time you want. I'll take care of the wire."

"How is your family?" Silk asked as we walked down the steps of the station. "Does Maude still make a good cup of tea?"

"Why, yes she does!" I said. We started toward the house. "She is seventeen now and should be home from school by now. I know she would love to see you."

"So you're a telegrapher."

"Yes, I am," I said as we walked. "I started working at the station the summer after the accident and fell in love with the dots and dashes. I have been there ever since. Full time since I finished school. It's a good job, and I can do it with one arm tied behind my back!"

Silk glanced over at me, caught off guard with my remark. I began to laugh and she joined in.

"Well, Ollie, I see you're comfortable with yourself. That's good."

"It's either joke about it or cry about it. I found that crying didn't help at all."

In a more serious tone, Silk asked, "Ollie, how has it been? Has it been hard?"

"I would be lying if I said it wasn't. But I'm okay. I've learned to adapt. And I am still learning. There are days when I would give anything to be whole again. But..." We were at the house—a good time to change the subject. I did not want to dwell on me and my problems.

The house was empty. Maude and Gussie had not made it home from school and I'm not sure where Lizzie was. We sat down in the parlor to visit. Silk picked up a linen pillow—the same one she had picked up eight years ago—smoothed it with her hand and placed it in her lap.

Silk looked around and saw the piano in the corner. "Who plays the piano?"

"Maude does," I said. "She's very good. In fact she is the pianist at church. Do you play?"

"Oh, no," Silk replied. "But someday I will learn. That is one of my goals."

"Silk, tell me about yourself. Where have you been for the past eight years? You look like you have been doing well yourself."

"It's been a long eight years." She rested her head back on the sofa and began.

"After we left Lockhart, we went to Macon. We were there only four months when Papa said it was time to move. This time to Montgomery, Alabama, but things there were no different and we moved again. I made up my mind that as soon as I could, I was going to leave. But Ollie, you can't just leave. You have to have a plan; otherwise you trade one bad situation for another.

"I was able to find work after school and on weekends and began saving every penny. My goal was a hundred dollars. That should be enough to get me to Birmingham or Atlanta, and keep me going for a few months.

"In two months I had ten dollars—a great start. Two years and I would be gone. But I made one mistake in my plan; I kept my earnings in a little box under my bed. A big mistake.

"Well, one afternoon I came home from work. Jasmine was on the front porch with her two little ones. 'Pa's drunk again. And it ain't even payday,' she said.

"It took me one minute to find that I had been robbed. Ollie, look at everything that happens as an opportunity to learn. And remember—a lesson learned early is a lesson of great value. It could easily have been at twenty-two months rather than two months. Pa never found it again.

"Two years later, on my sixteenth birthday, I boarded a train to Atlanta with one hundred and ten dollars in my pocket and a plan in my head. The first thing I did in Atlanta was to go to one of the best clothing stores in town and buy two dresses—expensive, fashionable dresses. It took the biggest part of my nest egg, but Ollie, when I looked in the mirror, I saw a new person—a person who could do anything she wanted. It was well worth the cost. My rags were left with the clerk. When she asked what to do with them, I said to burn them if she wished.

"The next step in my plan was to be where influential people are. Ollie, to become influential, you have to associate with influential people. No matter how well you are dressed, no matter how refined you become, if you don't meet the right people, opportunities will never come.

"I went to the most expensive hotel in the city and applied for a job. Here I almost made my second mistake. I had not considered my age being a factor in a job interview, but when asked how old I was, I suddenly aged four years. Twenty sounded so much more mature than sixteen. The first job was as an assistant to the check-in clerk. I worked hard, learned everything I could about the hotel business and the Atlanta area, and within a year had made my way to assistant to the concierge, helping with party reservations, plays, and the like.

"Then came my biggest opportunity. Ollie, there are many people who come to a big city alone on business, and at times are in need of a companion. Someone to accompany them to a party or to the opera. Many of them are very wealthy. It became apparent to me that there was a business opportunity here that someone with a pleasant face and a warm personality could capitalize on.

"And Ollie, I made it very clear that it was business and *not* funny business. In fact, I would only accompany registered guests, and all arrangements were made through the concierge desk. I was busy almost every evening, and the gratuities ... well, all I will say is it was not nickels and dimes. The hotel was also pleased with this service: requests for our hotel increased significantly.

"So that's what I've been doing. Right now I'm on my way to New Orleans to buy clothes. When the train arrived in Meridian, well, I decided to get off, come to Lockhart for the afternoon. I wanted to see how things were going here. It has been such a long time, and I have such good memories of my time here. And I wanted to see how you were doing, too."

Wanted to see *me*? This beauty wanted to see *me*? I didn't know what to say.

"Ollie, when I left this room eight years ago, I was so upset and so mad! Mad at my father, mad at you for being hurt, mad at Junius for causing it—mad at the world. I didn't know what to do. I thought about staying—leaving my family. I loved Lockhart. I loved the people who had been so good to me—treated me like a person, not like some stray dog that had to be tolerated. But I was only thirteen. As bad as my home situation was, I knew staying here would be worse.

"And I have thought of you, Ollie, worried about you. Wondered how you were doing after that horrible accident. And look at you! Eight years out and you have weathered the storm very well, better than most people would. You have accomplished so much."

She began to laugh. "Ollie, all my worry was for nothing! But that is not totally true. Everything is for a reason. If I had not worried … well, I wouldn't be here right now visiting with you. That would have been a terrible missed opportunity."

I was so surprised, so taken aback by what she said. Yes, I had thought of her through the years—dreamed about her, missed her. Thought of what life could have been like with her. But to think that she had kept me in her thoughts, had harbored the same desires as I had … Why, I could not believe it!

"Silk, I've missed you too, more than you can believe. When you left that day, when I thought I would never see you again—I couldn't bear it. I thought my world had ended, that my heart had died.

"I know that time changes us all," I continued. "We are not the same thirteen-year-old children of the past. But maybe we could…"

A sudden shocked expression came over her face, "Ollie, I'm so sorry. If I have given you the impression that … no, Ollie, I'm not here to…"

She took a deep breath. "Ollie, I'm engaged."

She stood up and walked over to the piano. She was silent for a minute, and then turned.

"I met someone at the hotel several months ago. He's from Philadelphia, from a very well known and respected family. We are getting married in two months in Atlanta, and then I will be moving. I'm on my way to New Orleans to get my wedding gown now. Ollie, I am so sorry! I did not mean to…"

She sat back down and took my hand in hers. "You were my friend. One of the most wonderful people I have ever known. At one time I may have thought of love, but we were thirteen. That was a long time ago."

Silk let go of my hand and leaned back against the sofa. The tenderness was again replaced with self-confidence and self-assurance. "Besides, it is not about love; it is about opportunity." She spoke as if she was speaking to herself, practically oblivious to me. "It's about opportunities. Setting goals and achieving them. Getting what you want. You have to seize opportunities or they are gone. It could never work for us. Your arm..."

Silk gasped and put her hands to her mouth, shocked at what she had allowed herself to say. "Ollie, I'm so sorry. I didn't mean..."

No words could describe how I felt at that moment. The embarrassment of having my love spurned was suddenly replaced by feelings of complete rejection and total worthlessness. I'm a cripple—useless and valueless, even to Silk. There are few times that I have felt as low as I did that day, so totally overcome with nothingness. And no, it did not make me angry. At that moment there was nothing in me, nothing to draw on. No desire to lash out, no feelings of anger to show. No, even the desire to live left me. If someone had come at me with a knife, I don't think I would have had the strength or the will to fight them off.

"Silk, you don't have to explain. It's okay."

Silk began to cry. "Ollie, I'm so sorry."

After a couple of minutes, she wiped her eyes, took a deep breath, and stood up. "Ollie, I think it's time for me to go."

We walked back silently. As we approached the station, Silk turned to me and said, "Ollie, I'm glad I came to Lockhart. I really wanted to see you. I care about you deeply, and I know that

I hurt you. That was not my intention. Please forgive me. But I am who I am, and sometimes I don't like it, but I can't change it. Please remember the good times we had, and try to remember the good in me."

It took me years to get over that day. But I did. And now I look back on that visit with warmth for the most beautiful—and the most determined—woman I ever knew. Yes, Silk was who she was.

After Silk, I decided not to actively pursue a wife. I never wanted to experience the pain and hurt of rejection again and was content to live my life as a bachelor. Getting over rejection once was difficult enough, but twice? I did not want to know. But matrimony was not totally ruled out. If a wonderful lady came along, if things fell into place, and if she could accept me the way I was, that would be great. But caution would reign.

And I did find a wife, but it was another nine years before she made herself known.

Chapter 10

The War

When I was born in 1877, the Civil War, or "the War" as it was called, had been over for twelve years. But throughout my youth, it hung over us like a dark cloud. Its aftermath was a part of everyday life, and even today, in 1945, its ghost is still felt.

My grandfather was fifty-four when the War started; my father was only eight. Both were spared the horrors of battle, but not the horrors of war. Papa occasionally spoke of the time Sherman came through from Vicksburg on his way to Atlanta, burning and looting everything in his path. Papa was eleven at the time.

When I was growing up the name "Sherman" was a curse word—equated with Satan himself. In the eyes of the South, it was well deserved. To break the backbone of the Confederacy he was merciless, and in his march across the South, what could not be hauled away was destroyed.

Because of the railroad, Meridian had a large Confederate arsenal, as well as a military hospital and a prisoner-of-war stockade. It was also the headquarters for several Confederate state offices. Its importance grew even more during the long Siege of Vicksburg.

When Sherman came through Meridian, there was really no battle. General Polk had evacuated the town when he realized he could not stop Sherman. But that did not soften Sherman's resolve to "scorch the Earth." As Sherman left, he is reported to have said, "Meridian with its depots, store-houses, arsenal, hospitals, offices, hotels, and cantonments no longer exists."

Tucked away ten miles north of Meridian and not on the path from Vicksburg to Atlanta, one would think that Lockhart would have been overlooked. But not so. Sherman and his men were very thorough. This little hamlet was not spared the wrath of Sherman.

Papa once said that the only time he ever heard his father curse was when they were standing in front of the old house watching it burn to the ground. But then his father bowed his head, asked for forgiveness, and thanked the Good Lord that he and his family had been spared and were still alive.

Lockhart and Meridian were resilient and after the War quickly began to cover the scars with new homes and businesses. Within a few years there was little visible evidence of war—except for the monuments that began to spring up on the courthouse lawns. But the scars that remained visible the longest were the bodies of the soldiers—those who were wounded and lived, but were too broken and maimed to carry on a normal life.

When I was young, there always seemed to be veterans gathered on the front porch of Papa's general store. They wouldn't always be there at the same time. Depending on the day of the week and on the weather, there might be just one or two or three. But on a beautiful spring Saturday afternoon, there would usually be five or six of them sitting around on the old wicker-bottom, straight-back chairs, reminiscing and rocking, and sometimes crying.

A few of them came under their own power, while others were brought by their children or grandchildren—an opportunity for them to have a little companionship, and an opportunity for the family to have a short reprieve.

Over the years the number gradually decreased as age and sickness took its toll, until when we moved to Meridian in 1902, there were none.

Before my accident, I really didn't pay much attention to them. When I would climb the steps to the store, I would give them a polite greeting and might stop and visit for a moment. But that was about it.

After my accident, things were different. I thought of those old veterans often, but rather than thoughts of compassion or sympathy or even empathy, my thoughts were thoughts of fear—fear that I would end up just like them. Sometimes I would dream that I was sitting on the porch. They would be around me, nodding their heads and rocking. I would try to get up and leave, but they wouldn't let me. They said that was where I now belonged.

Nathaniel Stephens was one of those veterans. He was usually there only on Saturdays and then only if the weather permitted. He lived with his daughter, Mary, her husband, Clyde, and their four children on a small farm near Topton four miles away, too far to come more frequently. By wagon it was a good hour and half trip.

Mr. Stephens had lost both of his legs. The right leg was missing from mid calf down, and the left just above the knee. I had always thought it so strange. Why didn't the doctor make them even?—not that it would make him more functional. But it would have looked better. Other than his legs, he appeared to be completely normal and healthy.

When Mr. Stephens's family would arrive at the store, Clyde would enlist the help of Papa, and they would lift him out of the wagon and carry him to a chair. The family would visit a minute or two, maybe look around the store, and then drive away. Late afternoon, they would show back up to take Mr. Stephens home.

Mr. Stephens was rather quiet. Several of the veterans would keep the conversation going, telling stories of the War, or of their youth, or of lost opportunities. But not Mr. Stephens. He seemed content to listen. But then, sometimes I wonder if he was listening at all. He never smiled and never laughed. For the most part he just sat there.

On a Saturday in May 1900, I stopped by the store on my way home from the depot. It was noon, and Papa and I usually walked home together for lunch. We had been doing that since I started working full-time at the depot four years earlier.

That day Mr. Stephens was the only person on the porch. In fact, the numbers had been dwindling for several years, and it was not uncommon to find him there alone on Saturdays. Mr. Stephens was now an old man, in his late sixties. The War had been over thirty-five years.

As I walked up the steps, I gave Mr. Stephens a polite greeting. He didn't respond. I shrugged my shoulders and walked on in.

Papa was busy with a customer and said to give him five minutes and he would be ready. I went back outside and sat down beside Mr. Stephens.

"It's a beautiful day, isn't it?" I said, trying to make a little conversation. From years of experience, I knew that with Mr. Stephens if there was to be conversation it would be me doing the talking.

Mr. Stephens nodded.

"Do ya'll hear much from Jake?" I asked. Jake was Mary's youngest son, and he and I were the same age. He had enlisted in the army during the Spanish-American War in 1898 and was still serving our country.

Mr. Stephens was silent for a moment and then said, "He's still down in Cuba, helping keep the peace during the military occupation. He says his duty is over in about six months, and then he'll be coming home."

I had expected him to answer a simple "Yes" or "No," and was surprised at his response.

"Well, that's good," I said. "It'll be good to see him again."

"He's a fool," Mr. Stephens said.

I was caught off guard with his statement. All I could say was, "Sir?"

"Anyone who would volunteer and take a chance of getting himself blown up is a fool. 'Want to serve my country.' 'Want to experience adventure.' Hog wash! You and I both know there's nothing worth having your body destroyed and your life made useless."

I didn't agree with him but felt it was best not to argue.

Mr. Stephens took a deep breath, shook his head, and said, "But then, I was a fool once, and I've been paying for it ever since."

I didn't know whether to respond or not, so I didn't. We sat there silently.

After a minute, Mr. Stephens adjusted in his chair, looked over at me, and said, "You don't know anything about me, do you?"

I was taken aback, and embarrassed. He was right. I had been passing by him for all of my twenty-two years and knew absolutely nothing about him. I didn't know what to say.

"You know, I once had a good life. A wife, two children, a nice little farm. We didn't make much money, but we got by—and we were happy."

Mr. Stephens shook his head. "Then the War came.

"Everyone was talking about joining up, wanting to fight the Yankees, not letting anybody tell us how to run our business, talking about saving our culture—whatever that meant.

"I got caught up in all the excitement and joined the Army of Mississippi under General Beauregard."

I was so surprised at the conversation. I had not heard Mr. Stephens say this much in my whole life.

He sat there for a moment and stroked his grey beard.

"Callie cried and cried," he continued. "Callie was my wife. She told me not to go. What was she to do with the farm? I told her this war wouldn't last long, and I'd be back in time for planting. Besides, her folks lived close and would be there to see about her. 'But what about the two girls?' she asked. Mary was ten and Rachael was six. 'They need their father here, not off somewhere fighting a war—and maybe not ever coming back.'

"Well, I came back—but like this," he said in disgust and pointed down at his legs.

"The first and only fighting I saw was at Shiloh. That's where it happened."

His eyes narrowed and he clenched his fists. He opened his mouth slightly, his lips tight, as if he were going to either scream or explode. He then took a deep breath and relaxed. He reached up and rubbed his forehead.

"Ollie, I want you to hear my story."

"In the spring of 1862, after only a little training, we were marched up to Corinth to protect the Memphis and Charleston Railroad. That railroad was a big supply route for the Confederacy, connecting the East and the West. When we got there, we found out that the Yankees under General Grant were already encamped at Pittsburg Landing on the Tennessee River.

"General Johnston took over the Army of Mississippi from Beauregard shortly after we arrived, and the plan was to make a surprise attack and drive the Yankees away from the railroad and the river. Within a few days there were almost forty-five thousand of us camped around Corinth. Men everywhere. More men than I had seen in my whole life.

"We surprised them all right. We attacked early on April 6. They didn't know what hit them. We thought it was going to be a rout, but things started to change. The advantage of surprise did not last long. Those Yankees were better trained and better outfitted than us. I only had my old hunting rifle with me. Some of the fellows with me were fighting with old muskets. A few didn't even have a gun—fighting with spears. We fought them good, but once those Yankees got organized they started fighting back.

"We were fighting at a place called the Hornet's Nest. Those Yankees were putting up a strong fight. Men were falling right and left on both sides. Men screaming and hollering in fear and in pain. Our unit was ordered to advance. I stood up and suddenly I felt like someone had knocked my feet out from under me. I fell to the ground like a rag doll, and couldn't move. It was horrible pain. A load of grapeshot had hit me, and my legs felt like they had been torn apart. If it had hit me higher, I would have been cut in half.

"I lay there all day, unable to move, fighting going on all around me. I found out later that General Johnston was killed about the same time I was wounded, and Beauregard had to take command again.

"Late afternoon the fighting at the Hornet's Nest was over. Men everywhere screaming and crying—and I was one of them. It seemed forever, but finally a stretcher came and carried me to a tent. All around the tent were men on stretchers. Many of them already dead, others crying for help.

"A man stopped in front of me, bent down, and cut my pants legs up to my thighs. He said, 'Soldier, I need to get a good look at your wounds.'

"I recognized that voice. It was Dr. Knox. He was a young man back then, not much older than me.

"I said, 'Dr. Knox?'

"He looked at me and said, 'Nathaniel? Is that you?'

A feeling of relief came over me. I thanked the Good Lord that someone I knew was there to take care of me.

"'Yes, sir, it's me,' I answered. 'Please, Dr. Knox, please help me.'

"'Nathaniel, I'm sorry. Both legs have to come off.'

"If he had rammed a knife in my stomach, I don't think it would have been any worse. Telling me that I was going to die might have been easier to take."

I remembered I had the same feeling ten years earlier when Dr. Knox told me that my arm could not be saved.

"A few minutes later I was in the tent. Thankfully he had some chloroform left. They ran out later that night and started cutting off arms and legs with nothing but a piece of wood to bite on. I guess I was lucky in that.

"Two weeks later I was on a train with dozens of other wounded headed back to Meridian. I was in the hospital there for two months. Thankfully I was close enough for Callie and the girls to come visit."

He started to choke up.

I was shocked. Mr. Stephens was actually getting emotional—opening up his feelings to me. I didn't know what to think.

"I was so glad to see them, but I wanted to die." He blotted his eyes with his sleeve. "The look on Callie's face—horror and pity and fear and love, all wrapped up together. I couldn't bear it. And the girls. Little Rachael was only seven and didn't under-stand. Even when I got home she couldn't understand that I was never going to walk again.

"They took me back home to the farm in Topton. I couldn't do anything. I couldn't even get myself out of the bed. I had to be carried from room to room. Callie's father put some wheels on a chair so they could at least roll me around the house. But I couldn't leave the house without being carried.

"When I had gone off to war, Callie's folks had moved in with her and the girls. Her papa kept the farm going and kept them fed. When I got home, they stayed on. If it wasn't for him, we couldn't have made it.

"But one day he all of a sudden fell over dead. He was healthy one minute and dead the next. It was mournful to see him die, but it was frightening to us. We were worried that we would starve to death.

"Ollie, you probably don't know this, but your grandfather saved us. When I thought that there was no hope, he came over with one of his slaves. Gave him to us to work our land and keep things going. He said we could keep him until things got better. But Ollie, things didn't get better. The War was long from being over. It went on another three years and the worst was yet to come.

"Then it happened. In 1864 Sherman's troops came through burning and stealing. They told us to get out of the house—that they were going to burn it down. I rolled out on the porch and begged them not to do it—that we had no place to go. They just laughed and said they had just as soon see a worthless Johnny Reb like me burn. One of them even aimed his gun at me and said that he had a mind to put a bullet right through my heart. I think he would have done it if the lieutenant with them hadn't told him to put it away.

"They burned the fields and ran their horses through our garden. Your grandfather's slave even ran away. We had nothing and nobody to help us get things back going. We had to live in an old shed behind where the house had been. It was the only thing the Yankees didn't burn down.

"And then Callie got sick." Mr. Stephens began to choke up again. "I think everything was just too much for her. She wanted to be strong, but she couldn't. When she got sick, I think that she just gave up. As she lay dying, she told me she was sorry. She asked me to forgive her."

Mr. Stephens began to cry uncontrollably. There was no one else on the porch but him and me. There was no reason for this old man to hold back.

"Ollie, she told me that *she* was sorry. Asked for *me* to forgive *her*. Oh, it was *me* that needed to be forgiven! I had abandoned my own family to seek adventure, to fight in a cause that I didn't understand and didn't really believe in. I had returned half the man I was and could no longer provide for my own family. I had failed them, and with that failure I had killed my wife."

Mr. Stephens continued to cry. I sat there silently. After a few minutes, he wiped his eyes again.

"Then Clyde showed up. The War was over. We were struggling to have enough to eat, living day by day. Mary was fourteen and Rachael was ten, and they worked all day in the garden and begged from the neighbors when there was not enough.

"Clyde was on his way home to Quitman from fighting in Tennessee, and happened to stop by, wanting something to eat. All we had was some greens which we shared with him. He was eighteen and seemed to take a liking to Mary. They spent the afternoon visiting, and then he left.

"Two weeks later he showed back up, and said he had come to stay. He wanted to marry my daughter.

"Clyde started farming the land, built a house where the old one had been, and before long was raising a family. And he's had to take care of me."

As he continued to speak, the openness began to disappear and a cold, hardness replaced it.

"Useless. For almost forty years unable to do anything—nothing but a burden on my family. Having to ask for everything. All I've been good for is taking up space."

He clenched his fists. "Nothing is worth that—no cause, no purpose. I should have minded my own business and stayed home. Things would have been good. I was a fool for what I did. And the way I look at it there are a lot of fools who have suffered and died when they should have minded their business and looked out for their own."

Mr. Stephens was quiet again. He then raised his head and looked at me. "Ollie, was it worth it to you?"

"Sir?" I said.

"Do you ever think you should have let him die? Junius would be gone, but you would be whole. Does that ever cross your mind?"

What is he asking me? I thought. *Don't make me think thoughts like that.*

"One day you will be old like me. Will you look back and think that you were a fool for what you did? If you hadn't done that, you wouldn't be living your life a burden to your family."

I couldn't respond. Am I a burden to my family? Is my life a waste? Was it really worth it?

At that moment Papa came out on the porch. "Ollie, you ready to go home for lunch?"

I sat there and didn't move. My mind was in a fog. I didn't know what to do.

"Ollie, let's go."

I got up without saying anything and walked down the steps with Papa. We walked along silently. I couldn't stop thinking—did I do the right thing? Is Mr. Stephens right—am I going to regret what I did someday?

Papa broke the silence. "Ollie, I'm sorry. Don't pay attention to what he said. He's just a bitter old man."

"But Papa…"

"No, son. Old Nathaniel has never come to grips with what has happened. I don't see how Clyde and Mary put up with him. All that they do for him … never a thank-you. Only complaining. He's been through a lot and I know it's been hard for him. But he should have found peace in his soul by now.

"I don't know why he opened up to you like he did. For a minute I thought that some good was going to come out of his story, but it didn't. He shouldn't have said what he said."

We walked along. I didn't say anything, my head hung low.

"Ollie, you and Nathaniel are as different as night and day. You're making something of yourself. You could have taken what happened to you and given up like he did, but you didn't. You've got a good life and a good job. Don't you ever think that you are a burden on us because you are not. You contribute just as much to this family as I do.

"And Ollie, no matter what Nathaniel says, there are things worth dying for. Things worth getting hurt for. And yes, you did the right thing. As Jesus said in the Bible, 'Greater love hath no man than this, that a man lay down his life for his friends.' Don't ever let anyone like Nathaniel, or even the Devil himself, make you think otherwise."

Chapter 11

Dallas

In 1908, I finally found my true love. I guess I can call it true love even though we divorced after twenty-four years of marriage. Deep down I still love her, love her very much. But I suppose that sometimes you can love someone, but not be able to live with her.

Her name is Anna Adrienne Therrel Parker. She goes by Adrienne. When we married I was thirty and she was sixteen. That may have been part of the problem.

In 1902, when I was twenty-four, my family moved from Lockhart to Meridian. Meridian was booming—thanks to the railroad—and had become the largest city in the state, boasting about thirty thousand citizens. Little Lockhart was slowly drying up.

Being single, I was still living at home, and when Papa made the decision to move, I saw no reason for me to stay behind. Papa bought a large two-story house on 25th Street, and I moved into one of the upstairs bedrooms. I continued to work for the M&O Railroad, but transferred to the Meridian station, doing the same thing I did in Lockhart—telegraphy.

Six years after the move I met Adrienne. She had come to Meridian from her home in Dallas, Texas, to care for a dying aunt. She was only sixteen but appeared mature far beyond her age. Since I was thirty years old, most people today would say that I had "robbed the cradle," but it did not seem that way to me. In fact, at that time it was not unusual for older more established men to court younger women. Even my father, at age thirty-one, married my stepmother, Lizzie, when she was only nineteen.

Adrienne was beautiful, but I have to be honest—not as beautiful as Silk. But unlike Silk, Adrienne had a warmth and a kindness that drew me to her. There were no motives, no "lessons to be learned," no "opportunities to take advantage of." Also my physical state did not seem to bother her at all. She would tell me that I was still a man, and "a wonderful man at that." Adrienne and I fell in love, and after her aunt died, we left Meridian for Dallas and were married in December of that year.

The initial plan was to go to Dallas for our wedding and then return to Meridian to live. Lauderdale County was my home. In fact, until I left for Dallas, I had never been outside of her boundaries and thought I never would. Here I would live, die, and be buried. Truth be known, I was more than a little apprehensive about leaving even for the short time it would take to get married. But things changed. Not only did I fall in love with Adrienne, I also fell in love with Dallas and the no frills Texas lifestyle.

Interestingly, Dallas and Meridian had very similar beginnings. Both owe their existence to the railroad: the Mobile and Ohio intersecting with the Alabama and Vicksburg in 1854 for Meridian, and the Houston and Texas Central intersecting the Texas and Pacific in 1873 for Dallas. Both cities were initially agriculturally based. At the turn of the century, both were the largest cities and the major business centers in their respective states. Their populations were comparable: Meridian with about 30,000 and Dallas with 40,000. But in the twenty-four years I lived in Dallas, 1908 to 1932, their paths diverged greatly. Meridian remained stagnant with no growth in population or business influence.

By 1930, Jackson, the capital of the state located ninety miles to the west, surpassed Meridian in population and business activity.

Dallas, on the other hand, saw her population skyrocket to 260,000 and her role shift from agriculture to banking and insurance, becoming the center not only for Texas but for the entire Southwest. With the opening of Neiman Marcus in 1907 and A. Harris and Sanger Brothers, Dallas also became a major fashion center. With the discovery of oil in 1930 in Kilgore, one hundred miles east of Dallas, she again saw herself in a new role as the center of oil commerce for the states of Texas and Oklahoma.

The weather was also similar, but different. Meridian and Dallas were about the same distance from the equator and at similar elevations. Summers in both were hot, but in Meridian it was hot and humid; in Dallas it was notably hotter and dry. In Meridian everyone was drenched with sweat in the summer. In Dallas sweat was usually not a problem. Winters in Meridian were mild and wet; in Dallas a little colder and windy.

And then there are the people. Both Mississippians and Texans are good people—honest, hardworking. They will give the shirts off their backs to help family and friends. But social structure was vastly different. Even though Meridian was less than fifty years old when I left in 1908, an almost aristocratic class had established itself. "Old money" is what it would later be called. Money from the railway and timber industry set those families a notch above the rest. Fashion and social entertainment filled the newspaper and the minds of the Meridianites. There was a constant awareness of who was who, the haves and the have-nots— where each person fit into the hierarchy of society.

Dallas was different. There was money. *Lots* of money! Railroad and cattle money, and later oil money. Dallas families had money that the Mississippians could not even imagine. But the people were different, less conscious of where they were in society, less likely to ask who your grandfather was or where you lived. Yes, there was fashion and social entertainment, but there were always the cowboy hats, the boots, the Levis, and the dust.

Finding work in Dallas was not a problem. Telegraphers were always in high demand and in no time I was working for the railway system doing the same thing I did in Lockhart and Meridian— but on a totally different level. Telegraphy in Lockhart had been a simple endeavor with few messages to be sent and received. Meridian had been busy but manageable. Dallas initially was not noticeably different from Meridian, but as the city grew, the workload became monumental. The telegraph key was never quiet, messages coming and going at all times of the day and night. New telegraphers were being hired every few months to keep up with the pace, and still we never felt that we caught up. But I thoroughly enjoyed it, and after a few years I was promoted to head telegrapher—hiring and firing and setting the work schedules.

Adrienne and I bought a small house not far from downtown Dallas, and we settled into life as Texans—well, I was a Texan with a heart for Mississippi. Life was good, and life was busy.

Church was a very important part of our lives in Dallas. We attended the First Methodist Church of Dallas, along with Adrienne's parents. We were there every Sunday morning, Sunday night, and Wednesday night. Here we found purpose and meaning in the Scriptures and sermons.

At church we also found friends. Our closest friends were the people we sang with, prayed with, and worshiped beside. I've always said that if a person wants a group of friends who will be with him and for him in good times and bad, go to church. And I don't mean just *go* to church, get involved. It surprises me when people come in the back door, listen to a message, and leave; and then wonder why no one knows them.

Chapter 12

Fatherhood

Eighteen months after we were married, we had our first baby, a beautiful girl named Margurite. A year later came Stephen, and two years later Elizabeth was born. Our son, Stephen—Stephen Decatur Parker II—we named after both my father, of the same name, and after Lizzie and Papa's first born, also of the same name, who died at fifteen months of age when I was twelve. It was to honor one and to memorialize the other.

I've often wondered why I had not been named Stephen Decatur Parker instead of the name going to my younger half brother. Typically if a child is going to bear the exact name of the father, it will be the oldest, the first born. I never asked Papa why. The only explanation that I can come up with is that it was a difference in Papa's wives. My mother must have wanted to name her son something other than her husband's name, but Lizzie either wanted to, or agreed to, pass on Papa's name.

When we were thinking of a name for a boy, we seriously considered giving him mine—Oliver Eras Parker. But truthfully, neither one of us liked my name. Oh, the name was okay for me, but for a child it seemed too old-fashioned. Also Stephen Decatur was a name that drew attention.

Commodore Stephen Decatur had been a naval war hero in the War of 1812, and through the years a lot of things, including children, had been named for him. My great-grandfather had fought with him during the First Barbary War against Tripoli in 1803 aboard the *Enterprise* and then the *Intrepid*. Papa said that his grandfather thought so much of the Commodore that he insisted on a grandchild being named after him. He would have given the honor to one of his own children, but he never had another boy.

Our youngest, Elizabeth—Adrienne Elizabeth—was named after Adrienne and after Lizzie, my stepmother. We decided to call her Elizabeth instead of Adrienne for two reasons. One was to prevent obvious confusion with her mother, and the other in memory of Papa and Lizzie's sixth child, Elizabeth, who also was named after Lizzie, and who died in 1903 at eleven months.

Our oldest child's name was a little different—Margurite—not Margaret, not Margarita, but Margurite. Adrienne's family had a housekeeper and nanny who essentially raised Adrienne and her siblings. Margurite was from Mexico and was in her fifties when she began working for the Therrels. She could barely speak English, but she loved those children as if they were her very own. Thanks to Margurite, Adrienne speaks perfect Spanish. Margurite died when Adrienne was seventeen, while we were expecting our first child. Adrienne insisted that if the baby was a girl, we would name her Margurite.

Fatherhood for me was a challenge, especially when the children were small. It surprised me how little I could do for them with only one arm. The simple task of holding them was difficult. When I was sitting, someone could rest an infant in my waiting arms—or rather arm—but I could do nothing else. There was no feeding the child as I held him, no adjusting his clothing, no pinching his little cheeks. If he started to squirm, all I could do was hold tighter, which made us both more uncomfortable.

I never once tried to walk around with a baby. The thought of dropping one of my little ones made me very cautious.

When they were a little bigger, I was able to help feed them, since Adrienne bottle fed all three. If the baby was in a bassinette or bed, or lying in my lap—and big enough to cooperate—I could hold a bottle without problem.

Burping a baby was difficult, but not out of the question. I learned to rest the baby in my lap, lean forward and with my hand behind his neck, pull him up to me and straighten up. I could pat his little back with my hand until the gas dislodged and then let him back down for more of the bottle. It was awkward, but doable.

Speaking of bottle feeding, I never quite understood the rapidly growing fashion of giving cow's milk rather than mama's milk to a baby. I would assume that God had made cow's milk to be ideally suited for the bovine species, and mama's milk for the human species, but the children seemed to do just fine and grew healthy and strong.

I think that one reason Adrienne decided to bottle feed was her obsession with cleanliness and order, which I will expound on a little later. The bottles could be sterilized and the milk was pasteurized and germ free. Powdered milk and condensed milk with all sorts of additives—flour, malt, potassium bicarbonate, vitamins, to name a few—were readily available. Just add water and ready to go. We bought cans and boxes of Carnation and PET Milk by the caseloads.

I still chuckle when I think about how Mr. Elbridge Stuart in 1901 came up with the name "Carnation" for his evaporated milk. He had founded the Pacific Coast Condensed Milk Company in 1899 and was doing quite well but wanted a catchier name. He happened to walk past a tobacco shop in Seattle and noticed the brand of one of the cigars—"Carnation." He thought it was catchier than "Pacific Coast," so he went back to his office and renamed his company the Carnation Evaporated Milk Company. He later came up with the slogan "Milk from Contented Cows" when he started his own breeding program for healthier cows.

Changing a diaper was out of the question. There was no way to hold up little legs with my only hand and accomplish the needed task at the same time. When I mentioned my inability to perform this duty to some of my friends, one of them exclaimed, "What are you complaining about? I've been trying to come up with a good excuse for years, but none of mine work." Everyone but me thought it was funny. I guess when you're unable to do something because you can't—even though it is a dirty, unpopular job—there is a feeling that you are missing out on part of life.

As the children got older and they could help do things themselves, my ability to help increased. Assisting a little girl in putting on her dress is a lot easier than dressing her when arms and legs go everywhere.

We enjoyed outings, and even with my limitations, we had some great adventures together—picnics on the banks of the Trinity River, visits to the Dallas Zoo and the State Fair at Fair Park. One of our favorite pastimes was taking the trolley to Love Field and watching the airplanes take off and land. Little Stephen particularly enjoyed these afternoon outings.

Love Field opened as a military airstrip in 1917 to train pilots who were destined for the aerial dogfights over France and Germany. We would go there on Saturday afternoons and watch the airplanes practice their maneuvers. There were several different types of airplanes at the field including Sopwith Pups and Triplanes, but my favorite plane to watch was the Sopwith Camel, a biplane that was well known for its combat abilities. The maneuvers that she could make, the dives and twists and turns, were truly amazing.

After World War I, Love Field continued to be a military installation, but it was not as busy. In fact, some days when we were there on our outings, there would be no planes flying at all. But we still went, if for no other reason than to have a nice little picnic.

In 1927 Love field was opened to civilian use, and the next year Delta Air Service began regular runs from Dallas to Jackson, with stops in Shreveport and Monroe. At one time I considered taking the flight from Dallas to Jackson, only ninety miles from Meridian. This would have made the trip so much quicker, but I decided I would stick with the railroad. The cost was one factor, and another factor was flying. Man has two arms and two legs and no wings for a reason. Well, most people have two arms.

Interestingly, Delta began as the world's first crop-dusting venture—Huff Daland Dusters in Monroe, Louisiana. When C. E. Woolman purchased it from Mr. Daland in 1928, he turned it into a passenger service, and changed the name to Delta, after the Mississippi Delta.

I have very fond memories of those days when the children were young. Each day I came home from the demands of work to a wife and three children who loved me and accepted me the way I was.

As the children grew, the demands of fatherhood increased, and at times my limitations were very evident, especially when dealing with a growing boy. It must be inborn, but if there is a ball close by, a boy wants to throw it and have it thrown back to him. I could do that. One hand was all that was needed.

But with the popularity of baseball—and its bat—difficulties arose. I could toss the ball to him and let him hit it without problem, but there was no way I could hit the ball to him. Other dads could hold the bat in one hand, toss the ball up with the other, and with both hands swing and hit it. But not me. I just couldn't do it.

At times, Stephen appeared disappointed at my limitations with baseball and other physical activities that required two hands, but overall he understood and accepted it.

Like so many boys in the United States, Stephen became almost obsessed with baseball. Every morning he would commandeer the sports section of the *Dallas Morning News*, memorizing statistics and checking on what was happening with his favorite team and his favorite player—the New York Yankees and Babe Ruth.

In the late 1910s and early 1920s, the "dead-ball" era of baseball was ending, and the age of the power hitters like Babe Ruth, Lou Gehrig, Rogers Hornsby, and Hack Wilson, was ushering in, making baseball a much more exciting game. In 1919, the Babe was traded by the Boston Red Sox to the Yankees and began hitting the balls out of Polo Grounds Park, packing the stadium like never before and making baseball the most popular topic of any conversation in the country. It seems that the Red Sox still haven't recovered from that trade!

In the spring of 1921, when he was ten, Stephen announced that he wanted to go to St. Louis to see a baseball game.

"Daddy," Stephen said with excitement, "the Babe's going to be in St. Louis in two weeks. The Yankees are coming to play the Cardinals at Sportsman's Park on that Sunday. Please take me. It will be great fun."

"I don't know, Stephen," I said shaking my head. "St. Louis is a long way from Dallas. It's at least six hundred miles. We can't just run up there for a ball game. It's too far."

"Oh, please," he begged. "We can do it. There's not a closer city with a professional team than St. Louis, and with the Yankees there, we have to go. I won't ever have another chance to see the Babe play. If we don't go, I don't know what I'll do."

I had heard that before—the old "if I don't get my way, I think I'll die" plea.

Stephen wouldn't take no for an answer. For days he pleaded and begged. He had to see the Babe play. Life would not be complete if he didn't.

He even researched the train schedule. We could leave Friday afternoon and get to St. Louis Saturday morning. We would have a day of sightseeing, go to the game on Sunday, then catch the late afternoon train and be back in Dallas Monday morning. For a young fellow, he certainly had it all planned out.

Finally I gave in, primarily because Adrienne got tired of his whining and said it should be a fun trip for the two of us.

On Friday afternoon we began our father-son journey to the city of St. Louis. Before leaving the house, I strapped on my prosthetic arm, wanting to blend in as much as possible. I didn't want to stick out like a sore thumb.

The trip on the Missouri-Kansas-Texas was nothing special for Stephen. For as long as he could remember, the family had been making yearly trips at Christmas back to Meridian. A train ride was old hat to him. After a light supper in the dining car, we retired to our two berths in the Pullman car and slept soundly, lulled by the "clickity-clack" of the tracks.

We were in St. Louis bright and early on Saturday morning and began our day of sightseeing. We took the trolley to Forest Park where the Louisiana Purchase Exposition of 1904 had been. About all that remained of that magnificent fair was the zoo and the art museum, both of which I thoroughly enjoyed.

Stephen, though, was too excited about the game to really enjoy seeing anything. All he did was talk baseball. He couldn't wait to see his Yankees and the Babe.

"Daddy," Stephen said as we walked around Forest Park, "do you suppose I'll be able to get an autograph from the Babe?"

"Well, son, I don't know." I hated to tell him the chances of that happening were about as good as my growing my arm back.

"Oh, I hope I can. It will be the biggest thing that ever happened in all of my life. Daddy, I bet we can do it!" Stephen exclaimed. "If we stand in the right place when he comes out of the dressing room, he'll see me and sign my baseball." He pulled his old baseball out of his pocket. "I will put it in a glass box and never hit it again. Everyone back home will be so jealous."

Again I tried to downplay it, not letting him get his hopes up. "Stephen, you have to remember that there are always a lot of people around him. I don't think that we will be able to get close enough to him."

"We can try! Can't we?"

I didn't know what else to say.

All afternoon Stephen talked and planned the best way to get the Babe's autograph while I stewed and worried about the disappointment he would most likely endure. But then, disappointment can be a learning experience. He will get over it.

As I tucked him into bed that night, Stephen said, "Daddy, there has got to be some way to get his attention. Something you can do so he will see me and give me his autograph. There's got to be. I know you can do it."

Oh! My! It has now gone from us to me. He's now expecting *me* to do it. What can I do?

As I undressed and unbuckled the harness holding my prosthesis, it suddenly came to me. This is it! Why not use my handicap to my advantage for once? All my life I have been trying to blend in, wearing this contraption so no one will look at me. Why not make myself stick out? By years of experience I knew that if I didn't wear it, people would look at me. Babe Ruth will look at me!

The next morning I was almost as excited as Stephen. It just might work. With a little luck and effort we may accomplish the impossible.

Late morning we left the hotel. It was a little cool, but I decided not to wear my coat: I wanted nothing to make my armless shoulder hard to see. I would carry it to wear after our deed was done.

As expected, we got the looks—the little glances and turns of the heads as we walked along. Instead of being self-conscious, for once I was delighted. When we boarded the trolley, a young man actually offered his seat to me.

We arrived at Sportsman's Park and got in line to buy our tickets. After a moment, the man in front of us turned around, noticed my incomplete state, and let us go ahead of him. Wow! This might work!

We bought our tickets and headed to find our seats. Sportsman's Park, or Busch Stadium as it was later called, was huge! When we walked in, Stephen said nothing; he just looked up and stared.

Sportsman's Stadium had been built in 1881 for the St. Louis Brown Stockings and would seat eight thousand fans. In 1902 it was enlarged to eighteen thousand, and in 1925, four years after our visit, it was again renovated and enlarged to accommodate thirty thousand. The increasing popularity of baseball and the fact that the Cardinals had begun playing there in 1920 made the bigger seating capacity necessary, and profitable.

We found our seats, left my coat, and headed to the dressing rooms. When we arrived, a large crowd had gathered—young boys, young men, and old men—all hoping to get an autograph.

Oh, no! I thought. *This is going to be impossible.*

We walked up to the crowd, and the most unbelievable thing happened. It was like Moses parting the Red Sea. Fellows would turn, see me standing there, step to the side, and usher us in with a kind, "Come on. Let me get out of your way."

It's interesting. When you are different, most people want to give you space. They don't want to be too close. I don't know if they think they may catch it, or if different equates to dirty, or if they are just uncomfortable being too close. I don't know, but it worked to our advantage. In no time we were at the front, right beside the door to the dressing room.

"Is he going to come out? Is he going to come out?" an excited Stephen repeated over and over as we stood there waiting.

"He will. Be patient."

I have to admit—I was as impatient and excited as he was!

After about ten minutes the door opened, and a steady stream of Yankee players emerged—Wally Pipp, Bob Meusel, Carl Mays, Waite Hoyt. Any of their autographs would have been considered a trophy. But we waited. We did not want our ball to be tied up when the Babe appeared. People started crowding around to get autographs on everything possible—hats, gloves, balls, hands—you name it.

Suddenly he was there! The Babe was right in front of us! As he walked by, he glanced over at me, or rather at my missing arm, and looked up at my face. This was my chance—my only chance!

"Mr. Ruth," I shouted. "Would you mind signing my son's baseball? He's one of your biggest fans."

The Babe smiled and looked down at Stephen. "Why, sure. I'd be honored to."

He knelt down and took the ball from Stephen's hand. "What's your name, big boy?"

Stephen didn't say a word. He was too stunned to do anything. He just stared into the Babe's face.

"His name is Stephen. With a *P–H*," I said.

He signed the ball and tossed it back to him. The Babe stood up, gave a fake punch to Stephen's chin, and said, "Wish me luck, big boy." Then he was gone.

For the next thirty minutes, the only thing Stephen said was "Wow!"

We took our seats in the stadium and enjoyed hot dogs and popcorn as we watched the Babe and his Yankees slug it out with Rogers Hornsby and his Cardinals. Both of them had a great game, but the Cardinals won with Hornsby's home run in the bottom of the ninth. The Yankees did go on to have a great season, winning the American League pennant, but losing out to the Giants in the World Series at the Polo Grounds, five games to three.

Late that afternoon we took the trolley back to the hotel, gathered our luggage, and headed to Union Station for our overnight trip back to Dallas. We were two tired but happy travelers. And yes, I did strap my arm back on for our return trip. My need for attention had passed.

When we arrived the next morning, Adrienne and the two girls met us at the station to take Stephen home. I had not wanted to take a day of vacation, so I stayed to work. As they left, Stephen waved good-bye, holding his baseball for everyone to see. I don't think he stopped talking about that trip for six months.

That trip to St. Louis was one of the few times in my life where being handicapped was an advantage. I almost felt guilty for using it for such a purpose, but when I thought about all of the difficulties and lost opportunities that my loss has caused, my guilt melted away.

Most of my memories of the children growing up, like the St. Louis adventure, are good. I think back on them with great fondness. But there are some memories that are not good; they are painful—and not in a tragic or disciplinary sense.

I suspect most parents have those memories: a time when a child hurt them deeply—and probably didn't even know it—and the parent has no alternative but to be silent, forgive, and try to forget.

It happened about three years after the St. Louis trip. Stephen was thirteen. He was still as obsessed as ever with baseball and spent his summers playing ball with the gang on one of the vacant lots. But he had also become interested in the Boy Scouts.

The Boy Scout movement had begun in England in 1907 and rapidly gained popularity throughout the world. In the United States, it grew like wildfire. With the migration of families from the farms to the cities, it was seen as a way to keep boys connected to the outdoors and also to instill in them "patriotism, courage, self-reliance, and kindred values." The Boy Scouts of America was officially incorporated in 1910 under the sponsorship of the YMCA, and within a few years every church and civic organization in the country had a troop, including our First Methodist Church. Young boys were seen everywhere dressed in dark green uniforms and bright neckerchiefs "doing a good deed daily."

Stephen joined our church troop in 1922 when he was eleven, and within two years had studied and worked hard on his advancements and had achieved the rank of First Class Scout. He and his buddies enjoyed some great times, camping out and going on nature hikes under the supervision of their scoutmaster Hayes Scott.

Another thing happened when Stephen turned thirteen—he became a thirteen-year-old. He suddenly was a teenager, experiencing all of the phases that teens seem to go through. He became moody; he didn't want to talk. He much preferred his friends' company over ours and acted as though he didn't want to be seen in public with his parents.

The teenage coldness bothered me. I didn't like it at all, but everyone said it was natural. He would grow out of it and become human again.

One morning I was busy as usual at the station when Stephen's scoutmaster walked in carrying a small suitcase.

"Howdy, Ollie. How are you doing?" Hayes said as he set his bag down and we shook hands.

"Everything's good," I answered as I looked down at his bag. "Looks like you're headed somewhere."

"Yea, a business meeting in Kansas City. A quick trip. I should be back in a couple of days. In fact, I'll definitely be back by Friday. I can't miss the campout this weekend.

"I'm sorry you're not going to make it," he continued. "Stephen told me that you have to work and can't get off. Sorry it didn't work out. It's going to be a great time. I've wanted to have this father-son campout since I became scoutmaster, and finally it's coming together. It will be a great experience for the boys and their dads.

"Hopefully the weather will cooperate. You know how March can be—either a perfect seventy degrees or freezing with icicles hanging off the tents. But either way, it'll be good."

He looked up at the clock and then picked up his suitcase. "Need to catch my train."

As he started to walk away, he said, "Oh, by the way, I told Stephen he could sleep in the tent with Billy and me since you won't be there. We won't let him feel left out. Maybe you can make it next year. See you later."

I stood there dumbfounded. I couldn't speak. Campout? Father-son? This was the first I had heard of it and was shocked that Stephen had not mentioned it to me. I didn't know what to think. Had I missed something? Surely there was a good explanation.

The more I thought about it the more confused I got. I was off that weekend, and Stephen had to have known it. He always knew. Why, he kept up with my work rotation better than I did. He had to have known.

And if he knew, then he lied. He lied to his scoutmaster. Lied about my working, and lied that I could not change my schedule. But why?

Was something going on that I didn't understand or didn't know about? I knew he had been acting strangely, but he's a teenager. They all tend to go through that phase.

Then it hit me. This has got to be about me. He doesn't want me to go because he's ashamed of me. There can be no other reason. He doesn't want to be seen with his one-armed father. He doesn't want the other boys to see what his father can't do. What use is a cripple on a campout? He can't do anything. Why, he won't even be able to put up a tent. How embarrassing it would be to have to ask another father to do it for him! And for activities that dads and sons are to participate in—he will only be a detriment. Daddy is okay at home and at work, but he doesn't need to be around my friends.

I suddenly felt empty—a sick feeling came over me that made me nauseated. It was a feeling that I had not experienced in almost twenty-five years, not since Silk had let it slip that it was my missing arm that made a relationship impossible. And now that feeling of rejection was coming from my own son.

I went back to my desk and sat down, confused at the thought of my only son being ashamed to be seen with me. What should I do? What should my reaction be?

For a moment anger gripped me. *I'll straighten that boy out, that's what I will do. I won't let him treat me like this!* But what would that accomplish? Anger would do me no good, and to voice anger at Stephen—why, he's only thirteen years old! It would accomplish nothing. It was best to keep anger completely out of this situation.

Should I talk to him? Bring it out in the open. Let him know how deeply he hurt me and how disappointed I am? Does he realize how much it hurts to know that he is ashamed of me? I have feelings, too. But again, he is only a child. He is thinking as a child. I really don't think it would accomplish anything but possibly cause a rift between us.

Or should I just tell him what happened? Tell him that I had heard about the campout from his scoutmaster and would love to go. Not give any hint of disappointment or hurt. But in all honesty, that could be the worst way to handle this. I did not want to put him on the spot. The last thing I needed was for him to tell me he didn't want me to go. That would be a horrible thing for both of us to experience. And then if he didn't tell me to stay home, would we both have a miserable time—him because he didn't want me there, and me because I knew it?

I struggled the rest of the day. I struggled with hurt and disappointment. I struggled with what to do.

I finally decided to do nothing. I would not bring it up. I would not even tell Adrienne. I would keep this hurt to myself and never let on that I knew anything about the campout. I had to remember that he was only a child. He would grow up. No need in making a problem worse when maturity would take care of it. I would hope and pray that I could forgive and try to forget.

As with Silk, it took me a while to get over that experience, but I did. And I am so thankful that I never said anything to anyone. Stephen did grow up. He began to think and act as an adult and our adult father-son relationship is good. Never again did I feel rejection at the hands of my son.

Chapter 13

Ship to Shore

A lot was happening in the world of telegraphy during the early part of the century, especially in the development of wireless communication. I was fascinated with the concept of radio waves and enjoyed watching the technology develop.

In late 1901 Guglielmo Marconi changed long distance communication forever when he was able to transmit the first wireless transatlantic message from Ireland to Signal Hill, Newfoundland. Within a few years ship-to-shore and ship-to-ship communication became standard, making the high seas less lonely and foreboding. Daily news, wired to ships at sea, was being read by the passengers as they enjoyed their morning coffee and toast. The world was becoming a much smaller place.

The importance of communication at sea was never more evident than on April 14, 1912, when the worst peacetime maritime disaster in history occurred. For several weeks there was little talk of anything else. The sinking of the *Titanic* and the loss of all but 706 of her 2,223 passengers and crew filled the newspapers and kept our wire humming.

A few days after the disaster, I was at my desk at the station in Dallas, sending a wire, when one of the delivery boys asked me, "Mr. Parker, what is *CQD*?"

The station in Dallas employed young boys to deliver messages in the Dallas area. They were paid a meager allowance and relied primarily on the tips when the message was delivered. This little fellow, George—I don't remember his last name—was always asking questions. He wanted to know everything about everything.

"Pardon?" I asked as I finished the wire and looked up.

"*CQD*," he repeated. "I saw it in the paper. When the *Titanic* was sinking, the telegraph operator on the ship kept sending *CQD*. What does that mean?"

"Oh! Yes, *CQD*," I said. "That's an international distress call. It's been replaced recently by *SOS*."

"Does it stand for something?" George asked.

"No, it doesn't," I replied. "I've heard people erroneously say it stands for Come Quickly, Danger! but that is not true. *CQ* has been around for years and is used to identify a message that is of interest to all stations on a line. Maritime radio also uses it as a general call signal, letting all ships know the message is of common interest or importance.

"Once maritime radio got started and the international shipping community realized how useful telegraphy was going to be, it was felt that there needed to be an emergency signal. For land lines there was none—no emergency signal was really needed. So Marconi added a *D* to *CQ*. Thus *CQD* became the distress call for maritime use. It was used worldwide for a few years, but in 1906, at the second International Radiotelegraphic Convention in Berlin, three dits, three dahs, three dits—*SOS*—was adopted as the international distress signal. It was easier for all people, with or without telegraphy background, to recognize. British ships still use *CQD* quite often.

"Why didn't it work for the *Titanic*?" George asked. "Why didn't it get help there on time? And why didn't he send *SOS*?"

"Well, George, the way it looks to me, there was a lot of miscommunication, or lack of communication, going on that night. And I understand the *Titanic* did start sending *SOS*.

"The information I have gotten while listening…" I paused in midsentence. "Now, George, you do understand that all news except local news comes through the wire. Every bit of news from the outside world is heard in this station, written down, and then given to the newspaper to print. Some of the information I'm telling you will be in tomorrow's edition of the *Dallas Morning News*." I chuckled and continued. "George, you should feel honored and privileged to get the news before everyone else."

"Wow!" George exclaimed.

In a more somber tone I said, "But you must not tell anyone. In fact, the rule is that you have to raise your right hand and promise that you will not divulge this information to anyone, not even your mother, until after the paper is printed tomorrow. Why, if news leaked out before its time … there's no telling what would happen!" I was having a hard time keeping a straight face.

George's eyes got big and he raised his right hand. "Mr. Parker! I promise! I promise!"

"George, I think you can be trusted." I looked around to make sure no one else was listening and motioned for him to come closer.

In almost a whisper I said, "George, according to the most recent wire, shortly after midnight on the fifteenth, when the captain of the *Titanic* realized the seriousness of the damage, distress calls were sent. Jack Phillips, the wireless operator, began sending out *CQD*. After awhile he began sending out *SOS*, but that was really irrelevant. Any wireless station, on land or on ship, would know that *CQD* meant distress. Several ships responded—the *Mount Temple*, the *Frankfurt*, the *Olympic*, and the *Carpathia*. Only one land-based wireless station at Cape Race, Newfoundland, received the message. The closest ship was the *Carpathia* which was fifty-eight miles away, and it was four hours before it could get there, too late to save most of the passengers. The water was twenty-eight degrees—a person can last only a few minutes in water that cold.

"George, the really tragic thing is that there was a ship much closer, the *SS California*. It was less than nineteen miles away. In fact, earlier in the evening the *California* had wired the *Titanic* warning them of icebergs in the area. The *California* had shut down all engines for the night and was waiting until daylight to continue, not taking a chance on hitting an iceberg. At eleven o'clock that night the wireless operator on the *California* turned his wireless off and went to bed.

"In addition to sending a distress signal, the *Titanic* also sent up flares. The *California* apparently saw them but did not think it was anything serious. They did try to communicate with Morse lamps, but got no response from the *Titanic*. Someone really wasn't using his brain. Those lamps are good only for about four miles. There was no way the *Titanic* could have seen or responded with lamps. And all the *California* had to do was wake up their wireless operator and send a wire to the *Titanic*. It makes me sick to think about it. I suspect the captain of the *California* is going to have a lot of explaining to do."

A few months later at the British Board of Trade's inquiry into the disaster, the *California* captain and crew were found to be at fault, having failed to give proper assistance to the *Titanic*. Revision and implementation of numerous safety regulations were recommended, including twenty-four-hour radio surveillance on all commercial ships and streamlining of radio communications in times of emergency.

"Now, George, remember our promise—not a word to anyone."

"Yes, sir, Mr. Parker," George nodded. "You can count on me."

Within two hours I think that every ten-year-old boy in Dallas was talking about the *California* and her sleeping radio operator.

Chapter 14

The Cowboy

As Dallas continued to grow, we not only saw an increase in telegraph activity at our depot, but we also saw a very rapid increase in railway traffic—trains coming and going from all over the United States, making our station an extremely busy place. Within a few years, other stations began to pop up around the city, and before anyone knew it, there were five depots scattered throughout Dallas.

To bring efficiency to the railway industry, the city decided to consolidate the five into one, and in 1916 the new Union Station Terminal, designed by Jarvis Hunt, opened to great fanfare. (Hunt also built several other stations, including Union Station in Kansas City and the Union Pacific Headquarters in Omaha.)

Dallas soon found herself as the transportation center for the entire Southwest, with as many as eighty trains stopping in the station each day. Thankfully the new station was close to where we lived, and my commute time to work by streetcar was about the same.

With the increase in rail traffic, there was an increase in the number and variety of people coming through the station—strange sounding people from all over the United States with accents that made English sound like a foreign language, and strange looking people from around the world with languages that I *knew* were foreign. Some were traveling through, some were coming to settle in the ever-expanding metropolitan city of Dallas, and some were coming to explore the mystique of the American West and the American cowboy—wanting to catch a glimpse of a real cowboy.

In 1903 the cowboy of lore was born when Andy Adams published his book, *The Log of a Cowboy.* It was the first book that really captured the essence of the life of the cowboy on a trail drive. Unlike *Buffalo Bill's Wild West Show* of the late nineteenth century which glamorized the settling of the West and the conflict with the Indians, *The Log of a Cowboy* was the cowboy's story. It was a work of fiction, but based on Adams's experience on a five-month cattle drive along the Great Western Cattle Trail from Texas to Montana in 1882. It was an instant best seller throughout the United States and had every young boy in the country dreaming about longhorn steers, rattlesnakes, and tumbleweeds. I was twenty-four when it came out, and I still remember the tug in my soul to leave everything, head west, and hit the trail—even though there probably wasn't a big demand for a one-armed cowpoke!

And in Dallas there *were* cowboys—plenty of cowboys—*real* cowboys—men who looked like they were made of stone—faces chiseled out of granite, and with skin the color of mahogany, cured in the sun and tougher than leather. They were in and out of the station at all times of the day, boarding trains headed farther West, or just checking on messages sent by wire.

I met several of them, and the ones who were in and out regularly were soon friends on a first-name basis. They all had in common a true love of life and the outdoors, and a genuine sense of honesty and fairness. I have to say that I envied them, wished that I could experience their unstructured, rugged lives—sleep under the stars as the cows moo softly, hear the coyotes howl in the distance, feel the relentless sun bear down on my wide-brimmed hat, experience the cold north wind on the open plains as it blows sleet and cold rain in my face, chilling me to the bone ... Well, not permanently—maybe just for a day or two!

There was one cowboy whom I got to know very well. His name was Buck. He must have been in his mid-sixties and was in the station every week or two on business. He was a short fellow, probably not over five feet tall, but he looked tough as nails. His back was as straight as a rod, but his legs were bowed—looked as if they had hugged a saddle for many a day. His Levis were always fresh and clean, his boots polished, and his shirt starched and pressed. When he walked into the station, his ten-gallon hat would come off, revealing a white forehead and scalp, so contrasting to his tanned face.

Buck always made a point of coming over to the telegraph booth, engaging me in conversation, and asking how things were going. His interest in me probably stemmed from the fact that we had something in common. Like me, he was an amputee. His left hand was missing—had been removed just above the wrist.

Oftentimes I would take my break when he came in, and we would go to the Rexall Drug Store down from the station for a cup of coffee. He took great pride in his cowboy heritage and loved telling me tales of the trail, keeping me captivated by his stories.

One day in the fall of 1916, he came by as I was breaking for lunch, and we were able to spend a good hour with each other.

"Ollie," he said in his rough voice that almost sounded like sandpaper rubbing together, "the life of the cowboy has changed a lot since I started out. Why, I was only twelve when I went on my first drive. That's been over fifty years—1866, if I remember correctly. We were living in Wichita Falls, Texas. My paw had died the year before on April 1, fighting for the Rebs at the Battle of

Five Forks in Virginia. That was the last major battle of the War. Lee surrendered eight days later."

Buck shook his head and took a sip of coffee. "Bad to die at all in battle, but to be one of the last, in a lost cause … It was hard to take.

"Well, after the War, my family was strapped for money. I heard about a trail drive that was taking about a thousand head of cattle to Kansas City.

"Ollie, after the War cattle was plentiful and cheap in Texas and the West—selling for only about four dollars a head. But in Chicago and the East, they were going for forty dollars a head. It didn't take a mathematician to figure out that it was well worth the trouble to get the herds to the north. At the time there were no railways in Texas, so the cattle were herded north to Kansas and transported from there to the slaughterhouses in Chicago.

"As a young greenhorn, I could make twenty dollars a month for the three month drive. That was half what the others made, but that sixty dollars sure came in handy for my family that winter.

"Ollie, it got into my blood. Living on the range, sleeping under the stars, out there with just the cows and the horses and the dust. I would look up at night and feel the presence of God like I had never felt before.

"The next year I couldn't wait to sign up again.

"By that time, 1867, the railhead had been extended to Abilene, Kansas, and we herded them there. I was with Jesse Chisholm that year when he marked out the route—became known as the Chisholm Trail. It was the major route for cattle drives from Texas to Abilene for years.

"Within a few years, though, the Missouri-Kansas-Texas Railroad reached into Texas from the north. The 'Katy,' as she was known, made it to Dallas in 1886, ending the drives to the north out of Texas. Also the Texas & Pacific Railway had arrived a few years earlier connecting Dallas and Fort Worth with the East and West. The Fort Worth Stockyards soon became a major holding area for cattle shipped all over the U.S.

"For the next ten or so years, I worked throughout the West—Montana, the Dakotas, Nebraska, Wyoming—herding cattle to the East. But before long, railways were reaching everywhere, making cattle drives a thing of the past. Last one I was on was a good twenty years ago—1895. Now there are very few drives, mainly to the nearest railroad. And barbed wire stretches everywhere, slicing up the once-open plains.

"Since my last drive, I've settled down north of here in Collin County, just south of McKinney. I've got a couple of thousand acres and a nice little herd of Angus."

Buck shook his head again. "Hated to give up the longhorns, but the Angus makes a much better piece of meat."

"Ever had any trouble with Indians?" I asked, hoping for some wild tale of scalping and warpaths.

"Naw," Buck answered. "Only problem we ever had was in Oklahoma. They didn't like us going through their hunting grounds. But we negotiated ten cents a head and they let us through. A hundred dollars per thousand head to prevent an Indian attack was well worth it.

"Yea, I miss those days on the open range." Buck sighed. "You're familiar with that song, *Home on the Range*, aren't you?"

"Yes, sir," I replied. "Everybody knows that song."

"Well, that speaks it all," Buck said. "Brewster Higley who wrote that song in the 1870s, really got it right. 'Oh, give me a home, where the buffalo roam, where the deer and the antelope play. Where seldom is heard a discouraging word, and the skies are not cloudy all day.'

"Ollie, that song really captures it. But one thing in that song is now missing—the buffalo. It has disappeared. In my first ten or so years on the trail, we would see thousands of them. But I haven't seen one in thirty years. Such a shame."

As he sat back in his chair and sipped his coffee, I looked at him and thought what a great life! Oh, to have experienced such a life, even for a day or two! But I knew I was fooling myself. With only one arm, I knew that even if trail rides still existed, the experience would not be mine.

Buck leaned forward and said, "Ollie, I've got a couple of hundred head of Angus that need to be driven from my ranch to the Fort Worth stockyards next week. How about you joining me? Why, you would get a kick out of it. It's only a forty-mile drive—two days on the trail and then back to Dallas on the train. How about it?"

My mouth dropped. I didn't know what to say. Ambivalence reigned supreme in my mind for several moments. Here was an opportunity of a lifetime that might never arise again—something that I had dreamed about for years. But I was scared to death! Why, I hadn't been on a horse in years. And my arm—could I do it?

"Buck, I—I don't know," I said. "What about my arm?"

My response must have hit a raw nerve, because Buck's demeanor suddenly changed. His eyes narrowed and he clinched his teeth. He held up his stump, shook it at me, and with a hint of anger in his voice said, "Don't you dare use that as an excuse! I won't let you!"

After a moment he smiled and leaned back in his chair. "Ollie, I lost this thing fifteen years ago. Everyone said I couldn't do it—couldn't keep up a ranch. But I've done just fine. Haven't missed a lick."

He then placed his right hand on my armless shoulder. "Don't ever let this keep you from doing what you want. If you let it, life will pass you by."

The next week I took a few days of vacation, left Adrienne and the kids, and had one of the most wonderful experiences in my life. For two days and a night, I was a cowboy—riding alongside *real* cowboys! I kept the 'doggies' moving, I wrangled strays, and listened to tales of the trail as I drifted off to sleep under the star-lit sky. I ate beans and brisket for supper, and I ate beans and bacon for breakfast—all cooked over an open fire by a man called 'Cookie.' From the back of a horse, I watched the sun go down in the west, and on the back of the same horse, I saw it rise again in the east.

When we reached Fort Worth and corralled our herd, I felt a sense of satisfaction that I had rarely felt before. It was a sense of accomplishment, of hard work and sweat and dirt, that my hand-icap has so often prevented me from experiencing. But for those two days, I learned the value and satisfaction of good, honest man-ual labor—work that makes a man proud to be a man. And at times, I even forgot that I wasn't whole.

Chapter 15

The Automobile

Then there is the automobile—not a friend to a one-armed man—a stark reminder that I am not whole.

I remember when the first automobile arrived in the state of Mississippi. It was at 10:00 a.m. on June 26, 1900. But Meridian did not get the honor; it was Biloxi, one hundred and seventy miles south on the Mississippi Gulf Coast. It was delivered by ship to a Mr. Frank Shaffer.

It was front page news for every newspaper in the state, including the *Meridian Star*. And wires were being sent continuously from Biloxi to keep everyone up to date on the progress of this important occurrence. I was twenty-two years old at the time, still in Lockhart, and the messages were even relayed to our little hamlet.

Mr. Shaffer's horseless carriage was an instant hit. Everyone came out to see it and many even paid to ride in it. He charged a whopping twenty-five cents to ride in it during those first few days and had a line of waiting customers every day. The third day saw Mississippi's first auto accident and the fourth day its first blowout. After the blowout, the entire wheel of Mr. Shaffer's automobile had to be removed and shipped to New Orleans for repair—there was no place in Mississippi to repair it.

The first automobile in Meridian arrived a few years later, thanks to my Uncle John. If fact, his 1905 Oldsmobile Curved Dash was the first horseless carriage I ever saw.

Uncle John Woods Parker, Jr., was Papa's older brother. He and his wife, Florence, had left Lockhart several years earlier to seek their fortune in the booming city of Meridian—and they succeeded. He began dabbling in the mercantile, railway, and timber businesses, and within a few years established himself as one of the most influential businessmen in the city. He eventually got into politics and served two terms as mayor of Meridian in the 1910s.

Unlike Papa, who was rather reserved, Uncle John was a glad-hander—he knew everyone and was everyone's best friend. He never met a stranger, and had a knack for never forgetting a name. He could tell you who your relatives were down to your third cousin twice removed, and he had a story about most of them that you had never heard before.

Uncle John surprised everyone with his purchase of an automobile. He told no one about it, not even Florence, until it arrived in Meridian. It was shipped from the Oldsmobile factory in Detroit, Michigan, arriving by train in early March 1905—gassed up and ready to go.

His new purchase caused quite a stir in Meridian and was the talk of the town for weeks—a similar response to the one Mr. Shaffer got in Biloxi a few years earlier. I was still in Lockhart at the time, and we were kept abreast of the happenings in Meridian by wire. The reaction to his new mode of transportation was quite varied. Some of the town folk equated this new arrival with the chariot that swept Elijah up to heaven—a miraculous gift from the Almighty Himself. Others saw it as a curse from the very depths of the fiery pit.

I saw his automobile for the first time about two weeks after he purchased it. We were having a quiet morning at the depot in Lockhart, when suddenly we heard the strangest noise coming from outside. "Put, Put, Pow! Put, Put, Pow! Put, Put, Pow!"

Everyone in the station looked up, wondering what in the world that could be! If it was a train engine, it was the sickest, puniest one that we had ever heard! We dropped what we were doing and headed outside.

In the distance was what looked like a carriage—a carriage without a horse—bouncing along on the rut-filled road that connected Meridian and Lockhart. And when I say it looked like a carriage, it did. It looked exactly like most of the two seat buggies of the time—minus the shafts for hitching a horse. The front of the vehicle, or dash, was curved up like a sled, and it was open-air with no cover for the sun.

As it approached, I recognized the lone passenger as Uncle John. Covering his eyes were strange looking leather-rimmed glasses (they now call them "goggles") and on his head was a tight-fitting leather cap that buckled under his chin. He had a wool muffler around his neck and a brown canvas duster that reached almost to the ground when he stood up. He had one hand on a metal shaft that projected up from the middle of the dash. This appeared to be the steering mechanism. (I later learned it was called a "tiller.")

As he passed us, he waved with his free hand and yelled "Howdy!" He didn't slow down and continued traveling up the road, finally stopping at Papa's general store about fifty yards away.

By the time we got to the store, there must have been seventy-five people gathered around Uncle John and his strange vehicle, most of them with their mouths open, gawking and pointing. Papa was standing at the top of the steps of the store looking down at the scene, scratching the back of his neck and shaking his head.

Uncle John dismounted his gas-powered steed, dusted himself off, and proudly said, "Well, Stephen, what do you think about it?"

"Where's the horse?" was Papa's response.

Everyone began to laugh.

"I know you won't believe it," Uncle John said as he pulled off his cap and goggles, "but there are seven of them—and they're right behind the seat."

Every jaw in the crowd dropped. Now it was Uncle John's time to laugh.

"Not real horses," he hooted, "but a gasoline-powered, single cylinder engine that has the strength and power of seven horses. They tell me it runs as if seven healthy steeds are pulling it. And an added feature—unlike a horse, it never gets tired. It will run all day as long as you keep the gasoline from running out. In fact, last year some brave soul rode one of these things from coast to coast in seventy-three days."

Uncle John's Curved Dash was a Model 6C, manufactured from 1904 to 1907. Prior to that, there had been a Model R Curved Dash made from 1901 to 1903 with only a 4.5 horsepower engine which had trouble making it up any significant incline. The Model 6C was a nice little run-about and surprisingly required little maintenance. The Curved Dash was discontinued when Ransom Olds sold his company to General Motors in 1908. The Ford Model T, which began production in 1908, soon replaced it as the most popular automobile of the time.

"Anybody want to go for a ride?" Uncle John asked.

No one said a word. There were no takers. We all shook our heads as if he had asked us to jump off a cliff.

"What's the matter? You afraid it's going to bite?" Uncle John reared his head back and began to laugh. "Why, these horses are as tame as can be!"

"Maybe so," someone said. "But I've seen plenty of 'tame' horses kick a man senseless!"

Everyone again began to laugh.

After a few more minutes of gawking and staring, the crowd started to thin out, and Uncle John said, "Well, I guess it's time for me to head back home."

He looked up at Papa. "Stephen, are you sure you don't want to ride with me back to Meridian? It sure is a lot of fun. Why, we should make it to Meridian in plenty of time for you to catch the afternoon train back here."

"No thanks," Papa said as he shook his head and laughed. "It looks like a pretty fascinating machine, but I will pass. Once those horses are broken in a bit, I may join you."

Uncle John put his cap and goggles back on, mounted his metal charger, waved good-bye, and headed back south, bouncing on the ruts as he went.

"Put, put, Pow! Put, put, Pow! Put, put, Pow!"

Within a few years several other Meridianites joined the ranks of automobile owners, but it would be years before the automobile would make an impact in Mississippi. When I left Meridian in 1908, there were just a handful of noisy, backfiring vehicles scaring the daylights out of women and horses alike. The Great War would come and go before they would be commonplace on the streets and roads of the rural South.

No one knew it at the time, but the arrival of the automobile would essentially kill Lockhart as well as thousands of other small towns throughout the nation. Being only ten miles from Meridian, Lockhart would see all business, except farming, dry up—thanks to good roads and the proliferation of inexpensive automobiles. It was just too easy to drive, and shopping in the big city was too much fun.

The inexpensive automobile owes its creation to Henry Ford. He streamlined production, cut production costs, and made cars affordable for the growing middle class. In 1908 the Model T began production, and in 1914 production lines in Detroit were spitting out a new one every fifteen minutes. They were coming out so fast that the decision was to paint them all black—because the black paint dried faster.

In the first decade that we were in Dallas, automobile owner-ship skyrocketed. Cars were everywhere. Everybody was buying one—everyone except me. I could not drive one. No one-armed man could drive one. The problem is steering the thing and shift-ing gears at the same time.

Prior to Oldsmobile's introduction of the Hydra-Matic drive in 1940, all cars were standard transmission. Gears were shifted by hand—by *one* hand, while the *second* hand held the steering wheel. There was no way a one-armed man could do it.

It was a little embarrassing how I came to find out that driving was out of the question. First off, when Adrienne and I decided to buy a car, I had never been in one. I had never even sat in the pas-senger's seat, much less in the driver's seat. I knew absolutely noth-ing about automobiles except that gasoline was required to propel them. That there were gears that needed shifting was foreign to me.

One evening I came home and Adrienne met me at the door. "Oliver," she said (she never called me Ollie). "Oliver, we need an automobile."

"Pardon?" I asked.

"We need an automobile. Everyone in the neighborhood is getting one and we cannot be the last."

We had been in Dallas for about six years, and it did seem that overnight motor vehicles were everywhere, even in our neighborhood.

"Mr. Taylor down the street drove one home today. Everyone was down there admiring his Model T, talking about how they were going to get one too. Mrs. Taylor says that the price of a Ford has really come down in the past year, and that they were able to get one for less than a thousand dollars. Everyone says that the upkeep of a car is actually cheaper than the upkeep of a horse. All you have to do is feed it gasoline and oil every few weeks."

"But Adrienne, we don't have a horse, and we don't need a horse. Public transportation does just fine. Streetcars take us anywhere we want. And if we don't need a horse, we surely don't need an automobile."

I lost the argument, and the next Saturday afternoon we took the streetcar to the Ford sales store. A nice young man met us as we walked in and asked us if he could help us.

"Yes," I said. "We are interested in buying a car."

"Well, you have come to the right place," he said with a smile. "Here it is."

He pointed to the lone car in the display room.

I was taken aback! This one is ours? Why, he doesn't even know my name and he had no idea that we were coming. How can he already have a car ready and waiting for us?

"Is that *our* car?" I asked as I scratched my head.

"This one or one just like it. They're all exactly the same. I can't tell one from another. In fact, I suggest that people place a little mark on their automobile, somewhere easy for them to see, so that when they are looking for their car among all the others, it will be easy to find. And they all drive the same too. Do you and the lady want to take it for a ride?"

"Well, that would be just fine. But I have to warn you, neither one of us has ever been in an automobile."

"No problem at all," the salesman said. "Driving one of these is as easy as riding a horse."

A big smile appeared on Adrienne's face. "See, what did I tell you?"

"Hop right in and I'll show you how it works."

Adrienne and I climbed into the vehicle: me in the driver's seat and Adrienne in the passenger's seat.

The salesman got quiet and scratched his chin. "Ah, sir, the young lady will need to be the driver."

"What?" I asked, a little confused at what he had said.

"Well, sir, you need two hands to drive a car. I assumed that you knew that. You will need to let the lady learn how to drive."

Adrienne's eyes got big and her mouth dropped open. "Me? Drive a car? You must me kidding!"

"No, ma'am," he answered. "There are a lot of women who are learning to drive. If you can handle a buggy, you can handle a car. Why, women, especially young women like you, are doing almost everything a man can do these days. They say that you will even be voting in a few years."

Adrienne stood up and quickly stepped out of the car. "This is not what I had in mind at all. Why, there is no way…" It wasn't that she didn't *want* to learn to drive; the idea scared her to death!

While their little conversation was unfolding, I sat there dumbfounded. "Another strike," I thought. "I cannot even drive an automobile. Everywhere I turn nothing but roadblocks."

I thanked the young man and told him that we were sorry for taking up his time. We needed to go home and discuss the situation.

"No problem," he said. "Come back anytime."

Adrienne and I departed with our tails tucked between our legs—totally embarrassed at what had just transpired. Adrienne never mentioned buying an automobile again. For the rest of our married life, the streetcar did just fine.

It's almost comical now, but when I went into the automobile store that day, I did *not* want to buy one. I thought, *What a waste of good money.* But when I left—when I realized that I was not going to get one of those noisy contraptions—I was disappointed! It was kind of like the dog chasing the bobcat, but in reverse. He likes the chase, but he really does not want to catch it—and the teeth and claws that go with it.

But I soon got over it. And I still have never owned a car. I did consider it one other time. When automatic transmission became available five years ago, I considered it only as long as it took me to read the advertisement in the paper! I was sixty-three years old and saw no need in complicating my life anymore than it already was.

Chapter 16

Junius

And then there was the Great War. When I learned that Junius had enlisted and was off to fight in France, I could not bear it.

Junius had never married. For a while he worked at the sawmill, and after his father died he took over the workings of the family farm. He was the only one of the Bludworth boys interested in farming; the rest moved away from Lockhart as soon as they could. Farming became his passion, and he spent most of his waking hours working the fields.

After his mother died, Junius lived alone in the old home place until he went to fight in France in 1917. When he returned two years later, he was a different man.

The interesting thing is that Junius really had no business enlisting. In 1917, when the United States entered the war, we were both almost forty years old, too old by most standards to be of any use on the battlefield: wars like to eat up the young, not men past their prime. But Junius wanted to go; he said he had no family depending on him, and he felt it was his patriotic duty to go and serve, and if necessary, die for his country. Also, he had never been out of Lauderdale County, and he thought this would be a cheap, easy way to see the world. So he lied about his age.

When we were born, there were no birth certificates. Everyone relied on his mother and father to tell him what day and what

year he was born. Not surprisingly, there were more than a few
people I knew who had no idea how old they really were. When Junius enlisted he stated his age as thirty-two, and he was sworn in
on the spot.

I was living in Dallas at the time and my sister, Maude, wired
me that Junius was on his way to Europe to fight in the war. I remember reading the message over and over, ashamed, and a little
envious, that it was he and not I who was going. My best friend
was off to the front, and here I was cooped up in an office. But
a one-armed man is a one-armed man whether he is forty or
thirty-two.

When Junius returned from the war, he was never the same.
He never worked, never held a job, rarely left the house—his life
destroyed by the war. But unlike the old Civil War soldiers who
were physically crippled, Junius's ruin was emotional. Yes, he had
been wounded, still walked with a limp, and had lost an eye, but
that seemed minor compared to what he suffered day to day in his
own mind. He would sit and cry for hours. Mostly his tears were
about the Great War and the horrors he endured, but sometimes
when I would visit, he would start crying and ask me, or rather
beg me, for forgiveness. I would say the same thing I had said a
thousand times before, "Junius, it wasn't your fault. You are not
to blame."

The first time I saw Junius after the war was in 1919. Adrienne, the children, and I were visiting in Meridian at Christmas,
a trip that we made every year until we divorced in 1932. We
would usually stay about a week before boarding the train back to
Dallas. The year before, 1918, Junius was not home. He was still
in a hospital in France.

The war ended for all practical purposes on November 11,
1918, when the armistice with Germany was signed, but it was

months before all the troops, the wounded and the whole, were home. Junius didn't get home until June 1919. He stayed with Papa and Lizzie in Meridian for a few weeks, but then went back to Lockhart—to the old Bludworth home place. He didn't go back to work the land; he went back to sit and cry.

Papa wrote me several times, telling me how difficult things were for Junius. For all practical purposes he had become a hermit. No one in Lockhart ever saw him except when he needed something at the general store.

Two days before Christmas I left the family in Meridian and took the train to Lockhart. The old depot in Lockhart looked the same—hadn't changed at all. Mr. Matthews had been dead for years, but several of the old depot crew were still around. Richard now ran the station. We had a nice visit—joking about how we were all starting to look like our fathers. It was hard to believe that it had been sixteen years since I had worked there.

I asked Richard about Junius. He shook his head and said, "Ollie, it's sad. I saw him at the general store a few months back. We had a nice little visit, but it was like talking to a shell of a man. You look in his one good eye and it's like you're looking into empty space. That war must have messed him up pretty bad. He's not the same Junius I used to know.

"And, Ollie, I haven't seen him since then. In fact, no one ever sees him, at least not in the daytime. Rumor is that he wanders the woods at night. And I emphasize 'rumor.' Truth is, no one has ever seen him out at night. In fact, it's probably not true at all.

"I hear the rumor got started by Ole Man McElroy teasing his grandson a few months ago. They were sitting on the porch at dusk when a bobcat let out a cry off in the woods. You know, a bobcat's cry can sound almost human at times. His grandson's eyes got real wide and he asked what that was. Mr. McElroy laughed and said that it was probably Junius Bludworth—roaming the woods, searching for his glass eye. Well, in no time every kid in town was talking about Junius and his wandering eye, and before long the adults in town were believing it too. Now every time there is a sound in the woods or a strange shadow in the moonlight, it's Junius."

I left the depot and made my way to the Bludworth home. The place looked pretty run down. It appeared that nothing had been done since Junius left almost three years ago. The house was in need of paint, and the yard was full of knee-high weeds. There were a few scrawny chickens scratching around the house and two mangy cats on the porch. The only bright spot was a small winter garden to the side of the house with a few rows of greens and onions.

With a little apprehension, I knocked on the door. After what seemed like five minutes, I heard someone walking to the door. As he got closer, I could hear a definite limp in his walk.

The door opened and a man inside said, "Yes?"

The man standing there couldn't be Junius, could it? Why, this was an old man looking at me. He looked sixty-two, not forty-two. His hair was uncombed, and his face had not seen a razor in several weeks. He was stooped and walked with a cane. There was a patch over his left eye.

I squinted, trying to get a better look in the dark house and said, "Junius?"

"Ollie?"

"Yes, Junius, it's me."

"Why, good to see you," he said as he shook my hand. "Come on in. How long has it been? Three or four years? Please excuse the place. Everything is kind of a mess. I haven't gotten around to cleaning everything up since I got back, but one of these days…"

I'm not sure what I had expected, but thus far he seemed pretty normal. I guess I had thought a crazy man was going to answer the door.

"I think it's been three years," I said. "Christmas 1916, if I remember correctly."

"Yes, that's right," Junius said. After he spoke, he was quiet. The silence lasted several seconds, the friendliness I felt when I came in seemed to fade. "I was in France 1917 and 1918."

For another minute he was lost in his thoughts, staring into space, oblivious to me and the rest of the world. His lip began quivering. I was starting to be uncomfortable when he took a deep breath, blinked his eye, and then looked at me. He smiled and said, "How are Adrienne and the children?" The cloud of the previous minute had disappeared.

"They're doing fine. They're in Meridian with Papa and Lizzie. Everyone would love to see you. In fact, you have a personal invitation from the entire family to join us for Christmas Eve and Christmas Day."

Junius shook his head. "Thanks, but no. Tell them that I appreciate the invitation, but I don't get out much. I pretty much keep to myself these days—I don't like crowds. I think I'll just spend the day here. Give everyone my best wishes, though. Maybe someday…"

Junius again seemed lost in his thoughts. We sat silently. Again it appeared that he was about to cry, and a tear formed in his one eye. It was as if he had forgotten that I was there. To break the silence, I asked, "How are things going here with the farm?"

"Okay, I guess," Junius answered as he looked over at me. "I've only been back a few months and things had gotten pretty run down. You know, it doesn't take long for everything to go to seed. And I really haven't been able to do much—my bum leg makes it a little difficult. Maybe when spring comes…"

Silence. Junius was again lost in his thoughts, staring across the room. He was staring so intently at the wall that I turned to see what he was looking at.

"Yes, maybe when spring comes," he said, coming back to life. "Maybe I will get some things done."

"It's a lot of work keeping a farm going," I said, trying to keep the conversation going. "Do you think you will need some help?" And I wasn't referring to myself as possible help. A one-armed man is about as much help on a farm as a wagon with three wheels. "You might be able to find someone to come and help you work the place."

"No, no—I'll be okay. Not sure if I want to do any farming anyway. Maybe keep up a little garden, that's all. I'll manage."

I thought about asking him if he had considered moving to Meridian, maybe moving in with Papa and Lizzie. They had that big house to themselves. But I thought better of asking—I was not about to volunteer their home without first asking them.

We continued to sit in silence. It was rapidly becoming apparent that conversation with Junius was going to be difficult— moments of almost normal conversation interspersed with total silence. I asked a few polite, general questions and got polite, to-the-point answers.

After a few minutes, I thought, *What am I doing here? This conversation is going nowhere. I have never been so uncomfortable with anyone in my life. How can I get out of here? Should I politely carry on for another few minutes and bid good-bye?*

But I can't do that. He was my best friend—I used to laugh and play with this guy all the time. We would do anything for each other. And now he is hurting. He is obviously an emotional wreck and needs help. But what can I do? What should I do? Should I get more serious in my questions? Should I ask about the war? Should I ask about his wounds?

I knew that it would be another year before I would be back in Mississippi, and I really wanted to have more than a "how do you do?" conversation. So I took a deep breath and asked.

"Junius, how are you really doing? Is there anything about your experiences or about coming home that you would like to talk about?"

Silence again. Junius was again drilling a hole in the wall with his one eye. But then his shoulders drooped and he looked down at the floor.

"Ollie, no one has asked me that before. No one at all. And, Ollie, the thing is—I don't have anyone. No wife. Mom and Pop are dead. Everyone has moved away. I have no one to talk to. Yes, Ollie, I do need to talk."

"Junius," I said, "I'm here. Tell me about it."

"Ollie," Junius paused a moment and then began to cry. "Ollie, I ran away."

Junius began to cry uncontrollably. He buried his face in his hands and sobbed. Again I was at a loss—in the most uncomfortable position I had ever experienced. I didn't know what to say or do, so I did nothing. I sat in silence. I would let him tell his story at his own pace.

After a few minutes he raised his head and said, "I ran away. My friends were dying—crying for help—and I ran away."

Junius stood up and walked over to the window. He wiped his eye and looked out at his little garden of greens and onions. After a minute or two, he said, "Ollie, I wasn't able to get in a summer garden. I didn't get here until the middle of July, too late to get anything planted. But my winter garden is coming along. Next summer I'll have some peas, corn, and okra. It'll be good to have some fresh…"

He dropped his head and began to cry uncontrollably again. After a minute he stopped and turned around. "Ollie, I'm sorry.

Controlling my emotions has become difficult. But I do want to talk. I think I can do it if I start at the beginning."

"That would be fine," I said. I was in no hurry to get back to Meridian and had plenty of time to listen.

He sat down across from me and wiped his eye and nose with his handkerchief. He took a deep breath and began.

"Ollie, I wanted to go. From that day in 1914 when Archduke Ferdinand was assassinated, I was ready to go. I, like so many other Americans, couldn't understand why we didn't join the French and British the very next day to defeat the Central Powers. But President Wilson did everything he could to keep us out of the war. Well, I still wanted to go.

"I thought about doing what some guys were doing—going to Europe and joining the Entente, fighting for the French before the U.S. was a part of the war. But those guys were pretty much on their own, and that didn't seem to be very smart, if you ask me. Plus they had to pay their own way to get there.

"Finally, in April 1917, America joined the Entente. Ollie, it's surprising what a difference three years can make. I was then almost forty, considered too old to fight. But I was not going to let that stop me. I told them I was thirty-two. No one questioned me at all, and I was in.

"We finally arrived in Le Havre in January 1918. Within a few weeks we were in the trenches, and within a few days the glamour of war was gone. Ollie, it was terrible. On the Western Front, where we were, there were trenches—hundreds of miles of trenches, two sets of trenches facing each other with No Man's Land between them. There were men in those trenches who had been there for months, living in filth and mud—living conditions that would have turned a hog's stomach.

"It was pure hell. Days of boredom, dealing with cold and stench and trench rot, interspersed with moments of sheer terror when bombs were falling or when the enemy made an attempt to run us over. And then there were the snipers. Every day someone would get careless—stand up or move into an open position—and get his head blown off. I thought I was going to go crazy with fear.

"The days stretched into weeks, and the weeks into months. We were living a subhuman existence, and what disturbs me, we were getting used to it. We began to adapt—felt a normalcy in the way we lived. The filth no longer seemed abnormal. We even started joking about ourselves, conversing and visiting like we were sitting on a park bench back home."

Junius was quiet—drifting back into his thoughts again. Silence again for several minutes.

"Ollie, I killed a man," he said softly. "And I'm not talking about the killing in battle. I killed a man for no reason—for sport—because of a dare." Junius paused, appeared to be on the verge of losing control, but then continued.

"Often times we would see the enemy across the open fields. We were in our trenches and they were in theirs. Usually it was just a moment, just a glimpse of them as they moved. Everyone on each side was too frightened of the snipers to be exposed for long.

"One day, a rainy, cold day, several of us were huddled together, bored and miserable. One of the guys got up. He said that his feet were about to freeze and he had to move around. He walked down the trench a ways and then climbed up on a mound of dirt to get a look at the enemy line. There were rows of barbed wire stretched as far as you could see.

"After a minute, he called back to us. 'Who's got the field glasses? Can you bring them over here? I think I see something.'

"We walked over to him and handed him the glasses. 'There's a guy standing in plain view over there. He is either a fool or wishing for death.'

"I asked for the glasses. Across the barren field was a man standing up in a trench with his shoulders and head exposed, smoking a cigarette and laughing with his friends.

"'I'm surprised a sniper has not picked him off by now. Someone is falling down on their job.'

"We began to laugh. Another guy picked up the glasses and took a look. 'How far away do you suppose that guy is?'

"'Oh, probably four or five hundred yards. Why?'

"'Oh, I was just thinking—it would take a good marksman to hit that guy from here.'

"'I bet I can hit him,' one of the guys said.

"'You're kidding yourself. You couldn't hit the side of a barn. Why, I've watched you shoot, and you're the worst shot in the whole U.S. Army. But I bet Ole Man here could do it. He's a pretty good shot.'

"Ollie, they called me 'Ole Man.' I was forty and most of them were in their late teens or early twenties."

Junius *was* a good shot. In our youth we would wander the woods with his .22 rifle looking for anything to take aim at. He could hit a sparrow in the head at fifty yards with no trouble at all.

"'Is that so?' the guy said. 'Well, let's have a shooting match. Ole Man, you take the first shot and if you miss—and I bet a dollar you will—I'll take a shot. Hopefully your miss won't scare him. In fact, I bet another dollar that you will be so far off that he won't even know someone shot at him.' Everyone began to laugh.

"I accepted the wager and climbed back up on the mound. I looked again through the field glasses and then handed them to one of the guys.

"'Here, you look while I shoot,' I said. 'You let us know if he falls because of a hit...'

"'Or ducks because of a miss!' the guy interrupted and laughed.

"I rested my rifle on the embankment. I looked through the scope and took careful aim. I slowly squeezed the trigger. A second later the man flinched and dropped out of sight.

"'You did it! What a shot! You hit that guy square in the temple! Ole Man, they're going to make a sniper out of you yet!' Everyone began to laugh.

"'Ole Man, good shooting and here's your two bucks. Don't know where you're going to spend it out here but you earned it.'

"Ollie, I killed a man for a two dollar bet! A stupid two dollar bet!" He began to sob uncontrollably. "Killing a man in battle—when it is kill or be killed—is one thing, but to kill a man like he is a mockingbird sitting on a fence post... Yes, he was the enemy, but that killing did nothing to further our cause. Nothing at all. It was just cold-blooded murder! And I will never forgive myself!"

I sat silently as he continued to cry. I was at a loss. I could think of nothing to say.

"And Ollie, that is not all. There is more." He composed himself and continued.

"Life in the trenches continued. Days of nothing, just sitting in the muck and stench, followed by moments of terror. In March things changed. We started hearing that the Germans were planning an assault. Thousands of American soldiers were landing on French soil every day, and the Germans knew that if they did not make a strong push, it would all be over.

"Our unit was alongside the British Third Army in Somme. Word got out that this was where it would happen—the German Eighteenth Army under General Von Hutier, the Seventeenth under Von Bulow, and the Seventh Army storm troopers would try to break our defenses. Problem for us was that the British had just taken over here from the French and were not well entrenched. The Germans knew this and took advantage of our weakness.

"That morning, March 21, the day the Spring Offensive began, was a cold, foggy morning—perfect cover for the Germans. The storm troopers were able to penetrate deep into our positions undetected.

"Ollie, the way the trenches were made—there were usually several rows of zigzagging trenches: a front trench, back supporting trenches, and interconnecting trenches to get from one to another. Because of the zigzag, you couldn't see more than ten yards in any direction, which was both good and bad.

"Well, that morning I had left the front trench and had gone back to the support trench for supplies. As I was making my way back to my unit, I heard gunfire and yelling. I came around the bend, and storm troopers were coming over the parapet by the dozens. My unit was being slaughtered! Men were screaming and crying, no match for the German guns and bayonets."

Junius stood up again and walked to the window. He stared into the sunlight for minutes. He then covered his face with his hands and began to cry.

"Ollie, I ran! I dropped everything in my hands and I ran! I left my friends. I left them there to die! All I could think was 'Get away! Save yourself! Get as far away as you can! Get away from this horrible hell!' I ran to the back trenches and climbed out and continued to run. I would have run forever, but a shell exploded in front of me, knocking me to the ground.

"The next thing I knew I was on a stretcher, being carried farther back. I was moaning and writhing in pain. The pain in my left leg was excruciating. I tried to look down at my leg, but as I lifted my head, my left eye began to throb terribly. I then realized I couldn't see out of that eye. It was as if there was something covering that eye, a cloth or something on my face. I reached up to remove it, but there was nothing there—nothing but clotted blood and a thick jelly-like substance.

"I began to cry out 'My eye! My eye! Please help me! I can't see!'

"One of the stretcher bearers said, 'Hold on soldier. We'll have you out in no time. You will be in the hospital before you know it.'

"I was in and out of consciousness, having a hard time staying awake. I continued to cry out about my eye and the pain in my leg as they carried me farther back.

"The stretcher bearer said, 'Soldier, there's nothing we can do right now. We're going as fast as we can. Soldier, where are you from? You sound like you're from the South.'

"'From Mississippi. Meridian, Mississippi,' I cried.

"'Well, how about that! I'm from Oxford.' Then he laughed. 'Not the Oxford in England—the one in Mississippi!'

"We arrived at an ambulance station and they loaded me in. The stretcher bearer said, 'Good luck, soldier, I'll be praying for you.' He reached into his pocket. 'Take this with you. It's a New Testament. It makes mighty good reading. Plus it's got my name in it. When you get back to the states, come visit me.'

"Then he was gone."

Junius walked over to a desk, opened the drawer, and pulled out a small book.

He tossed it over to me and said, "Here it is. The Testament he gave me."

The Testament was splattered with old dried blood. I tried to open it, but the pages were stuck together—Junius had not even opened it. I pulled a little harder and the front cover opened. There was writing inside. The name was smudged and illegible, but the rest could be read easily. "R— Q. —ell. Oxford, Mississippi. Genesis 31:49. Mizpah."

"Ollie, you can keep it," Junius said with contempt. "I don't plan on reading it."

His entire demeanor seemed to change in an instant. The sadness and self-guilt was suddenly replaced by anger and sarcasm. I was caught totally off guard.

"What?" I asked.

"I said I don't plan on reading it. It's just a book of lies. There is no God." Junius turned back to the window.

No God! Did he really say that? I was totally shocked! I had never heard anyone say that they did not believe in God. Why, this is the South—the Bible belt! Everyone down here believes in God. I know quite a few people who *live* as if there is no God, but none of them would dare deny his existence. But for Junius to say it— I couldn't believe it! Why, we had attended church and Sunday School together our whole lives. We prayed together. I remember when he trusted in Jesus, walked the aisle of our church, and was baptized. He never missed a service. He lived his faith much more than I ever did. I wondered if God would strike him down on the spot.

"Junius, you shouldn't say that," I said, not knowing what else to say.

"The God that is in that Bible doesn't exist," Junius continued. "Just a bunch of feel-good stories—empty, nothing. To think that there is a God who loves us and wants the best for us but then permits us to tear each other apart—no, I cannot believe that. Ollie, man is evil, and if man was made by God, then God is evil, or else He doesn't exist or He doesn't care.

"I have seen man at his lowest. I have seen man kill for no reason. I have seen man beg for life, and that life be taken with contempt. I have seen him plead to God for mercy, mercy that was never given. I have seen him cry to God for deliverance, deliverance that never appeared. And I have seen him ask for God's strength, strength that never came. No, Ollie, there is no God."

I thought, *God give me words and wisdom.*

"Junius," I said. "That's not right. There is a God, and He is good. Yes, there is evil in this world, and yes, you are right that man is evil—or rather he can be evil. The Bible says that sin is in all of us. All have sinned. None is righteous. But, Junius, evil is not of God, it is of Satan. And thanks to God, all is not lost. There is hope. Hope through the cleansing blood of Jesus. Through Him man can find forgiveness and salvation—become the person that God meant for him to be."

Junius turned from the window and looked at me. With anger he said, "No, Ollie. There is no caring God. If there was a caring God, I would not have murdered a man for a two dollar bet. And a loving God would have let me die with my friends instead of letting me live the life of a coward."

Oh, so that's it! That's what this tirade is about. This conversation is not about the existence or the goodness of God. It is about guilt. It is about overwhelming guilt and the inability to find forgiveness. And it is about blame—blame that is so easily redirected from the blamed to the Blameless.

Junius had turned back to the window. I stood up and walked over to him. I placed my hand on his shoulder.

"Junius," I said softly, "forgiveness never comes by denying the existence of God. It comes only by humbling ourselves, laying our burdens on the altar of God, and relying on His promise that we are forgiven."

Junius began to cry. The anger was again gone. But the self-forgiveness was still a long way off.

"Ollie, I think it is time to go. Thank you for coming, and thank you for listening. It means more to me than you know."

I picked up my hat and coat. "Junius, I'll write to you. And please write back. Adrienne and I would be honored if you would come to Dallas and spend some time with us. It's a beautiful part of the country."

"Thanks," Junius said. "I'll think about it." We both knew that the world would come to an end before that would happen.

I slipped my arm in the coat sleeve and then reached over my head to my back to pull the coat up onto my armless shoulder— an awkward appearing gesture, but the best way I had found to get my coat on. Junius was watching as I did my little dance and began to cry again. "Ollie, please forgive me. I am so sorry. It was my fault. It should have been me."

"No, Junius, it's okay. It was not your fault."

Mizpah. On the way back to Meridian, I couldn't get that word out of my mind. As soon as I got to Papa's, I pulled out my Bible. "Mizpah—let's see, where was it? It was in Genesis if I remember correctly."

I had left the Testament in Lockhart, hoping that Junius might someday pick it up. "Ah, here it is—Genesis 31:49. 'Mizpah; for he said, The LORD watch between me and thee, when we are absent one from another.'"

Chapter 17

Adrienne

Adrienne and I were married for twenty-four years. The first twenty-one were wonderful, happy years. The last three were not. It seems so strange—the contrast between those years. Children and laughter and love, and then frustration and confusion and fear. Those last three years were very difficult, more difficult than anything I had ever been through—even more difficult than those first few years of adjusting to my injury.

At times I thought our problems stemmed from our age difference. Fourteen years is a lot. There is a big difference in the desires and needs of a sixteen-year-old and a thirty-year-old, but there is an even bigger difference between thirty-six and fifty. At other times I thought it was the inheritance that Adrienne came into. "Mine" and "yours" can quickly force a wedge of suspicion and selfishness between persons who previously trusted and sacrificed for each other. But there was more, so much more.

Shortly after our twenty-first wedding anniversary I began to sense that something was not right, and within a year, our relationship rapidly deteriorated.

Adrienne was a wonderful wife and mother, but there was one trait of hers that was a little annoying to me from the first time we met. At the time, it seemed nothing of significance, but in retrospect it was probably a sign of things to come.

She was obsessed with cleanliness and order. We had the cleanest and neatest house. Everything had its place, and in its place it belonged. Our drawers were neatly arranged and the closets uncluttered. Clothes were worn once and then washed. The idea of wearing a shirt or pair of pants two days in a row—well, that did not happen. Food was prepared and eaten at that meal only. There were no leftovers. What was left was thrown away.

I'm no slob, but I do feel that everyone needs a place that he can throw things, stuff things, let things fall, and not worry about it—a place that he plans to clean up later, which may or may not happen. Not Adrienne. The entire house was perfect.

I adjusted to Adrienne's idiosyncrasy, and we did well. But I did have my "place." There was an old shed behind the house that was mine. It was off limits to Adrienne. The children also did well—they were born into it and knew nothing different. That is, until they were older. In the teen years there were more than a few confrontations between Adrienne and the children, confrontations in which I knew not to take sides.

In the spring of 1929 the first sign of trouble surfaced. Adrienne stopped leaving the house. Initially I didn't appreciate this change in behavior because it started out subtly. For several months Polita, our housekeeper, had been doing all the shopping for Adrienne. I typically got home at 6:00 p.m. and would not know that Adrienne had not left the house all day. The children were no longer at home, so there was no one else to see what was happening. Margurite was nineteen, Stephen was eighteen; both of them with jobs and on their own. Adrienne was sixteen and was away in boarding school. If they had been home, I'm sure that this odd behavior would have been brought to my attention earlier.

My first clue was when Adrienne stopped going to church. At first I didn't think anything about it. She had her excuses—she was too tired, or there was too much to do around the house, or the weather was too hot or too cold or too dry or too wet. I just shrugged my shoulders and went on. But after a few weeks, I became concerned. Adrienne loved our church and enjoyed going as much as I did, and it did not make sense. Had something happened that made her no longer want to worship at our church?

One morning while this was happening I ran into Polita on my way to work. I rarely saw her. Usually I was gone before she came and got home after she left. I was standing at the trolley stop when she came up.

"Buenos dias, Senor Parker."

"Good morning, Polita," I replied. "It's good to see you. Why, I haven't seen you in months."

Polita smiled and said, "Gracias, Senor Parker."

After a minute or two of polite conversation, I asked, "Polita, how has working for Ms. Adrienne been going? Anything different about her that you have noticed?"

She began to laugh. "Scrub! Scrub! Clean! Clean! She tell me all day."

I chuckled and said, "Yes, I know what you mean. But anything different?"

"Si, Senor Parker, she now give to me money for shop."

"What?" I asked.

"She give me list. She give me money. I go to store."

I was surprised! Adrienne had always enjoyed shopping, looking at new fashions and clothes. Also she was extremely particular about shopping for groceries. She only bought the freshest. I could not understand her turning this chore over to someone else.

"Polita, when was the last time she went to the store?"

"Oh, Senor Parker, long time. No remember." She threw her hands up. "Maybe three months, maybe four months."

I was becoming more concerned. "Polita, when was the last time she was outside the house when you were there?"

"She never leave house. Stay in all time. No sunshine. I tell her no good."

What is going on, I thought. *It's not just church that she is avoiding; she's not getting out at all. Something is not right.*

At the station I could not think about anything else the entire day. What should I do? What can I do? I decided I would lay it out in the open that night.

After dinner, we were sitting in the parlor. I was reading the *Dallas Morning News* and Adrienne was crocheting.

"I ran into Polita today as I was leaving for work," I said. "First time I've seen her in a while. She looks like she is doing well."

"Yes, she is," Adrienne said. "I don't know what I would do without her. She is a God-send."

I continued to read the paper, but after another moment I said, "She tells me she is doing the grocery shopping now."

"Yes, she is. She's been working for us long enough to know what we need. So I've turned it over to her."

I took a deep breath. "Adrienne, after talking to Polita, I get the impression that you're not getting out of the house much anymore."

Adrienne sat silently, continuing to crochet.

"When was the last time you left the house?"

Adrienne looked up and shook her head. "Ollie, do you realize there are germs everywhere? Germs cause sickness and disease. And no one seems to care. Everywhere you go there is dirt and filth and stench." She was right about the stench. If the wind was right, we could get a pretty strong whiff of the stockyards in Fort Worth.

"People don't wash their hands," she continued, "and they spread diseases everywhere. Scientists say that germs are even in our breath. Just talking to someone, especially if they have a cough, can make you sick. It's just horrible! The safest place is right here in this house."

So this was the problem—mysophobia, or fear of dirty things. I think now they call it germ phobia. I remember reading about it a few years ago. A Dr. Hammond, I think was his name, described it. He talked about people so afraid of coming in contact with something dirty and getting sick that their lives become paralyzed. They are afraid of doing anything.

"Adrienne, germs *are* everywhere. I agree that we have to be careful, but we have to use common sense about staying clean. I think you have carried it a bit too far. You can't just give up on the world."

"Well," she said as she continued to crochet, "you can never be too careful."

Over the next few months the situation worsened. I came home one evening and Adrienne met me at the door with a basin and towel.

"Oliver," Adrienne said as she reached for my hand, "I want you to wash your hand and your shoes with this before you come in. We cannot have you bringing germs into our clean house. No telling what kind of diseases come through that train station."

"What is in this?" I asked as she scrubbed my hand.

"Boric acid," she said. "It kills germs."

"What?" I said as I pulled my hand back. "You're using acid to clean my hand?"

"It won't hurt you," Adrienne said. "Just the germs. A lot of hospitals use it to clean and kill germs. Polita and I have been cleaning all our vegetables and fruits with it for weeks."

"What?" I exclaimed. "Our food, too?"

"Don't worry. It is safe. We rinse it off."

She began to use the towel to wipe my shoes. "Adrienne, you are going a bit too far," I said. "This is nonsense! You can't kill every germ in the world!"

"Maybe not every one in the world, but in this house I will do my best. And nonsense or not—if you want to come into this house, you will clean your hand and feet."

Within a few weeks it got worse. She would meet me at the door for my acid treatment, but would also have a change of clothes for me. I was not allowed to wear my "dirty" street clothes into the house. They would be left in a hamper next to the door, and Polita would wash them the next day.

I can't believe I let all of this escalate. I should have put my foot down and stopped this foolishness, but I guess it was easier to give in. Also as things progressed, I came to realize that this was not foolishness—it was a sickness that was rapidly getting out of control.

In the summer of 1929, Adrienne's mother died, leaving Adrienne and her siblings with a sizable inheritance. Her father, who had died a year earlier, had been in the mercantile business in Dallas, and had been very successful. He was also a very wise investor, and during the Roaring Twenties, he had invested heavily in the stock market and increased his wealth many times over.

Shortly after the estate was settled, Adrienne did something that at the time everyone thought was very foolish, but in retrospect was an extremely smart move. She cashed in her share of her father's stocks and put the money in government bonds. All of us—her children, her brothers and sisters, and even her banker—tried to talk her out of it. Stocks were going out of the roof, and she was settling for a measly three or four percent interest. But she would not budge. She said that she did not understand the stock market and was not about to leave her money in it. She understood interest, and that was good enough for her. Four months later, as everyone else cried, Adrienne smiled.

In early 1930, Adrienne fired Polita, a further sign that things were worsening. I came home from work one evening and Adrienne met me at the door for my "treatment" and my "change." As she helped me get my clean shirt on she said, "Oliver, we are going to have to get a new housekeeper. I had to let Polita go."

"Oh, really? What happened?" I was surprised because they seemed to have gotten along very well. Adrienne was depending more and more on her to do things, and Polita seemed to be enjoying the added responsibility.

"She tried to kill me today."

"What?" I exclaimed.

"I couldn't believe it either," Adrienne said as she dropped my "dirties" into a hamper. "At lunch today, she tried to poison me. The tomato that she gave me was bad. It obviously had been bruised and had a tear in the skin. I noticed it just as I was about to put it in my mouth. If I had eaten that … Oh I don't want to even think about it."

"Adrienne, a little tear in a tomato never hurt anyone. And besides, I know she didn't do it on purpose."

"Oh, yes she did!" Adrienne declared. "It was premeditated attempted murder. I've been trying to decide if we need to call the authorities."

I was flabbergasted! I shook my head and laughed. "Adrienne, you *are* kidding me, aren't you?"

"Of course not. And this is no laughing matter. She was trying to kill me. And she was doing it for my money."

"There must be some misunderstanding," I said.

"No, Oliver. It's true. Polita was talking to me about a moving picture that she and her sister had seen a few days ago. It was called *Monte Carlo*, about a countess who was engaged to a prince but fell in love with a count. Polita commented about all the wealth—what she could do with it—and then plopped that tomato down in front of me. She really had it all planned out. When I was dead, she was going to steal my bond receipts, go to the bank, and take everything." Adrienne crossed her arms and smugly said. "What do you think about that?"

My jaw dropped. "That's it?"

"Isn't that enough?" Adrienne answered. "It could not have been any clearer if she had pulled a gun on me."

"Adrienne, let's sit down and talk about this," I said as we walked into the parlor. "I'm sure that Polita meant nothing with that tomato, and as far as the bond receipts—there is no way a teller at any bank in the state of Texas would cash in those bonds for a Mexican housekeeper who can barely speak English. Think about it. She would have accomplished nothing by killing you, except that you would be dead. And she cares too much about you to want that.

"Now, tomorrow I'm going to get in touch with Polita, get her back over here, and we will get this straightened out. Polita has been the best housekeeper that we have ever had, and there is no way on Earth that we will find someone to replace her. No one else would do for you the things that she does. Hopefully she will not be too insulted to return to work."

Surprisingly Adrienne did not argue, and the next day Polita was back. But Adrienne was a little more cautious with her money and food around Polita for the next few weeks. Thankfully, Polita would just throw her hands up and say, "Aye, aye, aye!"

Within a few weeks, the relationship between Adrienne and Polita seemed to have healed, but my relationship with Adrienne began to deteriorate. As with most of her behavioral changes, it was subtle. I began to sense that our conversation was not as open as it had been. We talked freely, but there was a coolness in her attitude toward me that was developing. I didn't think anything about it initially—she was so caught up with making everything clean that I just thought she was in one of her "clean" moods.

One evening I was looking for our bank book and could not find it. I suspected that with her distrust of Polita, she had started hiding it. Adrienne was in the kitchen washing dishes, or rather scrubbing them down with her ever present boric acid, when I asked, "Adrienne, where is our bank book? I've been looking everywhere for it."

Adrienne continued to scrub, not taking her eyes off the dish. "Why do you want to know?" she asked.

Her question caught me off guard. Why did I need a reason to look at our bank book?

"I was just going to make sure everything was up-to-date and balanced," I casually said.

"You don't have to worry with that," Adrienne said. "I'll look after it."

"What?" I said, shocked at her response.

"I'll take care of the bank book from now on. Most of the money in there is mine, anyway. I'll take care of it."

"Adrienne," I said, trying not to sound too alarmed. "That money, and the bank book, is *ours*, not yours. And I have always taken care of the finances in this household, and for twenty-two years you have never even looked at it except when you needed some cash. What is going on?"

"Nothing," she said, still focusing on the dishes. "I just think I need to be more involved with our finances."

"But you are taking it away from me!" I exclaimed.

Adrienne continued to wash the dishes.

What in the world is happening? Where is the trust that we have always shared? I felt like I was going to explode, but I gathered my composure and calmly asked, "Adrienne, have I done something to make you question how I handle our finances? If so, please tell me."

She finished the dishes and dried her hands. "I think we have discussed this enough," she said as she took her apron off. "There will be no more discussion."

I was stunned. *No more discussion? What is going on?*

Within a few days, I realized that if I was to have any money at all, I would have to open up a separate account for my funds. Now things were hers and mine, and not ours.

Our relationship continued to deteriorate. Within a few months, I was sleeping in one of the children's rooms—I was not allowed in my own bedroom. Also my afternoon cleaning ritual was turned over to Polita. Polita was now staying late each day—Adrienne did not want her to leave until I was "cleaned," dinner was finished, and dishes washed.

Then one evening I had another big surprise. Polita had finished the dishes, but instead of getting her coat and leaving, she headed toward one of the bedrooms.

"Polita, what are you doing?" I asked.

"Oh, Senor Parker, I go to my room. I now live here," she said as she clasped her hands together. "Senora Adrienne ask me to live here. More money. Free room. Gracias, Senor Parker. You so good to me."

As she walked to her room I shook my head. Just a few months ago Polita was an attempted murderess. Now she was part of the family.

Adrienne continued to retreat from me. We rarely spoke anymore. I tried repeatedly to engage her in conversation but could not get anywhere. When we did talk, it was to the point—questions answered and that was it. There was a constant air of suspicion in her attitude toward me. I could not understand what was happening. It did not make sense.

Adrienne also began having bouts of what the doctor later called "melancholy." There were days when she would lie in bed, not wanting to do anything except lament about the plight of the world. She would have Polita sit beside her bed, and she would tell her how the world was rapidly becoming a cesspool of germs and dirt and disease. She would cry and say that no one except her and a few learned scientists understood how grave the situation was. For these respected scientists it was like crying in the wilderness with no one hearing or caring. Polita would sit there and nod in agreement, but she really didn't understand much of what Adrienne was talking about.

She also became obsessed with the idea that someone was going to break in and steal her money. Dead-bolt locks were installed on all the doors—doors that at one time were rarely locked now required three sets of keys to open. Windows which once allowed light and cool breezes to flow in were now closed and the curtains drawn. It was like living in a cave or prison.

I tried telling her that we had very little money in the house, only receipts and bank books, that everything was in safety deposit boxes at the bank, but she would not listen. It seemed that common sense and reason had left her.

Then the final blow occurred. In the fall of 1931, I was at work, sending and receiving messages as usual when Polita rushed in, out of breath, panic on her face.

"Senor Parker, Senor Parker!" she exclaimed. "What do I do? Please, what do I do?"

"Polita, what is wrong? What are you talking about?"

"Today Senora Adrienne, she give me money. She tell me to shop. But she tell me to buy gun! To buy pistol!" She threw her hands up. "Senor Parker, please, what do I do?"

Fear gripped me. Why does Adrienne think she needs a gun? For the first time her behavior was beginning to scare me. Things were much worse than I had imagined.

I tried to calm Polita as much as I could and told her not to go home until late afternoon—and then to approach cautiously. I left immediately for home, worried at what I might find or what might happen. But then I thought, "Wait, she doesn't have a gun yet, or at least she *shouldn't* have one."

We had never had guns in the house. I'm not a hunter, and safety in our neighborhood and city was never a factor. In fact, a rifle or shotgun was out of the question for me. A one-armed man and a shoulder weapon make for a very awkward and dangerous situation. I had not shot a gun since before my accident forty years ago.

And obviously, I thought, *Adrienne would not send Polita on that mission if she already had a gun.* And with her germ fear, there was no way she would leave the house to get one. Everything would be okay when I got there. I didn't have to worry about being met at my front door with a six-shooter aimed at my chest.

When I got home, Adrienne was in her room with the door closed. I knocked gently. "Adrienne, can I come in?"

"What do you want?" she asked.

"We need to talk."

A few moments later she opened the door, walked passed me, and sat down in the parlor. I followed and sat down across from her.

"Adrienne, I just spoke with Polita, and she tells me you want her to buy a gun."

"Yes, that is right," Adrienne said, eyeing me with suspicion.

"Why in the world do you need a gun?"

"You know very well why!" she exclaimed.

"What? I have no idea…"

She pointed her finger at me and shouted, "I've been watching you! I know what you are trying to do! But you are not going to get any of my money! It's mine! If you want your arm back, you'll have to find some other way to pay for it. You're not going to steal it from me!"

I couldn't believe what I was hearing. "Adrienne, what are you talking about? Getting my arm back? Stealing from you? Are you crazy?"

"I would be crazy not to see right through you. I know what you and Satan have been planning! He's promised you another arm! And he wants payment. You've already sold him your soul, but now he requires more. He wants money. That is the only way he will do what you want—and you plan to give him *my* money!

"Oliver, you are dealing with evil and you will burn in hell because of it! You've heard what the Lord says: 'If your hand offends thee, cut it off. It is better for thee to enter into life maimed, than to have two hands to go into hell!' You will not get away with it! My money will *not* be devil money! I will not allow it! Polita will be back soon, and then you'll know I am serious!"

Her eyes were wild with hate and insanity, and I realized there was no way to reason with her. She was completely out of control. My best option was to stay calm and try to calm her down.

"Adrienne," I said softly, "you are not making any sense. I think we need to get help for you."

"I don't need help! You're the one who needs help. The fires of hell are going to consume you because you are selling your soul for things of the flesh."

"Why don't we leave right now and go to the doctor," I said. "He will be able help you."

"And now you want to murder me!" Adrienne wailed. "Disease and sickness lurk outside of this house. Germs and filth are everywhere, and you are trying to entice me to leave my home so that I will get sick and die! No, I will not fall for your tricks."

I left the house in a quandary. What should I do? Adrienne was now obviously crazy, but with her not leaving the house, getting help was going to be difficult. If we were in Meridian, I would have found old Dr. Tatum and he would have come right over and talked with her. But in Dallas, house calls had gone the way of the horse and buggy.

I decided to go to our physician's office and talk with him. Maybe he could help me decide what to do.

Dr. Redmont had been our family physician for years, but since the children were grown, we rarely saw him anymore. He spoke in a very distinctive down-to-earth Texas drawl, but always seemed to be very knowledgeable and competent. It was late afternoon when I got to his office, and he was closing up, ready to go home—his ten-gallon hat already on his head. But he was kind enough to listen as I related Adrienne's strange behavior.

As I finished, he stroked his chin and said, "Well, Mr. Parker, what you describe is a very serious situation. I'm no psychiatrist, but it appears to me that she initially had obsession and compulsion, which is usually no big problem. We usually just laugh about the compulsions and go on. Sometimes, though, they can be pretty debilitating, as in the case with your wife—her not getting out of the house and such.

"But now she seems to have developed something much worse. She appears to have developed melancholia with bouts of mania. The new terminology for it is … let me think…" He took his hat off and scratched his head. "I think they call it … ah … manic depression. That's it. Manic depression. I would recommend her seeing a psychiatrist. I wouldn't be a bit surprised if they recommend that she be institutionalized."

"Institutionalized? You mean put her away in an insane asylum?"

"Yep, I'm afraid so," he said.

"This is horrible," I said. "The idea of putting Adrienne in an institution—I don't think that I'm ready for such a drastic solution. That would be such a harsh thing to do to my wife."

I sat down and rubbed my forehead. "Isn't there anything else we can do?" I asked. "There must be some other way to deal with this. A medication or some type of therapy.

Dr. Redmont shrugged his shoulders. "Not that I know of," he said. "Therapy is usually ineffective. She just needs to be removed from society."

"That's awful," I said.

"Mr. Parker, there is one other option. You could do nothing. Leave her be. If she won't leave the house and is no threat to anyone, let her stay where she is. That's the way a lot of families take care of situations like this—just take care of them at home. Why, she has essentially institutionalized herself anyway.

"But then," Dr. Redmont eyed me suspiciously, "if you are interested in getting control of her money—and I'm not saying that you are—that can only happen if she is diagnosed with insanity and committed."

"I don't care about her money," I said, a little irritated at his inference, "but there is one concern. She did threatened to do me harm."

"Why, yes, she did, didn't she," he said, scratching his head. "That is a problem. Well, if you don't commit her, I would not live in the same house with her. Not unless you can sleep with one eye open."

I thought, *Thanks a lot, Doc! That really makes me feel better!*

Maybe institutionalizing her would be the best option, at least for my health!

"Doctor, if I do decide to put her away, what do we do? She won't go in willingly. She'll fight us tooth and nail. Why, she will say we are putting her away just to get her money."

Dr. Redmont nodded. "You're probably right. But with a court order and a statement by a psychiatrist, you can have her involuntarily committed. The psychiatrist will need a face-to-face evaluation to determine insanity. It shouldn't be too difficult to get a psychiatrist to pay her a visit since you can't get her to leave the house."

He began to scribble down a note. "Here's the name of a psychiatrist at Parkland Hospital. I would recommend that you talk to him and get his advice."

As I walked home, I tried to come up with a plan. Should I talk to the psychiatrist or should I just leave her in her own confinement? I decided I would talk to the children in the morning and get their input.

As I approached the house, I stopped and thought, *Wait, what am I doing? I have no business going into that house. With the reception I got earlier, staying there would be paramount to suicide!* I decided to go stay the night with my daughter, Margurite.

The next day I met with the children, and we agreed that getting the opinion of a psychiatrist was best. We couldn't sit by and let Adrienne waste away in that house if there was something that could be done.

That afternoon I went to Parkland Hospital and visited with the doctor. As I related Adrienne's strange behavior, he said nothing except "Hmm" and nodded continuously. Occasionally he would make a note on a piece of paper.

After I finished, he sat silently for a minute. "Mr. Parker," he finally said, "your wife has the classic symptoms of manic depression. And it appears that she also has developed paranoid schizophrenia. Schizophrenia is a condition where the person loses touch with reality—has difficulty separating what is real from what is not. Paranoia quite often goes along with this break in reality, as in your wife's case. She thinks others are trying to do her harm. I'm afraid that her psychotic behavior will do nothing but get worse. There is no treatment. Whether or not to institutionalize her is up to you, as long as she is not a danger to the public."

After much prayer and consideration, we decided not to institutionalize her—we would let her confine herself to the house. If she ever started leaving the house, we would reconsider.

With Polita as her companion and live-in helper, we tried to interfere with Adrienne's world as little as possible. I moved into an apartment and rarely saw her. Whenever I would visit, she would point her finger at me and scream "Satan! Get thee away from me, Satan!" I don't know why, but as her condition worsened she thought I was the devil.

And by the way, I never got a new arm.

Chapter 18

Lockhart

Within a few months Adrienne and I divorced, and within a year I decided to move back to Meridian. After twenty-four years of life in Texas, I left Dallas never to return. The decision to leave was difficult, but it was the right thing to do. Dallas had been good to me, and I really liked the laid-back Texas lifestyle, but Texas wasn't as appealing without Adrienne. The bachelor's life was not for me: I didn't like living alone. I rarely saw my children. They were busy with their own lives. And deep down I really missed the piney woods of Central Mississippi.

Adrienne was well taken care of. Monetarily, there were no concerns at all. She never left the house as far as I know, living with the doors locked and curtains drawn. Polita continued to live with her, shop for her, and disinfect for her. The children were close by if ever needed. Eventually, though, she had to be institutionalized.

In early 1932, I was back home, back to my roots, back to my beginnings—back to Mississippi.

When I moved back home, our nation was experiencing the worst economic downturn in its one hundred and fifty year existence. The stock market crash of October 1929—initially felt to be a temporary correction—was soon joined by bank closures, job layoffs, foreclosures, and near starvation for millions of Americans.

Unemployment rose to fifteen million, almost one third of the non-farm workforce, leaving families throughout the country destitute and with no hope. The Great Depression lasted a horrible ten years.

Economic problems were not limited to the United States: the Depression was worldwide with joblessness and despair affecting almost every nation. Only Germany had a higher unemployment rate than the United States. Ironically, it took a war to get both economies back up and running.

Mississippi was not left out of the national suffering. When Franklin Delano Roosevelt took office in March 1933, forty percent of farms in Mississippi were in foreclosure, waiting to be auctioned off. Cotton—the white gold of the South—was selling for only five cents a pound, down from forty-three cents just a few years earlier. Farmers, both large and small, could not pay their debts, much less their taxes.

Mississippi's plight was made even worse because it had not yet recovered from the Great Mississippi Flood of 1927. Twenty-seven thousand square miles of the Mississippi River basin had flooded—not for days or weeks—but for months. Farms and homes were ruined; tens of thousands of people were displaced. Many of them never returned.

Thankfully I was able to find work doing the same thing I had been doing for the past forty years—telegraphy. There always seemed to be a need for telegraphers, even in the worst economic times. In Meridian I worked at the same depot and at the same desk that I had left twenty-four years earlier. The railroad was the same, but it was now the GM&O rather than the M&O. Gulf had been added to Mobile and Ohio.

Everything was unchanged except for the team of workers. The crew I left had all retired or died. The station was now staffed with new faces, most of them half my age. Even though I was the oldest member of the team and had been the head telegrapher in Dallas, I had to start at the bottom. I was the new kid on the block, taking orders rather than giving them. I settled into a peaceful life without stress: doing my job—doing what I loved best.

When I moved back, I initially lived alone in a small apartment in town, but within a few months I moved in with Lizzie and Junius.

Papa had died in 1931 leaving Lizzie alone in their huge two-story house on 25th Avenue. Junius was still in Lockhart living in the old home place—working his garden and doing little else. The Bludworth house was slowly falling down around him.

About the time I moved to Meridian the bank took over Junius's farm. Unknown to Lizzie or any other family, he had been unable to pay the taxes for the past three years. But even if it had been known, there wasn't anything she could have done. Money was tight for everyone.

Junius took it very hard. He had been living there alone for thirteen years and was distraught at the idea of moving. He vowed not to leave the house alive and threatened to kill himself, but Lizzie was able to convince him to come to Meridian and move in with her.

For me, though, living alone was not a lifestyle I enjoyed. I needed companionship, so I soon found myself spending most evenings visiting with Junius and Lizzie. When Junius was not in one of his crying spells, he was fairly pleasant to be around. And even though Lizzie was my stepmother, she was, and still is, a good friend—and a good cook. After a few months, she and Junius invited me to share their home, and I took them up on their offer and have been there ever since.

In April 1934 I decided to take the train up to Lockhart. I had been back in Meridian for two years and had not yet taken the time to go and see how my hometown was doing. In fact, I hadn't been to Lockhart since I was there with Junius fifteen years earlier.

I caught the early morning train. It was a beautiful Saturday—perfect for just looking around. When I got off in Lockhart, the conductor told me another train would be coming through later in the day and to just flag it down in order to get back to Meridian.

No trains stopped regularly in Lockhart anymore. The depot had closed a good ten years earlier when the GM&O had decided that there wasn't enough foot traffic or goods being loaded and unloaded to make the stop worthwhile. The meager farm produce being grown around Lockhart was now being transported to Meridian by truck for sale at the local market. Cotton was no longer being grown, and most of the fields lay idle, the only growth being weeds and thistles.

As the train pulled away, the conductor yelled, "Just stand at the north end of the loading dock and wave your hands. They'll stop for you."

I chuckled and thought, "Hand, not hands!" Little slips like that stopped bothering me years ago. I learned it was best to laugh to myself and let it go. To correct those slips—even in jest—would seem ugly and only cause embarrassment.

The station was deserted. Vines were starting to grow up the sides of the building and several of the window panes were broken. The loading dock was strewn with old newspapers and burlap sacks. Off to the side was an old cart, probably the same one that James, Junius, and I had used for loading and unloading over forty years ago. One of its wheels was broken, most likely explaining why it was still there.

The door to the building looked as if it hadn't been opened in years. There were cobwebs in the top corners, and the doorknob was rusty and dirty. It was unlocked, so I turned it and gently pushed. Gently didn't work. After a little more effort and a kick or two, it finally squeaked open.

As I walked into the room, there was a faint echo of the door opening: very little was left in the building to muffle the sound. The floor and countertop were dusty and littered with dead wasps and dirt daubers. I pushed open the swinging gate that separated the lobby area from the working area, stepped behind the counter, and looked around. The only pieces of furniture were an old wicker-bottom chair turned over on the floor and a desk pushed up against the far wall.

I walked over to the desk and dusted it off with my handkerchief. Why that was my old desk! I couldn't believe it was still there! But then, that desk was in pretty bad shape when I sat behind it thirty-five years ago. I guess they had decided it wasn't worth taking when they cleared everything out.

I picked up the chair, dusted it off, and sat down at my desk. I closed my eyes, and for a moment I was transported back in time. Mr. Matthews and Richard were there, laughing and talking. Townspeople were coming in and out, wanting to know if a message from a loved one had come in on the wire, or if there was any interesting news from the outside world. Mamaw came in with a fresh baked cake for everyone to enjoy. Even Silk made an appearance.

After a minute, I opened my eyes and took a deep breath. I reached down and started opening all of the drawers. In the bottom left drawer was an old telegraph key. I pulled it out and dusted it off. Why this is the key I learned on!—the one that Mr. Matthews let me take home those many years ago! I started tapping. THIS IS OLLIE PARKER IN LOCKHART. STOP. CAN YOU HEAR ME. STOP. For a moment I thought I heard a response. MESSAGE RECEIVED. STOP. I played with it for another few minutes, then stood up and put it in my pocket.

I walked outside and headed up the small incline to the church and cemetery. Since I had last been there, someone had placed a small sign on the southwest corner of the church near the only door to the building. LOCKHART METHODIST CHURCH. EST. 1885. I later found out that the church was still in use, but the membership had dwindled significantly. Services were being held only once a month by a minister from Meridian.

Behind the church was the cemetery. I opened the wrought-iron gate and again stepped back in time. Scattered around were markers for so many people that I had known as a youth: the Browns, the Perkinses, the Hobgoods, the Jarmans, the Matthews.

In the center of the cemetery was the Parker plot. I walked over to it, and the first stone I saw was Mama's, Georgia S. Parker. It had been almost fifty years since she had died, and a twinge of guilt hit me as I realized that I could not for sure remember what she looked like. My sister, Cornelia, whom I don't remember, was to her right, and to her left were all seven of Lizzie's angels. Had it really been twenty-four years since the last one died? In many ways it seemed only yesterday when our family was nearly destroyed by the mystery surrounding those deaths.

And above Mama was buried my sister, Gussie. Such a shame—hers was a life filled with problems: selfishness, rebellion, and a failed marriage. She finally straightened herself out and found the love of her life—only to die in childbirth at age thirty-four in 1918.

I turned around to look at my grandfather's and grandmother's graves. They were not in the Parker plot but just a few feet away. Mamaw, how I miss her hugs and her words of wisdom—and her apple pies! And my grandfather: a true pioneer of this area—I wish that I had been old enough to remember his stories of the early settlers, when there was nothing but vast forests and wild animals and Indians.

There was a stone bench in the shade of an old oak tree, and I walked over to it and sat down. I looked out over the cemetery: so much life and death represented in this acre of land, so much happiness and grief—all spanning fewer than fifty years.

Sitting there alone, among the memories of the past, it was hard not to be a little sad—hard not to be a little choked up. Memories can be so sweet, but memories can also make the heart hurt, especially when the memories are only memories—and can no longer be touched.

I left the cemetery and walked down the road to the general store. I passed several houses. Some were vacant and caving in: others were still inhabited and struggling to stay alive. There had never been more than twenty-five or thirty houses in Lockhart, but now I counted only ten. Lockhart was slowly disappearing.

Mamaw's little cottage was gone. The only reminder was a pile of bricks where the chimney once stood and a stone walkway leading from the road to nowhere.

Papa's old general store was boarded up and the roof had caved in. When we had left thirty-two years ago, he had continued to run the store from Meridian, making trips once or twice a month to check on things. But after about ten years, business was so slow that he closed it.

Our house was located a hundred yards farther down the road, the only house beyond the store. We, or rather Lizzie, still owned it and the five or so acres around it. Papa had not been able to sell it when we moved to Meridian and had rented it out to various families over the years, but it had been vacant for the past five. And unlike Junius and the Bludworth house, taxes were up-to-date.

As I approached the house, I was surprised to see an old Ford truck parked beside it and smoke coming out of the chimney. Someone was living there! Had Lizzie found a tenant and forgotten to tell me? I decided to go check things out.

The house looked to be in pretty good shape. Even though it was in need of paint, the roof and windows all appeared to be intact, and the yard was well kept and free of litter. There was a small winter garden to the right of the house in the same spot that we used to have ours. The rest of the fields and pastures were overgrown with waist-high weeds.

As I got closer, I could see a few old toys and dolls scattered on the front porch, and leaning up against the side of the house was my old Crescent bicycle. I had left it behind when we had moved: I was twenty-four at the time and had not ridden it in years. I chuckled, thinking that someone had been able to get that forty-year-old relic up and rolling.

The front door appeared to be open, but the screen door, in remarkably good condition, was closed. As I stepped on the first step, a dog from inside the house began to bark, and a second later a man shouted, "One more step, Mister, and I'll shoot!"

I stopped dead in my tracks. I felt as if my heart were either going to beat right out of my chest or stop at any moment. I raised my arm. "I don't mean any harm, sir."

I squinted, trying to make out who was talking, but it was too dark in the house for me to see in.

"Mister, what do you want?" the voice called out.

"I used to live here," I said. "I'm just looking around."

I wasn't about to tell him I still owned the house. I didn't want anything to provoke this guy. He might think I was there to collect rent, or maybe even to evict him.

The screen door opened and a thin young man stepped out. Thankfully there was not a gun in his hand. He appeared to be about thirty years old, but had a worn, weathered look about him that hinted of very hard times. It was a look that had become very commonplace throughout Mississippi and the rest of the country. It was a look that said hope was almost gone.

"My name's Ollie Parker," I said.

The young man nodded. "I've heard old folks around here call this the Parker House. You can come on up and have a seat if you want. Sorry for how things started. Can't be too careful, though."

"Thanks," I said.

There were a couple of straight-back chairs with the bottoms almost gone leaning against the house, and I pulled one up and sat down.

"My name's Henry Luke," he said as he pulled up the other chair.

"Good to meet you," I said. "My family moved out of this house over thirty years ago. We live in Meridian now. I haven't been out here in years."

He nodded.

"How long you been here?" I asked.

"Six months," he answered. "Moved in early October."

It became obvious that he was a squatter. If Lizzie had found a tenant six months ago, I should have heard about it.

The screen door squeaked, and two little faces appeared. Both were girls and looked to be about five and seven years old. Their dresses were not much more than rags, but were clean and pressed. Their hair was combed, and there were small barrettes in each head holding up beautiful blond bangs. They both began to giggle and the younger one pointed at me.

"Judy, look! That man has a arm gone!"

"Girls! Show your manners!" their father said sternly. "You two've been brought up better than that."

"Sorry, Papa," the older girl said as she looked down at her younger sister.

"That's okay," I said. "No harm done."

The two little faces disappeared back into the house.

I looked around and eyed the old bicycle again.

"That used to be mine when I was a boy," I smiled and pointed. "Can't believe it's working."

"I found it in the barn," Henry said. "Hope you don't mind. Can't afford to buy gas no more."

"No, no," I said apologetically. "You can keep it. An old man with one arm doesn't have much use for a bicycle."

We sat there for a minute in silence.

"Where you from?" I asked.

"North of here, 'round Brooksville. I'd been working some land for a man up there for the past few years, but he stopped planting. He said the government was paying him to leave his land fallow. Said he could make more money by doing nothing." Henry shook his head. "Don't make no sense to me."

I had heard about that program—The Agricultural Adjustment Act. It was put into effect in 1933 to try to boost agricultural prices. The government was paying farmers to leave some of their land uncultivated: decreasing the supply in hopes of increasing the demand. It was the old "supply and demand" theory. It sounded good on paper, but it didn't take into consideration the workers in the fields who ended up with no work and no pay. It actually hurt the ones who could afford it the least.

"He wouldn't even let me grow a vegetable garden on his land. Afraid it might mess up his government check. With no work, we headed south hoping to find something. We ran out of gas here in Lockhart. Found this old house empty and moved in."

"It *is* in pretty good shape," I said proudly.

"Wasn't when we moved in," he said, and my bubble of pride began to deflate. "We patched the roof and was able to find glass from empty houses around to fix up the windows. Everything's coming along fine now. Scavenged some screen, too. Don't want the mosquitoes getting us when it gets summer."

It sounded like they were there to stay.

"I was able to get in a little winter garden," he continued, "kept us going with turnips, greens, and carrots. We've been able to catch a rabbit or two for some meat."

Henry stood up and walked over to the porch rail. "I'll be planting a real garden in the next week, and in a few months we'll have some peas and corn and okra."

"You think you will try to plant anything else?" I asked.

Henry was quiet for a moment, and looked out toward the overgrown fields.

"I'd like to. Maybe an acre or two of corn. That's selling pretty good right now. Cotton's out of the question—you can't hardly give it away." He shook his head. "I could sure use some money. The few dollars I had when we got here have just about disappeared."

Henry turned around, and with a sadness in his eyes like an old dog that had been kicked around more than once, he said, "But I don't think I will. I'd hate to put in all that work and get run off by whoever owns this place."

A twinge of guilt came over me. All this time I had been look-ing at this fellow as a trespasser. But this guy was destitute. He had nothing—nothing but his pride and a desire to keep his fam-ily from starving.

"I see you have a couple of little girls," I said. "Any other family?"

"Yea, my wife, Lois, and a little boy, Luke, Jr. Luke's two. He's been having a time with a cough lately. We can't afford to take him to a doctor."

The screen porch squeaked open, and the two little faces appeared again. After a moment the girls eased outside, and stood there looking at me. I had gotten used to that look years ago and didn't let it bother me.

The five-year-old came a little closer, put her finger up to her chin, and asked, "Were you born without a arm?"

"Sarah!" her father exclaimed.

"No, that's okay," I said. I then pointed down the road. "See the railroad track down there? Well, Sarah—now, that is your name, isn't it?"

She nodded and smiled.

"Well, Sarah, I got run over by a train right down there when I was a boy."

Her eyes got big and a look of horror came over her face.

"I bet your father has told you never to play down there, hasn't he?"

She nodded.

"Well, you need to mind him. Because you don't ever want a train to run over you, do you?"

Sarah shook her head. She and her sister didn't say anything else. They just stood there with their mouths open.

After a little more visiting, I bid them good-bye and as I started walking away, Luke called out, "Mr. Parker, just want you to know—I don't own a gun. Sorry I scared you."

I left there without ever telling them that we owned the house and property—or rather that Lizzie owned it. I hated to say anything without first talking with her.

The next Saturday afternoon my brother-in-law, Arthur, Maude's husband, was kind enough to drive me to Lockhart with a nice little bundle of clothes and house goods. Dr. Tatum also came along for the ride and brought his medical bag. He said a nice ride in the country in April would do him good. I also delivered some news, with the blessings of my stepmother. If Henry could make enough profit to pay the taxes, he and his family could stay there and farm the land for as long as they want. I also told him there was a mule and an old plow in town that was his, and he could pay me for it when he was able.

The Lukes stayed on the Parker Place for several years, making enough to get by. Our table was kept well supplied by fresh vegetables. And corn was soon coming out of our ears.

When the war started in 1941, the Lukes moved on. Good work and good pay could be found in the factories that suddenly had more work than they could keep up with. Millions of families moved from the farms to the cities—never to return.

Chapter 19

The Skies over Meridian

In early May 1934 I was busy at my desk, sending and receiving messages when Al Key walked into the station with his brother Fred.

Al and Fred ran the Meridian Municipal Airport. In fact they built it, maintained it, and had been keeping it in business for the past six or seven years. The airport wasn't much to look at. There was one small hangar and a dirt airstrip that had originally been a cotton field. Al and Fred had leveled out the furrows and beaten down the dirt by dragging a railroad iron around behind a truck. Delta Airlines was the only commercial outfit that used it, making a stop twice a day on its route from Dallas, by way of Shreveport and Jackson, and then on to Tuscaloosa and Birmingham, and then back.

The Key boys had one small plane and would occasionally charter it, transporting dignitaries who needed to get somewhere faster than the train would take them. But for the most part they were aerial performers—barnstormers at county fairs and circuses throughout Mississippi, Alabama, and Louisiana. Al had started flying in 1924 when he was twenty; Fred in 1927 when he was eighteen.

"Ollie," Al said, "I need to get my hands on a radio code transceiver. You know where I can get one? I need it for a plane."

Barnstormers never used instruments or radio contact with the ground. Everything was done by visual contact, following roads and landmarks, waving their hands—flying by the seat of their pants.

"What do you need it for?" I asked.

"We are getting ready to set a world record endurance flight," Fred answered, "and we need to be able to communicate with the ground. We'll be in the air for about a month."

My mouth fell open.

I soon learned that the city of Meridian had been talking about closing down the airstrip. The Depression was drying up what little air traffic there was, and the cost of upkeep was more than the city was willing to pay. The Key boys were trying everything they could to keep it open and thought that a little national publicity might do the trick.

Their goal was to beat the record set in Chicago by the Hunt brothers in 1930—five hundred and fifty-four hours—or twenty-three days and two hours.

"We've borrowed a Curtis Robin monoplane from W. H. Ward in Oxford and are getting it outfitted," Al said. "Our plane could never last that long. Ward wants some of the credit when we finish..."

"And the plane back in one piece." Fred butted in and began to laugh.

W. H. Ward was an aerial photographer, and his business was also in a slump. He had kindly loaned his plane, named *Ole Miss*, and was allowing them to do whatever outfitting was needed.

After I got over my shock, I said, "Al, I don't have a radio transceiver on hand—it's not something we use in the depot.

We transmit by wire. But I should be able to order you one. It ought to be here in a week or two."

Over the next few weeks, the Key boys were hard at work converting that plane into an endurance machine. Dave Stevenson, a welder in town, built a catwalk on both sides of the engine to allow maintenance in flight. Frank Covert designed an oversized fuel tank which almost filled up the baggage compartment. There was a little room for a mattress behind the tank, but stretching out to sleep was going to be impossible.

The most ingenious development was the refueling mechanism. The engine burned about ten gallons of gasoline per hour, and the seventy-five gallon tank would need to be refilled every six to seven hours. There was a spare sixteen gallon tank in case of an emergency—which came in handy several times.

When the Hunts in Chicago had set their record, they had used a common hose to refill, but there was always the worry of a spill and a fire. A. D. Hunter, a mechanic here in Meridian, came up with a nozzle that would automatically stop flowing when the hose separated from the tank. It worked wonderfully. In fact, his design is still being used by the Army Air Corps for military refueling today.

The upcoming event was the talk of the town, and I was soon caught up in all the excitement. Telegraphers were needed to help man the communication center—which turned out to be one corner of the old hangar. Before long everyone in Meridian who knew telegraphy had volunteered to help and take turns.

The Key boys, however, didn't know Morse code, and we had to give them a crash course in communications. They got by, but were never very good.

On June 21, 1934, several thousand people gathered at the field to watch them begin. The *Ole Miss* was painted bright silver, and a Mississippi flag adorned each side of the fuselage. A small band was there to send them off, and with a wave of the hand the two brothers were off.

To everyone's disappointment, the flight lasted only five days. Two of the cylinder heads began erupting in flames, and they had to bring it down.

Over the next month they did several modifications, replaced the engine, and replaced the code transceiver with a two-way radio voice transmitter—they could speak much better than they could code! The telegraphers were no longer needed, but we still cheered them on.

A month later in July, they were ready for flight number two. A crowd of about a thousand showed up to bid them a good flight.

Again things didn't go well. Weather was a problem, and they were dodging thunderstorms all day and night. During one storm they came out of a cloud bank and found themselves over the Mississippi River near Vicksburg, one hundred and fifty miles away. They headed back toward Meridian and connected with the refueling plane and continued.

In another storm, the exhaust pipe was jarred loose, and there was fear that the heat would cause a fire on the wooden fuselage. After only seven days, they were back on the ground again.

The excitement died down, but their quest for a record continued. Over the next year they undertook several modifications, learning from their mistakes. They were able to get a gyro compass and horizon indicator. The engine was overhauled and light aluminum exhaust pipes were installed. Even a team of doctors got into the act and developed exercises to keep them healthy.

A year later, on June 4, 1935, they set out again. This time only about a hundred Meridianites showed up to see them off. In fact, the *Meridian Star* barely noted the event on a back page. It was "Here they go again!"

But the third time was the charm. Everything was going well. Refueling was down to a fine art, and transfer of home cooked food from the refueling plane in a canvas bag, fresh from their wives' kitchens, kept their spirits high. Even Henry Weidmann furnished a continuous supply of fresh orange juice from his restaurant for the adventurers.

After ten days, everyone started getting excited. It looked like this time they were serious. Several reporters started checking into the local hotels, and national newspapers started covering the flight. The reporters were in and out of the depot, keeping us busy with wires to New York, Philadelphia, and Chicago. Even a few European papers began reporting it.

For another seventeen days, they circled Meridian, going a steady ninety to one hundred miles an hour. The brothers would take four-hour shifts at the controls, trying to get a little sleep when they could.

There were two major crises in their otherwise uneventful adventure. The first was a tooth abscess. On day twenty, Al began having a toothache and soon an abscess developed. The pain became severe, and Al desperately needed to get it seen about. But rather than abort the mission, a local dentist sent up a lance and instructed Fred on how to drain an abscess. Fred performed the surgery admirably, with Al achieving almost instantaneous relief.

The other was when Fred was on the catwalk, greasing the engine. The plane suddenly hit some turbulent air and Fred was thrown off. Thankfully he was wearing an electrical linesman's harness which saved his life. Fred was able to pull himself back into the plane by himself: Al couldn't help and fly the plane at the same time. Later Al told me that that really shook them both up. He said he still gets a chill when he thinks about it.

On June 27 the Key brothers broke the Hunt brothers' record, and announced by radio to the crowd of several thousand that they would continue until the Fourth of July. The world was watching, and they were not quite ready to relinquish the spotlight.

On June 29, while they were still in the air, the airport was renamed Key Field to honor Meridian's newest heroes.

Two days later they began experiencing difficulty in controlling the plane, especially during refueling. The left stabilizer fittings were wearing out, and if they failed, they would have no control. It was time to quit.

That morning Fred radioed that they would land late that afternoon. News spread rapidly and by six o'clock thirty thousand people—and I was one of them—had gathered at Key Field. At 6:06, July 1, 1935, Al and Fred Key landed, having logged over fifty-two thousand miles in six hundred fifty-four hours, or twenty-seven days and six hours. Six thousand gallons of gasoline and three hundred gallons of oil had been used, having been delivered during four hundred thirty-eight refueling and supply contacts.

When they crawled out of that plane—and I mean they had to crawl out—they looked terrible: unwashed and unshaven, groaning with pain as they stretched out their legs. Not even their wives and children wanted to be near them—they smelled so bad. There were no hugs and kisses until they'd had a bath.

A few weeks later Fred was in the depot waiting to board a train to Memphis to give a talk. For several months the two celebrities made numerous appearances throughout the country, telling about their magnificent adventure, captivating the imagination of men and boys alike.

"Hey, Ollie," he called out, "thanks for the help with the transceiver."

"You're welcome," I said. "I'm sorry it couldn't have been of more help."

"Yea," Fred shook his head. "I couldn't ever get that Morse code down. Those dots and dashes were driving me crazy. I don't see how in the world you can do it."

"Well, how does it feel to be a celebrity?" I asked.

"It's great! I haven't had this much fun since I did my first loopity-loop ten years ago. Everybody's patting me on the back and wanting my signature. And paying me to tell my story. It sure beats sitting in a cramped monoplane for twenty-seven days."

Still a barnstormer at heart. But now the attention without the danger.

"Would you do it again?" I asked.

Fred laughed. "No way! I'm glad to have my name in the record books, but it was miserable! I couldn't straighten out for a week.

"Ollie, when are you gonna take a ride with me? You know I've been trying to get you in the air for months, and you can't say no forever. Why, you would get a kick out of it. It's a blast!"

"No, thanks," I said. "I plan on keeping my two feet on the ground. I still think that if the Good Lord had meant for man to fly, He would have given him wings."

Al and Fred went on to serve in the Army Air Corps during the war, flying bombing missions in the Pacific Theater. Both had distinguished careers and thankfully came home intact. They recently returned to Meridian. Al is talking about staying in the Army Air Corps, but Fred plans to get the Key Brothers Flying Service at Key Field back up and running.

Chapter 20

The Second War

Shortly after Thanksgiving in 1945, I sent a wire to Mobile letting them know that I would retire. PARKER IN MERIDIAN. STOP. NOTIFYING COMPANY OF RETIREMENT. STOP. EFFECTIVE LAST DAY OF 1945. STOP. I decided not to tell my coworkers, partly from pride, but mostly from fear. I was afraid that I would get emotional, and maybe even cry. No one wants to see a blubbering old man with teary eyes and a quivering lip. They would just hear about it from the GM&O headquarters.

Yes, it is time to retire, but to stop what one has poured his very life into for over fifty years is not easy. It is extremely difficult. In my early days, when I saw men struggling with retirement and trying to find new purpose and meaning in their golden years, I was puzzled, almost amused. Why, there is so much to do outside of work! Enjoy the time you have left! Relax and do whatever you wish! But as I have aged, I have found that it's not as easy as I thought.

It's strange how our view of work changes. Initially we work for the pay, and possibly for the challenge. Deep down, though, we often wish that we were somewhere else—anywhere but at our desk or at our work station; doing something—anything but what we are doing. But there are bills to pay and mouths to feed, so we continue to work. As time passes and the demands of life diminish, the work takes on a new meaning. Without our even realizing it, we no longer work for the pay, or even for the challenge. We now work because it's part of us; it has become part of our very soul. It really doesn't matter if we enjoy it, we work anyway. The thought of stopping work now frightens us: stop and a part of us will cease to exist.

And with the passing of time, something else even more frightening begins to happen. No longer are we given the difficult and challenging tasks. We see younger coworkers solving the problems, getting the job done faster—and better—than we can. When we express our discontent about being passed over, or maybe we even lash out, it is not anger that seizes us, not even envy—it is panic. We suddenly realize that we are not indispensable. Youth is taking our place; and we can't do anything about it. We feel useless. And more terrifying, the next step in this journey of life is death.

And then another fear: what do we do with all that extra time? There is just so much rocking and fishing a guy can do. And in my case, what is a one-armed old man to do? There is not a lot of physical activity that I *can* do. How can I possibly fill up an entire day with activities? I'll go crazy with boredom!

But it is time, I have no choice: either retire with dignity, or wait until I'm incompetent and am asked to leave.

Funny thing is that no one knows how close I came to retiring four years ago. I never told anyone, but at sixty-four, with fifty years of service to the railroad and telegraphy, I was considering stepping aside and maybe doing a little traveling. I envisioned seeing the country—traveling around, getting to know this mighty nation of ours.

Having been divorced for several years and with all the children grown and on their own, I had built up a fairly substantial nest egg and had nothing to tie me down except my work. As a retired railroad employee, I could board a car going wherever, as long as there was a seat available and as long as I was willing to get off if one was needed. But I changed my mind about retirement one Sunday in early December 1941. In fact, the plans of our entire nation changed forever that Sunday afternoon.

On that tragic day in December 1941, I was living with my stepmother, Lizzie, and Junius. That Sunday started out as any other Lord's Day in most small towns in the South: a leisurely breakfast of eggs, bacon, pancakes, and grits, followed by a couple of hours of worship. The service at Hawkins Memorial Methodist Church in Meridian was no different from the one last week—singing led by the choir and a sermon expounding the wages of sin and the gift of salvation.

Around 3:30 that afternoon, I decided to walk downtown and check on things at the depot. Even on my days off, I tended to migrate to the station, especially when Junius was having one of his crying spells. Sunday afternoons seemed to be particularly difficult for him, and over the years I learned that there was no consoling him—it was best to just let him cry.

Not much was going on at the depot. Harris, the telegrapher on duty, said that the wire had been silent for most of the day. He shook his head and said he would have been able to read the Sunday paper if it weren't for a lady waiting for a train. She wanted to talk: wanted to tell someone her whole life's history and he was unlucky enough to be one of the few people around.

Harris and I were enjoying a cup of coffee when the wire suddenly came alive. URGENT. STOP. PACIFIC FLEET IN HAWAII ATTACKED BY JAPANESE. STOP. MORE INFORMATION WHEN AVAILABLE. STOP.

The next several days can only be described as chaotic. Our nation was trying to figure out what had happened in a place that most of us had never heard of: Pearl Harbor. On December 8, we gathered around the radio and heard the president declare a state of war on the nation of Japan.

Over the next few days more information came through about that "day that will live in infamy"—2,388 young Americans were killed—thirty from Mississippi and one from Meridian. I was at the depot three days after the attack when the wire came through addressed to the local Navy liaison officer. NOTIFICATION OF NEXT OF KIN. STOP. RICHARD P. MOLPUS OF MERIDIAN. STOP. ABOARD USS ARIZONA. STOP. MISSING IN ACTION AND PRESUMED DEAD. STOP. This was the first of 208 similar messages that we received over the next four years, messages notifying Meridian and Lauderdale County families of the personal horror of war.

Saturday afternoon, December 13, 1941, I visited the Molpus family. It was a difficult visit, but I felt that I had to go. I had known his parents, Lewis and Mattie Molpus, for years and had watched Richard and his two brothers and four sisters grow up attending Hawkins Memorial Methodist Church. Mattie welcomed me graciously, and between tears asked me if I would like some tea or coffee. I declined and said I would only be a minute, just wanted to come by and give my condolences.

Richard's two younger sisters, Lucy and Minnie, sat quietly staring at the floor. Richard's father, Lewis, sat in an old rocking chair in front of the fireplace, his eyes lost in the yellow glow of the flame. Mattie said that Richard's young widow, Sherrie Renee, was in the back room in bed. She was almost due with their first baby and had taken the news very hard. Baby Sherrie Molpus was born three weeks after my visit.

I had not known that Richard was married, much less that he was about to be a father. It broke my heart to think about it. Sadly, this was the first of many young widows of Meridian who would raise their children alone, their husbands having paid the ultimate price for our freedom in that second of the "war to end all wars."

After a few minutes of silence, I said what a fine young man Richard had been and how everyone would miss him. Mattie cried softly and then began to tell me all about her youngest son. An hour later I bid them good-bye. Mattie thanked me and told me how much the visit meant: meant more than I would ever know. As I walked to the door, Lewis, who had been silent, looked up at me and said, "I wish that I had told him more how much I loved him and how proud I was of him."

It soon became obvious that retirement for me was not an option. Within a few days everyone was enlisting, ready to fight the Japanese, and later to fight the Nazis. Emotions were high and patriotism was never more evident. Staffing of the depot, as well as most other businesses in Meridian, was left to the elderly and the handicapped. I fit both categories. Most of the young and healthy were gone to war, only a few were left to work the factories and fields to keep their brothers equipped and fed.

And over the next few months life became very busy for the station: men in uniform coming and going, and the telegraph staying busy with messages being sent and received. (The telephone was slowly becoming popular, but most communication was still by wire and post.) As more of our boys left Meridian and headed to their training destination, the number of messages we were sending and receiving became astounding. Boys were letting their families, and girlfriends, know that they had reached their destination. Mothers and wives were reassuring their sons and husbands that everything at home was fine, but that they were greatly missed.

Harris and several other young fellows at the depot were soon gone—good telegraphers were like gold to the military, and

Harris was in Europe before he even knew how to salute. Staffing for us was down to a minimum, enough to keep things going but with little time off. Sixty-hour work weeks became the usual for us: ten-hour work days with one day off each week. Unlike before the war when weekends were the slow times at the station, Saturdays and Sundays soon became the busiest days of the week.

As the war progressed and our boys were deployed to Europe and the Pacific, the dreaded messages addressed to the Navy and Army liaisons slowly started coming in. We at the station were always the first to know, a burden we had not asked for and did not want.

The Navy and Army liaison officers shared an office in the Threefoot Building in downtown Meridian, and I soon got to know them very well. Lieutenant Charles McDonald from upstate New York was the Navy officer; Captain Steve Lent from Indiana, the Army officer. Both men were initially assigned to Key Field with the 153rd Observation Squadron, but their offices were moved downtown after war was declared and the dreaded messages started coming in. When I would open the door to their office and walk in with a note in my hand, they would not speak. They would look at me with a look that said "Please, not again." Then they would bow their heads and cover their faces with their hands.

McDonald and Lent usually went together. Each needed the other's support in relating the worst news that any mother or father would ever get. A knock on the door and then the dreaded words, "I'm sorry to inform you that your son..."

I found it almost ironic that these soldiers, fortunate to have been assigned a stateside duty, had one of the most dreaded, difficult missions of the entire military. On those days when I would deliver the message, I sensed that battle on the front lines would have been easier.

They did their jobs well and were very professional, but I soon sensed that there was something missing. Not being from Meridian, or even the South, they didn't know the people, and they didn't know the culture. The news was terrible enough, but to have it related by a total stranger, and one whom you could hardly understand ... They soon began enlisting the local clergy to accompany them on their visits.

As in the case of Richard Molpus, I made it a point to visit each family several days after the message had been delivered. I felt that it was the least that a one-armed old man could do: in my own way be a part of the war effort at home.

At most homes there were family members and friends present twenty-four hours a day to comfort and console. At others, I would find no one there but the immediate family. These poor families were mourning their losses alone: no support group, no church, no close friends to help guide them through their anguish. Several told me that I was the only person, except for the soldiers and a preacher, to visit.

Initially I would think what is wrong with people? Don't they know that these people need help, need a shoulder to cry on? But then, to be perfectly honest, to have a friend, one has to be a friend. I don't mean to sound cruel, but people can't expect others to help if they don't even know that they exist. People need to get out, go to church, meet the neighbors, join a club. Develop those friendships so that when the need arises, they can console, and in turn have people console them in their time of need.

Other dreaded messages also came pouring in from the War Department: loved ones wounded in battle. However, unlike the killed-in-action messages, these did not go through the liaisons. They went directly to the families, which posed another difficult problem.

For most wires, there were young boys always available to deliver the messages to families and businesses, working primarily for the tips at the time of delivery. Most of them were twelve to fifteen years of age: an age not known for having a lot of understanding and tact. We quickly learned that with the wounded-in-action it was best for us to make the calls personally.

Families needed more than just a piece of paper with a message on it, delivered by a kid eager for a tip. They needed to ask questions, needed to get more information, needed someone to offer hope for their son. We would tell them that we knew no more than what was in the message, but promised that as soon as we did we would let them know. They were very grateful: appreciative that someone was at the depot looking out for any information on their child.

Chapter 21

Arthur

The war raged on. The weeks turned to months and the months into years. The wire continued to deliver messages of hope, messages of love, and messages of heartbreak.

One day in January 1945, I received a wire that brought me to my knees. A message was especially difficult when we knew the person, and even more difficult when it was a family member. ARTHUR SIMPSON COBURN. STOP. WOUNDED IN ACTION. STOP.

Arthur is my sister Maude's oldest child—Arthur Simpson Coburn, Jr. He was thirty years old when the war started. Now at age thirty-four, he has been in an Army hospital for almost a year. Two months ago he was transferred to the Army Hospital in Tuscaloosa, Alabama, only one hundred and ten miles away, and a few weeks ago he came home for a weeklong furlough.

I was working at the station the afternoon Arthur came home and wasn't surprised to see his parents get there a good hour before the train. They were so excited and anxious to have their oldest boy home—even if it was for only a week. Maude had been cooking and crying all morning, getting ready for his return. Arthur, Sr., had been busy setting up a bed downstairs, knowing that climbing a flight of stairs would not be possible.

The word had gotten out that Arthur was coming home, and a fair-sized crowd of family and friends began to gather. Someone even painted a nice little banner with WELCOME HOME ARTHUR on it.

The train pulled in and, as we anxiously waited, several people got off. But there was no Arthur. Everyone was silent—wondering what had happened to our Arthur—when we heard a faint "Hello, Mother and Daddy!" coming from one of the windows midway down the coach. There was Arthur smiling down on us.

"Would someone mind helping me get off the train? I'm afraid the steps may be a problem."

A couple of the guys climbed up the steps to help him. I stayed on the platform—I didn't think a one-armed old man would be much help. As they helped him maneuver the steps with his crutches, Maude covered her mouth and began to cry. This was the first time she had seen her boy in almost four years. I know she was overjoyed to see her son, but she was also heartbroken to see him so weak and frail. There wasn't a dry eye in the station as they hugged and kissed.

I only had a chance to welcome him home that day, but I was able to have a nice long visit with him later.

I stopped by late one evening after work for a visit. Arthur was resting in bed with his legs propped up, reading the *Meridian Star*, our local newspaper, when I walked in.

"Ollie! Good to see you!" Arthur dropped the paper and reached out his hand. He had a way of smiling one-sided, like one side of his mouth didn't work just right, and that grin hadn't changed. "Hope you don't mind if I forget my manners and don't stand up. Come on in and have a seat. Haven't seen you in almost four years. Why, you haven't changed a bit!"

"Arthur, you haven't changed either."

I was lying, but what was I to say? He was thin, pale, and looked fifteen years older than the last time I saw him.

"How are you doing?" I asked.

He shifted in bed, grimaced, and said, "Doing pretty good. The doc in Tuscaloosa said that in another month or two they're going to discharge me and send me home. Said that any further care I needed could be done at the V.A. in Jackson."

He smiled and continued. "It sure will be good to be a civilian again. Didn't want to be in the Army in the first place, but when Uncle Sam called, I went. You want a cup of coffee? I'm sure Mother would be glad to brew up a pot for us."

"No, thanks," I replied. "Can't drink coffee at night the way I used to. Keeps me up. And besides, Maude and Arthur were headed to bed when I came in and said that I could let myself out when we were through visiting."

"Sure is good to be home, even if it is only for a week," Arthur said. "I'm to report back to Tuscaloosa on Sunday. Lots of friends and family have been by, letting me know that they have been praying for me. How are Lizzie and Junius doing?"

"Lizzie's doing well, but it's been pretty difficult for Junius. His crying spells have been pretty bad since the war started, and I don't think he has been out of the house in six months. No one talks about anything except the war, and everywhere you go there are men in uniform. It must bring back too many bad memories for him."

The smile on Arthur's face suddenly disappeared. He sat silent for a minute, staring at the sheets covering his legs. He then softly said, "After the Civil War, General Sherman once said that 'War is hell.' Ollie, he was right.

"You know I didn't want to be a part of all this," Arthur continued. "After December 7, when everyone was enlisting, I stayed at home. Sure I was willing to go, but I wasn't about to go asking for it. I'm no conscientious objector. I'm just as much a patriot as the next guy, but I had no desire at all to go to war.

"But my desires soon took backseat to the desires of the United States Government. On January 27, 1942, I got my

'Greetings' and on February 7, I was loaded on a bus headed to Camp Shelby for induction into the United States Army—became a bona fide nephew of Uncle Sam.

"Ollie, things changed in a hurry. One minute I'm on the sideline watching the game get started, the next minute I'm on the starting team in the middle of the game!"

Arthur paused a moment and said, "Well, I don't want to bore you with my story." But he had a look on his face that said, "I'll be glad to tell you more if you are willing to listen."

"Arthur, what happened after you left Meridian?" I asked. "I'd like to hear all about it."

He leaned forward and continued. "From Camp Shelby we were sent to Leesville, Louisiana, to begin training in tank warfare. From there we were shipped to California for desert training and then to Georgia for training in hilly, wooded terrain—all the while learning military tactics, use of weapons, and survival skills. We studied about places I had never heard of: Algeria, Tunisia, Libya. This went on for over two years until finally, on June 6, 1944, our unit boarded the *Queen Mary* in New York Harbor and headed across the Atlantic to Scotland. You know, that is the very day that the invasion of Normandy was taking place—D-Day.

"We were in Scotland and England for two months preparing to join in the European campaign, and on August 11 we crossed the English Channel and landed on Omaha Beach." Arthur shook his head. "Ollie, the destruction on the beach was unimaginable! There was wreckage of ships and landing craft everywhere, and disabled tanks and land equipment were strewn on the beach as far as you could see."

Arthur paused a moment. Quietly, almost reverently, he said, "Two months earlier 34,000 American boys landed on that beach. Three thousand of them never walked away."

After a moment of silence, he continued.

"Over the next several months we slowly advanced inland, experiencing fierce fighting as we made our way through France, Belgium, and Holland. As we advanced to the German border our casualties began to mount. Ollie, the carnage was horrible—the killing and being killed. I can't describe the horror. Three of my closest friends lost their lives in those days of fighting: Lewis Keith, Roy Fowles, and Weldon Bailey."

Arthur was silent, and his lip began to quiver. "While I've been laid up in the hospital, I've written to all of their families, told them as best I could how they died." Arthur began to choke up. "Lewis was from Purvis, just outside Hattiesburg. Yesterday his two sisters came to visit. We had a nice visit. They were so appreciative of my letters. Roy's wife wrote me back a few weeks ago. Said that she was going to save the letter and give it to their four-year-old boy when he turns fifteen."

Arthur pulled the sheet up and wiped his eyes. After a moment he let out a big sigh and continued.

"Ollie, I was wounded on January 27, 1944. The Battle of the Bulge had begun a month before, and our unit was on patrol near the German border. It had been snowing all day and the cold was numbing. We were walking in single file, spaced several yards apart. I was third from the end.

"Suddenly there was a tremendous blast behind and to the right of me. I felt like I had been hit in the back and on the legs with a baseball bat. I fell right straight back in the snow.

"I must have been unconscious for a minute or two—not really sure how long, but it couldn't have been very long. When I woke, there was ringing in my ears and spots before my eyes. My head cleared fairly quickly, probably due to the cold air, and being the soldier I am, I looked around for my rifle. It was about ten feet away. I remember thinking, 'How did it get that far away?' As I looked closer, I could see that the butt of the gun was shattered. It must have been hit by the blast, probably saving my life.

"I knew I was hit too, but I didn't know how badly at the time. Later I learned that I had several deep lacerations on both of my legs and feet, and a chest wound that resulted in a hemopneumothorax—or blood and air in my lung cavity.

"I tried to get up, but realized that I could not move. I then tried to get to my first-aid kit which was on my pistol belt, but I couldn't find it." Arthur began to laugh. "It strikes me funny now, but what in the world was I going to do with a little first-aid kit when my legs were almost blown off? The only things in that kit were a bottle of aspirin, a box of Band-Aids, and a bottle of mercurochrome."

In a more somber tone, he continued. "But, Ollie, when you think you are going to die, you will grasp for anything that will give you hope.

"While I was lying there, the shelling continued. I thought that if I could turn over, then I could crawl to the ditch alongside the road and find cover. I turned to my left and surprised myself by rolling onto my stomach. But the exertion took all my strength and there was no way I was going to be able to crawl. My chest was hurting so badly that I could hardly breathe.

"I looked back to where I had been lying, and the white snow was stained with my blood. Ollie, I thought I was going to die." At that moment Arthur began to cry. "All I could think of was home and Mother and Daddy. Oh, how I wanted to feel my Mother's arms around me!"

Arthur shook his head and began to chuckle. "Well, Ollie, instead of Mother, I got Pete Sunich. 'Corporal, I'm coming,' I heard Pete holler, 'and the medics are on their way.' When he got to me, he asked what he could do. I told him that my hands were about to freeze and could he please rub them. Pete said he could take

care of that, and he pulled off our gloves and rubbed my hands between his. He then slipped his own warm gloves over my hands.

"Within a few minutes, the medics were there and I was
loaded up and carried to a clearing station for wounded, and then
further back to an evacuation hospital where a chest tube was
placed and my legs were bandaged. Ollie, I have only praise for the
medics and doctors. Thanks to them, I am alive today.

"Over the next few months I have been taken from hospital
to hospital, getting closer and closer to home, all the while having my wounds cared for. I've had multiple operations on my legs,
and this chest tube in my back is still there and still draining.

"Now I'm only a hundred and ten miles away in Tuscaloosa.
Since I've been there, the nurses have really been working hard
with me, helping me regain my strength and function. It had been
six months since I had been able to put any weight on my legs,
and they got me up and walking. PT twice a day, every day of the
week. There are still numb areas in my legs, and some of my leg
muscles don't work right, but it's getting better. I'm just now
starting to move the toes on my right foot. I've really made good
progress. Look."

Arthur pulled back the sheets. His legs looked bad—scarred
and discolored. I'm glad he was looking at his feet and not at me.
I know the expression on my face was one of horror.

"I can wiggle my toes!" he said. "I'm still on crutches, but the
doc said in a few months I should be able to throw them away.

"Ollie, it sure is good to be home and on the road to recovery.
But being home has been a little hard—good, but hard. The doc
told me the wound on my back has to be cleaned and dressed every
day while I'm here. It's still open and draining, and the chest tube
is still in. Mother has been cleaning it for me. She cries the entire
time she is doing it—says she hates to see her boy like this."
Arthur began to tear up. "No mother should have to do that."

Arthur paused a moment and wiped his eyes. "And, Ollie, no man should go through what I have been through. It was horrible. And they tell me I can now return to civilian life. Go back to life the way it was. But how? How do they expect me to get over seeing my friends die? How do they expect me to get over being a part of killing? Can anyone really expect me to go on with life as usual now that the war is over? And how do I get over lying wounded in the snow a thousand miles from home, snow that was stained with my own blood, begging God to let me live? And Ollie, I'm one of the lucky ones—I *did* live. How do I get over the fear I may never walk again? How do I get over the months of surgery and rehab and pain? Ollie, I would give my right arm…"

Arthur stopped in mid sentence and looked at me. "Ollie, how old were you when you lost your arm?"

"Thirteen," I answered.

"How old are you now?"

"Sixty-eight."

"Fifty-five years. That's a long time. But Ollie, I would gladly trade places with you. I would gladly have cut off my own arm if it would have kept me from going to war. You may not agree, but you are blessed—blessed to not have memories of hell on Earth. Blessed to have a clean, pure heart—unstained by the guilt and horror of war. Yes, you have suffered and have been limited, but you have had a good life, a peaceful life—a life without nightmares that make you cry out in terror."

I was not about to tell of my own horrible nightmares. After his story, my dreams no longer seemed to be significant.

Arthur leaned back on his pillow and closed his eyes. After a minute he took a deep breath and let it out slowly. Exhaustion seemed to have taken over him completely, every ounce of energy gone. For a moment I wondered if he would say anything else—if he had fallen asleep. But then he raised his head and opened his eyes. "Ollie, thank you for listening.

"And Ollie, I'll be okay. I know I will. As bad as it was, as horrible as the memories are, and as much as what I participated in was man at his lowest—killing and being killed—I know I will find peace." Arthur bowed his head and closed his eyes. "Yes, I will find peace: it will come—it has to come. Because I already know that I am forgiven."

He lifted his head and opened his eyes. "The Bible tells us that 'In Him we have redemption through His blood, the forgiveness of sins, according to the riches of His grace.' That's in Ephesians. It has become my verse—the truth that I cling to. God has forgiven me, not because I deserve it, but because of His mercy and grace. And at some point peace will come."

Arthur rested his head back on his pillow. Within minutes he was asleep, snoring softly. I stood up, quietly left his room, and let myself out the front door. I looked at my watch. It was three o'clock in the morning.

Chapter 22

The Injury

Years ago my grandmother made the comment that it's a wonder that any boy makes it into manhood. How he lives through all the falls, broken bones, busted lips, cuts, bruises, and near drowning was a mystery to her.

There is a lot more truth to her comment than she may have realized. Child mortality was extremely high when she was alive, but most of the deaths were due to the ravages of disease and sickness, not due to the foolish harm that boys are known to inflict on themselves and each other.

But stupid things do happen, and boys do die—or are severely injured and live on. With some injuries, even though the damage is sometimes horrific, even though the chance of survival is often slim, boys do pull through and live—live to be old men. But the injuries are sometimes permanent and debilitating, and the old question "Why did I do such a stupid thing?" will haunt them for the rest of their days.

And I have to admit that I am no different. For fifty-five years, since the summer of my thirteenth year, I have often thought "What if…" and "If only…". I know that wanting to redo or undo what has been done is a waste. But I can't help it. It must be human nature to wish to turn the clock back—make things right again. But as time passed, I finally resigned myself to the fact that things were not going to change.

Funny thing, I'm not really sure when it happened, when that resignation took hold. It's not like one day I was wishing and praying that I would get my arm back, and the next day I wasn't. It was gradual—a gradual acceptance that things would never be the same.

The accident happened in July 1890. That summer I had my first job—or rather my first *paying* job.

At age thirteen I had been helping around Papa's general store for several years, but with no payment expected. Like all other children in rural Mississippi, from the time I could walk and understand simple instructions I was expected to contribute to the well-being of the family. Most of my friends, being from farming families, had been in the fields planting and hoeing long before they had lost their first baby tooth.

Since Papa owned the general store and had no farm land to speak of, my contribution—besides helping Sam with the weeding of our small garden, milking the cow, feeding the chickens, hauling in firewood, cleaning out the fireplace, etc.—was to sweep the floors and restock the shelves at the store. Papa would say that my payment was the food I ate and the clothing I wore. Occasionally, though, he would toss me a penny at the end of the day and tell me not to spend it all in one place. Funny thing, unless I went to Meridian, about the only place to spend my penny was at his general store!

That summer, the summer of the accident, Papa decided it would be a good idea for me to get some experience doing something else. Restocking and sweeping was not a full-time job, and he felt that a thirteen-year-old needed to be kept busy. I was too old to spend my summers playing, and swimming, and fishing, and hunting, and … Oh! The penalty of growing up!

He made arrangements for me to work at the depot—loading and unloading boxcars and doing whatever else Mr. Matthews could come up with. I was paid a dime a day, and at the time I thought I was overpaid.

Mr. Bludworth had the same idea for his youngest two sons, and James and Junius were also hired. It was hot, sweaty work but we loved it. At that age every boy wants to look like Atlas, and we just knew that all that heavy lifting and exercise would put muscles on top of our muscles. But in the six weeks I worked—up until the accident—my skinny little arms were still skinny little arms. But then, the bulge in our pockets and the little jingle of coins did make up for the lack of bulges on our biceps.

We were not always busy. There were times where nothing needed loading or unloading, and Mr. Matthews would try to keep us busy with other chores—sweeping and cleaning and rearranging. But with the three of us, he had a time finding enough busywork. When everything was done that could be done, he would sometimes tell us to go have fun, go swimming or fishing, and be back in an hour or two.

On that day in July we had finished loading the few cartons into the boxcar and were waiting for instruction from Mr. Matthews for something else to do. The train had not yet left, and we were standing around, admiring the steam engine with all its bells and whistles as it was about to leave.

Junius pointed to the front of the engine and said, "Have you ever seen one of those in action?"

"What are you talking about?" James asked.

"The cowcatcher. Have you ever seen it push a cow out of the way?"

The real name for a cowcatcher is a "pilot." It looks like a large sieve, but instead of filtering, its purpose is to move things off the track. It will move not only animals, but also logs, fallen trees, and rocks. Without it, a train could easily be derailed if a large object made its way under a wheel. Some cowcatchers are even outfitted as large snowplows. As a young child, I had always thought a pilot looked like gritted teeth, ready to gobble down anything in the train's path.

"No, I haven't seen it in action," said James. "But I have seen the final result. When we were in Tennessee, one of the neighbor's cows got hit. One of my friends saw it happen, and he said instead of a push, it was more like the cow bounced off of it. That cow was pretty messed up; all four legs were broken. They had to put her down, put her out of her misery. I saw her after she was already dead. It was not a pretty sight."

As we were standing there, Mr. Matthews came out and said, "Boys, it looks like it's going to be slow for the next few hours. Go have fun but be back in time to load up the noon train."

It was a cloudy day and looked as though it might rain at any time, not a good day for doing much of anything. We just stared at each other and shrugged our shoulders. What could we possibly do to keep ourselves from complete boredom for the next few hours?

As Mr. Matthews turned to go back inside, Junius suddenly perked up and snapped his fingers—as if a light had just gone off in his head.

"Mr. Matthews," Junius said. "You don't suppose the engineer would let us ride with him to Meridian and then catch the next train back. We would be glad to stoke the boiler for him—let him and his fireman have a leisurely trip. I've never ridden in a loco-motive before. Do you think he would mind us going with him?"

Mr. Matthews looked up at the engineer, who was busy get-ting everything in order to leave, and then looked back at us. "Let me ask. I bet it would be okay."

"Oh, boy!" we shouted.

For the next forty-five minutes, James, Junius, and I had more fun taking turns shoveling coal and blowing the whistle. The engineer said that the whistle had more use that day than it had in the past five years! We waved and hollered at every farmer, cow, and pig between Lockhart and Meridian and were hoarse and exhausted when we finally arrived. We were in Meridian for about two hours and then caught the train back, having the same fun, but in reverse.

We got back to Lockhart at noon, loaded up that train with boxes destined to head north, and waved it good-bye as it headed to Columbus. There was nothing else for us to do until the next train came through at three o'clock.

We tried to at least look busy, straightening up the platform, sweeping a little, but boredom was setting in. It was also getting hot. The cloudy morning had given way to a sunny, humid afternoon and we were dying to head up to Ponta Creek for an afternoon swim. We kept hoping that Mr. Matthews would come out and tell us we could leave for a couple of hours, but he never did—and we never asked. It was an unwritten rule that breaks had to be offered, not asked for. Even to give little hints, verbal or nonverbal, was frowned upon. After a while, I pulled out my bag of marbles and we played "ringer" and "rolly" for awhile, but we soon tired of that, too.

At about two-thirty, Junius let out a sigh and said, "Thirty more minutes! I can't stand it." He stood up and wrung his hands. "I'm about to die! I'd rather be digging in the fields at home than sitting here doing nothing. There has got to be something we can do."

After another few minutes he jumped off the ramp onto the tracks and said, "Why don't we flatten some pennies when the next train comes through?"

It had been a practice of ours, as well as most boys who grew up close to a railroad track, to place pennies or other small metal objects on the train track and watch as the train ran over it. The result was often a piece of metal as thin as a piece of paper.

I shook my head. "I better not. Mamaw was pretty upset with me the last time I did that," I said. "She said it was a waste of good money."

"Well, let's do just one," Junius said. "And so you won't get in trouble, we'll use one of my pennies. I think it is so much fun. When they are flattened, they are the size of silver dollars."

"I'll stay here," James said. "Ya'll go ahead. I'll start loading when the train gets here, and you can come help as soon as you pick up the penny. I wouldn't want Mr. Matthews to come out when the train gets here and find nothing being done."

The train would be coming from the north, so Junius and I walked up the track about fifty yards, sat down, and started throwing rocks into the woods.

"Did you hear that ol' Miss Brown died last night?" Junius asked as he picked up a rock.

"Yea," I said. "Mamaw told me this morning. She was pretty old, wasn't she?"

"Yea. She was ancient," Junius said as he threw the rock at the nearest tree. "She must have been at least sixty."

"Mamaw was over there late into the night with the family," I said. "She said Miss Brown had been sick for several months— consumption is what she had. Mamaw said it's a pretty terrible way to die. Coughing and gasping to the end."

"Yea, that's what I hear. Ma says the funeral is tomorrow, and that she is going to be buried in her red flannel nightgown."

"Really?" I said.

"Yep. She told her family that she had been in that gown for so long, that to be dressed in anything else when she met Jesus— why, it just wouldn't feel right."

We both began to laugh.

About five minutes until three, we heard the train in the distance, blowing her whistle to alert everyone of her arrival.

"There she comes," I said.

Junius placed the penny on the rail, and we scrambled down the embankment.

We were lying on our stomachs, watching in anticipation as the train got closer when suddenly the rail with the penny on it started to shake. The spikes must have been a little loose, allowing it to vibrate as the train approached. After a few seconds the penny began to bounce and bounced right off the rail onto the gravel.

Junius started to get up.

"What are you doing?" I asked.

"I'm going to put the penny back on the rail."

"No! Junius," I said as I grabbed his arm. "The train is getting too close."

"I've got time!" Junius said and shook my hand loose. The train was a good fifty yards from us and had been slowing for several hundred yards in order to stop at the depot, but it was still going fifteen to twenty miles per hour.

When the engineer saw Junius scrambling toward the track, he pulled the whistle cord and didn't let go. With the loud high pitched sound so close and so long, Junius took his eyes off the ground and looked over at the train. As he did, he missed his footing, slipped, and landed face down with his body right over the rail.

Junius didn't move.

"Junius!" I screamed. "Junius, get up!"

He still didn't move. The brakes on the train started squealing, but there was no way the train would stop in time. I jumped up and ran to Junius. "Junius, get up!" I screamed.

I pulled on his shoulder, rolling him to his side. There was blood on his forehead.

"Junius! Wake up! Please, wake up!"

He began to moan and reached his hand up to his head. The train was no more than twenty yards away, coming fast. I grabbed his arm and with all of my might I pulled him into a sitting position and pushed him as hard as I could off the track. He went rolling down the embankment.

I looked up, and the train was barreling down, less than ten yards away with her brakes squealing and whistle blowing. I leaped with all the strength I had left. My body cleared the rail just as the train got to me, but the cowcatcher caught my arm, and I started being dragged down the track. My arm was trapped in the slits between the metal beams. I heard a snap and felt a horrible pain in my left shoulder. Everything then went black.

Next thing I remembered I was lying on the gravel beside the train. It was no longer moving. Several men were standing over me. One of the men took off his shirt and pressed it against my left shoulder. I screamed in pain.

"Ollie, be still. Don't move. We've got to stop the bleeding."

"Someone find Dr. Knox," another man shouted. "Tell him to get here as fast as he can."

My shoulder was hurting so badly I could hardly stand it. I looked down at my left hand and tried to move it but nothing happened. The fingers would not move.

The man who had taken off his shirt whispered to the other men, "It's almost torn off!"

"God help him!" someone else exclaimed.

I started feeling weak and dizzy, as if I were going to blackout again.

As I lay there in a half-conscious state, James's words from that morning began to replay in my mind. "Cowcatcher ... had to put her out of her misery ... not a pretty sight ... all four legs were broken … she bounced off … messed up pretty bad … had to put her down…" I suddenly became frightened. They're going to put me down! They're going to put me out of my misery!

"Please, don't shoot me!" I began to scream and fight. "I'll be all right! Please, don't!"

"We're not going to shoot you," I heard Mr. Matthews say. "But Ollie, you've got to be still."

After that everything was a blur. I was in and out of consciousness. Occasionally I would hear someone talking, but I couldn't make out what they were saying. I remember someone carrying me, running with me in their arms. It was Sam.

"Mister Ollie, you gonna be okay. We gonna be at the house in no time, and Doctor Knox is gonna fix you up."

As he ran, the pain in my shoulder was excruciating.

The next time I was aware of what was happening, I was on our kitchen table. Someone was talking softly. It was Papa and Dr. Knox.

"Can you save his arm?" Papa asked.

"I wish I could," Dr. Knox said. "But there is no way. The arm is mangled pretty badly. The bone in the upper arm is shattered and pieces of it are sticking through the skin. We call it a compound fracture. If infection sets in—which it most surely will— he'll die. I was with General Beauregard at Shiloh, and we saw a lot of injuries like this from cannon fire. We found that it was either amputation or death."

"I understand," Papa said.

"I'll have to take it off at the shoulder. But he'll pull through. I've done dozens of amputations like this. He'll make it."

"What are they talking about?" I thought as my head began to clear. "Amputation? Pull through? Someone must be hurt pretty badly."

I opened my eyes and Mamaw was standing there, wiping my forehead with a cool cloth. "Ollie, be still, you'll be okay. Be still."

Suddenly I panicked. "Mamaw! It's me they're talking about! They're talking about me, aren't they? Mamaw, don't let them do it!"

Papa turned toward me, "Son, there is no other way."

"Papa! No! Don't let him take it off!" I screamed. "Please, Papa! I'll be okay!"

"I'm sorry, Ollie," Dr. Knox said. "I wish we could save it ... but we can't." He covered my face with a cloth. "There, now ... Breathe deeply. We're going to get you through this. That's it ... Slow, deep breaths."

The room was spinning. "No, Papa! Please, Papa! Please..."

I don't remember much that happened over the next two weeks. I have faint memories of Mamaw feeding me soup and telling me to swallow. There are memories of my shoulder being wrapped and unwrapped. That's about it. I don't even remember much pain during that time.

Later Mamaw told me that for several days it was touch and go. Dr. Knox had initially been very optimistic; but when I began running fever, he was very concerned. It was so hot that July and August, and with the fever I was delirious. For days Mamaw sponged my face and used moist towels on my legs and chest, anything to try to break the fever. When they could get it, ice was used to cool me down. The ice had to be sent from Meridian. We had no means of making ice in Lockhart. Thankfully—with the care of my grandmother and the prayers of the entire town of Lockhart—the fever broke, and I began to improve.

I was in bed for weeks. No one was allowed in except family and Dr. Knox. Very little was spoken to me, and then only in hushed tones: whispers. Everything was quiet and dark. As I gained strength, my consciousness began to improve.

I slowly began to realize the seriousness of my injury. My arm was gone, but then, I thought, *It can't be permanent, can it? Why, this is all some mistake. I'll wake up and this will have been a dream, won't it?* But I never woke up from that nightmare. It was real. And in the quiet of my room, I had plenty of time to think and cry. And acceptance was slow—it took years.

During those first few weeks, I remember having dreams—many of them of the accident. In one of the dreams I was being pulled down the track, and the train never stopped. For hours I was dragged and dragged. No relief in sight. In another I saw Junius lying on the track, unconscious, and I did nothing—I was frozen in fright and covered my eyes as he was swept away.

Junius! I thought. *How is Junius? Is he okay? No one has said anything about him! Is he dead?*

I was afraid to ask. For several days I was tormented with the thought. One day as Mamaw changed my dressing, I guardedly asked, "Mamaw, is Junius okay?" I held my breath.

"Yes, he is," she said as she dabbed my shoulder. "He had a nasty bump on his head and some scrapes and bruises, but he's just fine."

I sighed in relief.

"Ollie, you saved his life," she said as she continued the dressing change. "If it hadn't been for you, he would have died. Hopefully through all of this, you will remember that. You paid a big price for saving him. It was a brave thing that you did. I'm very proud of you."

As I gained strength, Dr. Knox started allowing visitors. One morning James and Junius came to visit. I heard Mamaw whisper to them before they came into my room. "He's very weak. Don't say or do anything that will upset him. You won't be able to stay long. He needs his rest."

The door opened, and James and Junius tip-toed in and stood at the end of my bed.

"Hey, Ollie," James said. "We've been praying for you. Are you doing okay?"

"Yea," I answered. "Just tired. I wish I could get up, but Dr. Knox says it's too soon."

James and I continued to visit for a few minutes. Junius stood there and didn't say a word. He would stare at the floor and every so often look up at me for a moment and then look down again.

Mamaw came in and said, "Boys, it's time to go. Ollie needs his rest. Ya'll can come back and visit another day."

As they were leaving, Junius said, "Mrs. Parker, is it okay if I stay a minute longer and talk with Ollie alone?"

"I guess that would be okay," Mamaw said. "That is, if it's okay with Ollie."

I nodded yes. James and Mamaw left, closing the door behind them.

Junius continued to stare at the floor for a minute, and then looked up at me; tears were in his eyes. "Ollie, thanks." He walked around to the side of my bed. "Ollie, you saved my life. If it wasn't for you..."

He began to cry, "Oh, Ollie, I'm so sorry! I shouldn't have been so stupid! It's my fault. If I hadn't been so..."

"Junius, it's okay. You didn't mean to."

"But if I hadn't..."

"Junius, please don't."

Junius dropped his head and continued to cry.

A twinge of anger suddenly came over me. *Junius, I don't need this*, I thought. *I'm suffering as it is, trying to come with grips with what happened, and I don't need your guilt to weigh me down even more.*

But then, I thought of Junius's side of this tragedy. Guilt does hurt. And guilt and the injury to the soul that it brings can sometimes be more of a burden than physical injury—a fact that became more apparent with Junius as the years passed. Some people, like Junius, can never get over the scars of guilt. No matter how hard they try, no matter how hard they pray, guilt consumes them and destroys them.

I began to tear up. "Junius, you're my best friend and will always be my best friend. If you weren't around, well, I don't know what I would do. And I'm glad I was there. And you know what?"

I began to chuckle.

"What?" he asked.

"I'd much rather have you than my arm." We both began to laugh through our tears.

As Junius was leaving, I said, "Where is the penny?"

Junius looked at me with a confused look on his face.

"The penny on the track," I said. "I hope you haven't spent it."

"Why, it's probably still out there," Junius said. "I haven't thought about that penny since the accident."

Two days later Junius and James paid me another visit. As they were leaving, Junius again wanted to visit for a minute after James left. After the door was closed, he reached in his pocket and pulled out a penny. There was a hole drilled above the Indian's head with a string threaded through it. He handed it to me.

"Here you are. A souvenir," Junius said.

I still have that old penny, somewhere. I wore it around my neck for a few years, but then retired it to the back of a drawer.

Chapter 23

Acceptance

As time passed and the reality of my loss sunk in, all types of fears and doubts and emotions began to enter my thoughts. The one that consumed me the most was a feeling that somehow I deserved what happened—that I was being punished for something that I had done. "Punishment comes to the wicked," I had always been taught. But what was it? What had I done to bring the wrath of God on me? What had displeased Him so much that he would take my arm? Yes, I knew that God was a good God, but He was also a God of judgment, and the Bible says that he will judge and punish the wicked. But what wicked deed had I done? Or could it have been a wicked thought?

I began to pray for forgiveness of an unknown sin that I had committed. Even though I didn't know what it was, I prayed fervently for forgiveness. Maybe if I prayed hard enough and long enough, God would forgive me, right the wrong that I had done, and give me my arm back.

For days as I lay in my bed, I prayed for hours at a time, but nothing happened. Maybe I'm not praying long enough, or fervently enough, or maybe it's because I can't get down on my knees. There must be something that I am not doing right. I began to beg, "God, please tell me what I can do. What is it that you want? What will please you?"

Guilt—guilt of a sin I didn't know—began to consume me.

Or maybe this was a test, I thought. Maybe it's like the story of Job. Maybe Satan and God got together one day and they decided to hurt me, to test me to see if I would break, as they did to Job. The only reason Job honored God, according to the devil, was because God blessed him and gave him everything he wanted. Why, if enough was taken away from Job, he would surely reject his God. Eventually everything was taken away from him, even his family.

I remember feeling sick at my stomach and beginning to sweat. "God! Please don't take my family! You wouldn't do that, would you?"

Oh, the turmoil that a thirteen-year-old mind can generate!

One day I was all worked up—worried, anxious, feeling guilty—pondering all my problems, as Mamaw changed the dressing. *Mamaw should be able to help me*, I thought. *She always had the right answers.*

"Mamaw," I said. "How do you find forgiveness for something you don't know you did?"

"Pardon?" she asked, as she finished the dressing change.

"I think I've done something to displease God," I said as I lay back down, "but I can't think of what it was. And Mamaw, I've been asking Him to forgive me, but how will I know He forgave me if I don't know what I did?"

"Ollie," Mamaw said. "I don't know what in heaven's name you are talking about."

"My arm," I said. "There must have been something that I did for Him to punish me."

Mamaw sat down on the side of my bed and took my hand in hers. "Ollie, God is not punishing you. Why, that's not how He works. He's not some ogre in the sky waiting to pounce on us every time we do wrong. And when bad things happen it doesn't mean we did something wrong either.

"Tell me, if you stump your toe, is it because you did something wrong, and God is punishing you?"

"No, ma'm," I answered.

"Now, if you cut your toe, and Dr. Knox has to put some stitches in it, is that punishment from God?"

"No, ma'm," I answered again.

"Right again. It just means you were clumsy, or you didn't see the object, or it was dark ... or numerous other possibilities. Likewise, if you cut your toe off, do you think that is punishment?"

I sensed a pattern in her questioning. "No, ma'm."

"Then how about your foot? Your leg? Do you see what I'm saying? At what point is an injury bad enough that you say that it is punishment from God?"

"I don't guess there is one," I said.

"That's right. If you go around trying to link injury—or sickness, or bad crops, or bad weather—to punishment from God for something you did or didn't do, you can't draw a line. You can't pick and choose.

"Now, Ollie, I'm not saying that God does not punish. There are consequences to our sins, and He does punish. But to say that all of our suffering is a result of a particular sin ... That's just not so. And Ollie, don't you ever think that losing your arm was the result of sin.

"Stupidity—yes. But sin—no." Mamaw shook her head. "Putting pennies on a railroad track. Of all the things..."

I have to agree with her.

Mamaw stood up, pulled out a bottle from a pocket in her apron, unscrewed the top, and poured a spoonful. It was cod liver oil.

"Open up. It's time for another dose."

"Oh, Mamaw! That stuff is horrible!"

"I'm sorry," Mamaw said. "Doctor's orders. We need to do everything we can to get you healthy."

I held my nose and swallowed. It was nasty! While still holding my nose with my right hand, I started looking for some water to wash it down. A glass was on the table beside my bed, and I reached for it with my left hand.

A sudden shock of reality gripped me when I realized I couldn't do it! My left arm was gone! This was the first of many times when I forgot and tried to use my left arm. As time passed I learned to laugh at myself when it happened, but this time I began to cry.

Mamaw immediately realized what had happened and sat back down on the side of my bed. There were tears in her eyes, and for several seconds she didn't say anything. She just patted me on the leg.

She then looked over at the glass and with a chuckle said, "You want me to hold your nose or hold the glass?"

We both began to laugh. One thing that Mamaw would never let happen was for me to wallow in self-pity.

"I'll hang onto the nose," I said.

After I drank a sip of water, I asked, "Mamaw, why does God allow us to make bad choices? He knows what's best for us but still allows us to do wrong."

"Ollie, that is one of the great mysteries of God and his relationship with man. God is in control of everything and nothing happens that He is not fully aware of and does not have complete control over. But within that control, He has given man the ability to choose. Not only to choose different paths of good, but also to choose paths that lead to nowhere or paths that lead to destruction. And with our bad choices there are consequences—and punishment.

"And an even more fascinating mystery—a truly wonderful mystery—is that no matter what happens, no matter how bad things are, no matter if what happens is due to the consequences of sin or is just something bad that happens, God can use it for good.

"But…" Mamaw glanced over at me as if she was about to tell a secret.

"But what?" I asked.

"There's a catch."

"A catch?" I asked, puzzled at what she said.

"Yes, a catch."

She walked over to my chest-of-drawers and picked up my Bible. She began to thumb through it.

"Here it is," she said as she pointed to the scripture. "The 'catch' is found in Romans 8:28. It says 'And we know that all things work together for good to them that love God, to them who are called according to his purpose.' There it is. Ollie, what does that tell you?"

"It tells me that if I want something good to come out of something bad, I have to love and trust God."

Mamaw smiled and closed the Bible. "That's it. You hit the nail on the head. How can anyone expect God to help make things work for good if we blame Him, ignore Him, or fail to trust Him? You have to trust with all your heart and make living for Him your primary purpose in life. If you do, then no matter what is thrown at you, you will have the peace and hope and knowledge that good can ultimately come out of it."

She sat down on the bed again and held my hand. "Ollie, right now I know that you feel that losing your arm is horrible and bad and makes no sense. And I fully agree with you. I don't pretend to understand or try to explain why it happened—except that it was the result of a wonderful, brave boy willing to risk his life to save his friend. But I do know that if you love and trust God, one day when you are old and gray, you will look back and see that He was in control and that He did have a plan for you. 'For I know the plans I have for you,' declares the LORD, 'plans to prosper you and not to harm you, plans to give you hope and a future.' That's in Jeremiah.

"And Ollie, good can come out of suffering. It's difficult to see right now. No one likes to suffer, and in the midst of suffering it is almost impossible to see the good, but as Paul tells us in Romans, in suffering we develop endurance, and endurance gives us character, and the result of character is hope. 'And hope does not disappoint, because the love of God has been poured out in our hearts through the Holy Spirit who was given to us.' Even in suffering, never give up hope, because when hope is gone, despair will take its place."

Mamaw leaned over and kissed me on the forehead. "God has a plan, and someday you will see it."

She stood up and fluffed my pillow. "Now, you lay back and try to get some rest. I'll be back in a couple of hours with supper."

"I hope it's not liver again," I said under my breath.

Mamaw began to laugh. "How does fried chicken sound to you? And mashed potatoes and butter beans?"

"That would be great!" I exclaimed.

As Mamaw closed the door, she looked back at me and said, "Remember what I said. And pray that God will give you peace and understanding. He will honor your prayers, and He will give you 'exceedingly, abundantly above all that you could ever ask or think.' "

Fifty-five years later I remember that conversation as if it were yesterday. Those words of wisdom and understanding have helped guide me through many difficult and trying times. And she was right. God did have a plan for me, and my life has been good. Oh, it's had its ups and downs, and I will never say that I'm glad it happened—that I lost my arm—because I am not. What I would do to be able to go back and change that! But my life has been fulfilling and rewarding. God has taken a horrible, tragic situation, and through his infinite love and mercy, made it good. It's been a wonderful journey.

And retirement? Tomorrow I start a whole new adventure, and I have to admit that it scares me to death! But I'll manage. A rocking chair?—no. A fishing pole?—yes!

Epilogue

In late 2007 as I was finishing my first book, *The Angels of Lock-hart*, I learned that Ollie, the narrator (and my wife's great uncle), had lost his left arm. None of the family had any knowledge of how or when it happened. I considered rewriting that manuscript, incorporating his loss in the first book, but decided against it. I felt that the life's story of a man who lost his arm as a boy could stand alone. Plus I did not want to distract from the original intent of *The Angels of Lockhart*.

Although no one knows how Ollie lost his arm, most of the stories within the story are based on real events. All historical references and dates are true.

The following is information that the reader may find interesting.

Ollie's life, as depicted in this book, is basically a true story. His family, life in Lockhart, Meridian, Dallas, and back to Meridian are real. The main liberty I took in his story was that he actually died in 1943. In the book, he is still alive two years later so that he could experience the Second World War in its entirety.

Adrienne's story is also basically real. In her adult years, she developed mental illness, most likely schizophrenia. Treatment at the time was limited and she ultimately was institutionalized. She and Ollie separated sometime in the late 1920s or early 1930s, and he returned to Mississippi.

Ollie's grandfather, John Woods Parker, Sr., was one of the early settlers of the land ceded by the Choctaw in 1830. He had a large plantation somewhere in north Lauderdale County, but the family doesn't know where it was. He and his second wife, Augusta, Ollie's "Mamaw," are buried in the Lockhart Methodist Church Cemetery next to the Parker family plot. I have no information about Mamaw. She died in 1904.

Ollie's father, Stephen Decatur Parker, moved from Lockhart to Meridian in the early twentieth century and became a successful businessman dabbling in mercantile, railway, and timber. He died in 1931 and is buried next to his second wife, Lizzie, in Magnolia Cemetery in Meridian.

Ollie's Uncle John, John Woods Parker, Jr., was also successful in business and became one of the movers and shakers of Meridian in the early twentieth century. He served two terms as mayor when Meridian was at its political and business zenith. He and his wife, Florence, are buried in Magnolia Cemetery in Meridian.

Junius Bludworth fought in France during the first Great War and was wounded. He lost an eye and walked with a limp for the rest of his life. His actual battle experience, no one knows. He outlived all of the characters except Arthur, Jr., and died in 1964. He never married, lived with Lizzie until she died in 1952, and is buried in Lockhart in the Bludworth plot located just south of the Parker plot.

The chapter, "Arthur," is the actual war experience of my wife's father, Arthur Simpson Coburn, Jr. His memoir, entitled *A. S. Coburn. My Story. 1942–1946*, was found while cleaning out some old files in 2007. He had died twelve years earlier. The fifty-page typed single-spaced account—a truly fascinating read—was condensed to ten pages.

The Key brothers' record for the longest subspace flight, twenty-seven days and six hours, has never been broken. The in-flight refueling nozzle designed by A. D. Hunter for the flight is still in use today by the military, with minimal alterations.

Silk, Sam, Buck, and Nathaniel are fictional.